TIMELESS
WESTERN
COLLECTION

Calico Ball

TIMELESS
WESTERN
COLLECTION

Calico Ball

CARLA KELLY
SARAH M. EDEN
KRISTIN HOLT

Mirror Press

Copyright © 2018 Mirror Press
Print edition
All rights reserved

No part of this book may be reproduced in any form whatsoever without prior written permission of the publisher, except in the case of brief passages embodied in critical reviews and articles. These novels are works of fiction. The characters, names, incidents, places, and dialog are products of the authors' imaginations and are not to be construed as real.

Interior Design by Cora Johnson
Edited by Haley Swan and Lisa Shepherd
Cover design by Rachael Anderson
Cover Photo Credit: Period Images and Deposit Photos #14433931

Published by Mirror Press, LLC

ISBN-13: 978-1-947152-43-4

Enjoy our Timeless Regency Collections

Autumn Masquerade
A Midwinter Ball
Spring in Hyde Park
Summer House Party
A Country Christmas
A Season in London
A Holiday in Bath
A Night in Grosvenor Square
Road to Gretna Green
Wedding Wagers

And our Timeless Victorian Collections

Summer Holiday
A Grand Tour
The Orient Express
The Queen's Ball

Table of Contents

The Keeper of the Western Door
by Carla Kelly

A Convenient Arrangement
by Sarah M. Eden

Isabella's Calico Groom
by Kristin Holt

The Keeper of the Western Door

Carla Kelly

In memory of Henrietta Blueye, who once told me that every girl should have the Radcliffe experience.

"Remember that some of the greatest needs may be those right in front of you."

Bonnie Oscarson
October 2017

Prologue

BLAME IT ON Mrs. O'Leary's cow, although the jury is still out on the matter, and the cow wasn't talking. On October 8, 1871, around nine o'clock at night, the unnamed cow kicked over a lantern in the O'Leary's barn, located on DeKoven Street in Chicago, Illinois.

The fire spread rapidly through the mostly wooden city, dry from summer drought. After two days and nights, the flames wore themselves out, moving north and helped along by rain. Three hundred people died, with 17,500 buildings burned and 100,000 rendered homeless.

News of the disaster reached Fort Laramie, Wyoming Territory, via a telegram, which was admittedly brief. Since the Union Pacific Railroad now passed through Cheyenne, 110 miles south, more detailed newspapers made their way to the fort when troopers rode south for mail and supplies.

"My word, Chicago is suffering," Mrs. Gertrude Hayes told her husband over breakfast on Officers' Row one morning in mid October.

She handed the paper to Captain Hayes, G Troop, Fifth Cavalry. He read it with his porridge. Oatmeal was his least favorite breakfast, but that was the army. There was a current overabundance of oats and raisins in the commissary. Too bad there was never a surplus of eggs.

When Captain Hayes left for guard mount, Mrs. Hayes began to wonder what to do for Chicago. She knew the city well enough, with its rows of wooden houses, most with shingled or tarred roofs. A woman of some imagination, Gertrude Hayes could picture desperate women fleeing with babes in arms and little more. Newspaper in hand, she walked next door to the post surgeon's quarters, where she found Mrs. Stanley staring at *her* newspaper.

Gertrude plunked herself down. They were friends of great standing, having moved together from garrison to garrison since before the War of the Rebellion. "Augusta, how can we help these pitiful folk?" she asked.

Augusta Stanley was cut from the same army cloth. "Let's have fun and do some good at the same time. We should hold a calico ball."

"I've heard of them," Mrs. Hayes said. "Heavens, who hasn't?"

"Granted, we are pretty small potatoes out here," Augusta Stanley said (she was regrettably prone to slang). "If every lady made a calico dress and wore it, we could send the dresses to the poor women in Chicago. We should include the sergeants' wives in this ball."

"Would we charge the men one dollar admission?" Mrs. Hayes asked.

"At least. We can donate refreshments. The regimental band will play."

The women looked at each other, thoughtful, because the next matter loomed. Neither was prone to much exertion, and rank did have its privileges.

"Who should be in charge of this event?"

"Who is the lowest-ranking lieutenant in the garrison?" Mrs. Stanley asked.

"Lieutenant Yeatman, I Company, and a bachelor. He won't do."

As the sound of the band faded away, indicating the end of guard mount, Mrs. Stanley and Mrs. Hayes thought a little more.

"I have it," Mrs. Hayes declared. "Lieutenant Masterson's wife. He is my husband's brand new second lieutenant. I'll grant you Victoria Masterson is self-centered, but she has what we need."

"Come again?"

"Augusta, think a moment. Can *you* sew a dress?"

"Certainly not. That is what the lower orders are for."

"Precisely," Mrs. Hayes said. "Victoria Masterson's maid—you know, the one with the silly name—is a seamstress without equal. She sews all of Victoria's clothing, and you know smart *she* always looks."

"Yes, Mary Blue Eye," Mrs. Stanley said. "My husband says that is a Seneca or Mohawk name. But will she do it?"

"Of course! It's time Victoria Masterson learned how things are done in the army. The Blue Eye maid has no choice."

· 1 ·

MARY BLUE EYE was no snob. It was an unlikely title for someone serving as a maid to a friend. To be honest, maybe less of a friend than Mary had thought last summer, when she grudgingly agreed to accompany newly married Victoria Masterson from New York to Fort Laramie.

Yet here she stood in front of the dining room mirror, staring at a woman sort of tan, with dark hair and eyes. True, she was Seneca, but far superior to the luckless Sioux and Cheyenne lurking around Fort Laramie, begging for handouts. Wasn't she?

Sergeant Blade was the only person in the entire garrison who might understand her growing doubts, but he wasn't available for idle chat. She didn't even know his first name. She couldn't ask Victoria's husband, Lieutenant Silas Masterson, if he could send G Troop's first sergeant over for cookies and milk when there was nothing better to do.

The best Mary could hope for was to run into him in the sutler's store, which so far hadn't happened. She did enjoy watching the sergeant lead new recruits through the mysteries of equitation on the parade ground. He had a brisk air of command that brooked no disobedience from man or beast. He was also not a man to idle away his time anywhere appropriate for Mary to meet him.

Not that she ever wanted to recreate the one time when she had him all to herself, albeit briefly. They were a day out of Cheyenne, traveling to Fort Laramie in an army ambulance, which amused Victoria Masterson until she realized it was the common mode of transportation for army dependents, and not as comfortable as her father's carriage back home.

They had bumped along over nasty trails, mashed together in the ambulance with the wife of G Troop's first lieutenant and their three children, the wife growing more irritated with each mile that her darlings were crowded tighter than clams in a basket.

Ignoring Mary, the woman finally addressed Victoria. "Mrs. Masterson, tell your maid to ride with the baggage so Anthony can stretch out before he pukes."

Startled, Victoria had nudged Mary. "Would you mind?"

"*Mind?* Mrs. Masterson, she is your servant," the woman said. "Tell her."

Victoria spoke to the driver through the canvas barrier. He stopped his horses, and Mary got out without a word, humiliated.

Sergeant Blade had been riding beside the ambulance. He dismounted and asked what the problem was.

"Where's the baggage wagon?" Mary asked. "Not enough room in here for me."

"Lieutenant Caldwell's wife is not known for tact," he said as he walked her to a blue-painted wagon with red wheels. "Let me help you up."

The help-up meant hands on her waist and a boost that landed her beside the driver, who saluted the sergeant with a casual two fingers to his cap. "I'll look after her, Sarge."

"See that you do," Sergeant Blade said. Coming out of *his* mouth, it was no suggestion.

That was that, almost. The sergeant mounted and rode beside the wagon, pacing his horse. "I'm afraid you have to eat dust back here. I'll see what I can do."

When she didn't say anything because she was too embarrassed, he side stepped his mount closer to the wagon. "May I help you?" he asked.

She saw so much concern on his face. She knew there was nothing he could do, but he was kind to say it, and so she told him. He nodded.

"You're not used to being a maid, are you?"

"No, sir," she said, not sure how to address a sergeant. "I thought I was a friend."

She looked away so he wouldn't see her tears, and he rode to the top of the detail after one backward glance. It was then that she understood something about the army—sergeants were in charge of everyone in the command. The knowledge warmed her heart and made the dust almost bearable.

They had camped that night beside the Chugwater. Lieutenant Caldwell's wife had included a cook in her entourage, so the Mastersons fared well enough. Unsure of herself, Mary stood close to Victoria.

"Should I take a plate?" Mary whispered.

"I don't know," her childhood friend whispered back. "I don't see any of the other servants eating here."

I'm hungry, too, Mary thought. She looked around until she saw another woman who had been riding in the other baggage wagon. Nothing ventured, nothing gained.

She walked to the other campfire and waited there, not sure what to do. The woman glanced at her briefly, then glanced away, hunching her shoulder as if she didn't want to know her.

Startled, Mary walked away. If she could find a water barrel, at least there would be something to drink. She remembered longhouse elders smoking their pipes and talking about starvation marches as they fought with the British against the American colonists.

I should have brought along some pemmican, except I can't stand pemmican, she thought, which made her smile. *I'm a pretty poor Seneca.*

She found a water barrel with a tin cup beside it and dipped herself a drink. She relished the coolness, even though the water tasted of wood, with just a hint of tar, probably from the lining. She rolled it around in her mouth, thinking of Papa and his favorite brandy, an annual Christmas gift from Victoria's father, Judge Wilkins.

"I can offer you something better," she heard behind her, and knew she was about to be cared for.

Sergeant Blade held out a tin plate with what looked like smashed hardtack. She took the plate, her mouth watering from the bacon that the mangled crackers were cooked in.

He handed her a fork and indicated a log. She sat down and he joined her. Too shy to speak and hungry, she ate in silence, relishing the odd combination.

"Why does this taste so good?" she asked, knowing about manners and conversation, and after all, he had found her a meal.

"One of two things," he said. "You're either really hungry, or food cooked over a buffalo chip fire is well ... uh ... seasoned."

She laughed out loud. "Doesn't even need pepper."

"Good to hear you laugh," Sergeant Blade said. "You were looking pretty glum earlier." He was silent for a moment, then, "And I don't blame you."

Her stomach was full. She wasn't thirsty. The sky had

darkened, and Mary felt bold enough to ask the man seated beside her something that had been bothering her since she and Victoria Masterson had seen their first Indians in Nebraska.

"Sir, do I look like an Indian?"

She asked it quietly, partly because it seemed like a frivolous question, and partly because she doubted she should even mention the matter.

"Everyone calls me Sarge," he told her. "You can too."

"Very well." Maybe he wasn't going to answer her question.

"Yes, you do," he said, "but you don't. Tell me more."

"Are you certain?" she asked, doubtful. Maybe it was time for her to return to the ambulance and see if Victoria needed her for anything. But that would mean walking past the other servant who had turned away, and facing the lieutenant's wife again.

"I'm interested. I've never met an eastern Indian, if that's what you are."

"I am Seneca," she told him. "My family is descended from Mary Jemison, a captive who chose to stay with the Keepers of the Western Door. Her second husband was Hiakatoo, a Seneca. Their daughter Jane is my grandmother. We live in a nice house on property belonging to Victo . . . Mrs. Masterson's father, Judge Wilkins. My mother is his cook, and my father is the judge's secretary. We're Methodists." *So maybe I am not much of an Indian*, she thought.

"If I'm not being rude, do most Seneca look like you?" he asked.

"Some do, some don't," she said, hearing nothing in his question but curiosity. "There's been some marrying back and forth." She looked toward the other campfire. "I suppose I had better go over there."

"Do you want to?"

That was precisely what she had been asking herself ever since she was evicted from the officers' ambulance. She glanced at Sergeant Blade and again saw nothing but goodwill in his expression.

"Part of me does, and part of me doesn't," she said, which made him chuckle. "I don't think I belong in the West, but I promised Mrs. Masterson I would stay for six months, and so I shall. Goodnight, Sergeant."

She didn't ask, but he walked her back to the officers' campfire. "I'll tell the teamster to shift around some boxes in the baggage wagon," he said as they came closer. "Throw your bedroll in there. You'll be safe, and I won't worry."

"Why would you worry at all?"

"You're part of my job, and I like you," he said simply. "Good night, Miss Blue Eye. Things will go better tomorrow."

· 2 ·

THEY DIDN'T, EXCEPT that Mary learned something about herself on that last day's travel to Fort Laramie. She also learned more about Sergeant Blade.

She had resumed her place in the baggage wagon, seated this time on the open tailgate because it was cooler. To console herself, Mary indulged in a hearty round of self-pity, wondering how soon she could leave. Mama had sent her West with enough money for a return ticket.

Here she was now, hanging on for dear life to the chain that lowered the gate. Mary hadn't dangled her feet over the edge of anything in years. She was happy to face away from trail dust and breathe better air.

She hung on tighter when the wagon began its descent into what was probably a reluctant creek that had been emboldened by a recent series of gully-washing rains. Muddy water swirled around the wheels, and two things happened at once.

The nearest crate slid off the end of the wagon and pulled her with it, plopping into the water and sucking her down. Frantic, she tried to scream and ended up gargling mud. She bloodied her fingers, feeling for a hold on the rough wood of the crate, then forcing her fingers through a small opening.

Trouble was, the crate held china—she felt sodden newspaper and ceramic—and began to sink as it bumped along. She turned her attention to worming her fingers out of the slat, ready to strike out for the bank. The weight of her dress wore her down, too. Her shoes were already gone, which helped, but the dress was heavy.

She shrieked when a horse blocked her view, then realized salvation loomed. She yanked her hand free and held it up, to be grasped by Sergeant Blade, who leaned down and grabbed whatever else was handy, which turned out to be her shirtwaist. With no ceremony, he threw her stomach-down over his lap and transferred his spare hand to the back of her skirt, working his gauntleted hand into her waistband.

"Hang on."

To what? she asked herself, then grabbed his leg, which he obligingly raised a little so she could put her forearm between his thigh and the saddle.

"Damned steep bank," he muttered, then up they went, after crossing the swollen stream and charging up the other side.

Safe now, she let him gently lower her to the ground, her sodden dress and petticoats sticking to her, and the buttons gone from her shirtwaist where he had grabbed her. She didn't care. She was alive.

She covered her face with her hands. Perhaps it was vestigial memory—heaven knows the Seneca had little to fear recently except prejudice—but her mother had taught her never to cry in times of struggle, never to invite unwelcome sound into any fraught situation. She stood there in silence, alone until Sergeant Blade dismounted and pulled her close.

"You all right?" he asked.

She nodded, not all right a bit and wanting her mother in the worst way.

"Liar," he said, which made her laugh, too. Maybe she *was* all right.

Victoria Masterson came running, but not too fast, because she was a lady, and not too close, because of all the mud.

Then Sergeant Blade astounded Mary, amazed her, and warmed her heart to a profound degree. "Mrs. Masterson, Miss Blue Eye leaped into the water to save your china."

Two thoughts seemed to collide inside Victoria Masterson's admittedly roomy brain: Her china was gone. Her servant-friend had risked her life for it.

Victoria gasped and started to cry. She didn't go so far as to embrace her soaking wet servant, but she held out her hand. "Thank you, Mary," she said. "I'll never forget this."

Yes, you will, Mary thought, even as she wanted to laugh at the sergeant's adroit interpretation of the event. *And you, Sarge, should be a diplomatist.*

"Do you have dry clothes in the baggage wagon?" Sergeant Blade asked.

Mary nodded, her face warm because it was a delicate subject. He helped her into the wagon, told the driver to back away, and organized a few troopers to travel downstream to see what they could salvage from the crate, if anything.

Dry except for her hair and at least partly clean, Mary took a seat beside the driver, who looked at her with some awe now as the selfless attempted rescuer of a doomed china crate. She watched Sergeant Blade ride to the head of the column beside his officers, touched in her heart that his artless lie had made her a heroine and smoothed a path.

She was certain the army didn't pay him enough.

· 3 ·

BUT HOW DID a body find an opportunity to get to know such a man better? Mary still stood before the mirror, which was not getting any silver polished. She sat down at the dining room table and applied herself to tarnish.

It wasn't a dining room. Second lieutenants were entitled to four rooms, if available, and none were. The Mastersons had crammed the table into a corner of the tiny parlor. Victoria had made quite a show of insisting that they call this side the dining room and the other side the parlor.

Mary knew better than to argue. She had known Victoria all her life, well aware that once she dug in with an idea, it was there to stay, no matter how ridiculous. A new husband, Silas hadn't learned his lesson yet. Mary had to pretend she didn't hear a spirited argument that night. By morning, he was calling that corner of the room the dining room, and peace reigned.

Mary's room was a curtained alcove off the kitchen, probably meant for a cook. Once a bed had been crammed into the small space, there was room for little else.

A cook. Another lively fight involved a question from the

lieutenant, sounding both aggrieved and aghast: "You can't cook *anything*?" At least, that was all Mary heard before he slammed the bedroom door.

The Mastersons had solved that thorny issue by hiring a corporal's wife from G Troop who claimed she could cook. The wary woman appeared for dinner, but took Mary aside to give her a shake and order her to manage breakfast and luncheon for Mrs. High-and-Mighty. "Boil eggs and make biscuits," she snapped, then made it worse. "Even an Indian can do that."

Mary had set the last of the spoons in warm water when Victoria Masterson came home, quite the reverse of the confident woman earlier, answering a summons from the company commander's and post surgeon's wives, acknowledged leaders of Fort Laramie's elite, at least according to them.

The lady of the house sank into a chair and stared at the dishpan holding her spoons. Mary waited, confident that her friend/employer/who knew? would eventually speak.

A massive sigh came first, followed by the drama. "I do not know what I have got myself into," she said.

Mary remained silent. Her mother had taught her the virtue of silence when dealing with "those of lighter skin," as Mama put it. She waited.

"Or rather, what two perfectly capable women have got me into," Victoria amended, and glared at Mary, probably because she was handy.

Silence still seemed wise to Mary.

"Mary, have you heard of a calico ball?"

Mary thought of an excruciating time ten years ago when she was eleven and her tribe had suffered through a poor harvest, followed by diphtheria. The Blue Eye family had been largely immune, since they lived on Judge Wilkins's property, away from contagion.

"Yes, I have," she said. "Remember that bad winter when so many babies died?"

Victoria shook her head, which came as no surprise to Mary.

"Some of the ladies in the First Presbyterian Church held a calico ball, with proceeds and dresses going to my people," Mary told her. Mama had politely handed back the dress Victoria's own mother thought to give her, after the ball. She didn't need it. When Mrs. Masterson insisted, Mama cut it down for Mary, who didn't need it either.

"I remember now. That was so kind of the church ladies," Victoria said. Another sigh, then, "Mrs. Hayes and Mrs. Stanley are organizing a calico ball, with dresses and proceeds for the poor of Chicago, who lost everything in that fire."

Mary had a sudden vision of thousands of poor ladies lined up for perhaps twenty dresses headed their way from a four-company garrison in the middle of nowhere. "It might be a worthy project," she said cautiously.

"*Might* be," Victoria said, with barely controlled distress. "Who is put in charge but the wife of the lowest-ranking officer on post? Me!"

"Hmm," seemed like the wisest reply.

Then came The Look, which Mary recognized. She steeled herself.

"I assured those two biddies that I have the perfect solution to calico dresses on demand. Surely you can guess."

"No, I can't." Mary said. Dread began to loom over her shoulder like a perched vulture.

"You can make the dresses!"

Mary stared at her employer and perhaps by this time, former friend. "But ... With only a needle and thread? Victoria, I ..."

"Better call me Mrs. Masterson. I know it seems so formal, but you do work for me now," Victoria said. "Mrs. Stanley has already corrected me about that."

Definitely former friend. Thank goodness the Union Pacific ran both west *and* east throughout the coming winter. "How many dresses?"

"Perhaps fifteen. That would take care of the officers' wives, who, I scarcely need tell you, don't sew." She laughed. "Don't look so stunned! Heaven knows why, but Mrs. Hayes has a sewing machine. You have plenty of time. The dance is in four weeks."

Four weeks. Mrs. Masterson obviously had no idea how long fifteen dresses would take. "And my other duties?"

"Oh, pish posh. You'll have time." Victoria looked at the clock. "Let's go to the sutler's store and look over the calico."

After which I will run away, Mary thought. Too bad Fort Laramie was surrounded by hostiles who wouldn't stop to politely inquire if she had any Indian blood before scalping her.

The sutler's supply of calico proved to be nonexistent. Mary watched Victoria stand in front of the dry goods counter and stare, as if hoping that bolts of fabric would suddenly—poof!—materialize. Alas, no.

Next stop was Mrs. Hayes's quarters, where Victoria gave the captain's wife the sad news.

Mrs. Hayes took it in true army stride. "Simple. We'll send uh—Mary, is it?—Mary to Cheyenne with a cavalry troop in a day or two. She can pick out fabric, hurry back here, and start sewing."

Mary knew better than to look around. *Am I invisible? Can you ask me?* she thought.

"I should go, too," Victoria said.

"Heavens no, my dear! Hostiles are out and about. It would never do if something happened to you," Mrs. Hayes said. "Mary can go."

Mary realized two things: first, she was expendable; second, perhaps Mama and Papa shouldn't have spoiled her so much, going so far as to assure her that she was as good as a white woman. Maybe there was a third matter. In the eyes of these people, Victoria Masterson included now, she was an Indian servant in a place with no use for Indians.

· 4 ·

THE WALK BACK to the Mastersons' quarters featured nothing beyond the crunch of shoes on gravel, Victoria well beyond her usual languid stroll. Indecisive, she stood in the tiny alcove they laughingly called a foyer. Her mind made up, she mashed her hat down more firmly.

"Start luncheon, Mary. I'm going to find Lieutenant Masterson."

Mary warmed the soup and buttered the bread. When they first arrived at Fort Laramie, the two of them had sat down together for lunch and chatted. That ended after Mrs. Stanley popped in unannounced one day and found them sitting together.

Almost, but not quite, in a whisper, Mrs. Stanley set the new bride straight as Mary listened from the kitchen, hearing enough words to be chastised, which was probably the entire intention of the surgeon's wife: "Not done . . . she's your servant . . . remember her place . . ." Mary heard the unkind words long after Mrs. Stanley flounced away.

Mary ate in the kitchen, then went onto the porch to watch for Victoria. "I could have told you, had you asked me, that it's bad form to go traipsing after your husband in a garrison," Mary said under her breath.

She sat in a rocking chair and indulged in her favorite fantasy of imagining herself aboard an eastbound train. She heard a small noise and glanced over the railing to see an Indian woman with a little girl and a baby on her back. Mary had noticed them last week at the slaughtering floor behind the commissary storehouse. Some of the more bedraggled women stood there during the slaughter, begging silently with their eyes for whatever the army didn't want.

Victoria had sent her to the storehouse for another pound or two of the endless raisins that some harried clerk had sent their way from Omaha, perhaps mistaking an order of one hundred pounds for one thousand, which meant enough raisins to see them into the twentieth century.

The private in Fort Laramie's storehouse was equally harried and insisted that she needed ten pounds instead of the more modest two that Victoria had requested. "I don't care what you do with them," he said, then gestured toward the slaughterhouse. "Find some Indians." His face grew solemn. "They're always hungry."

Mary had done precisely that. She stopped a woman carrying a bloody bucket of entrails and brains and handed her small daughter a brown paper parcel bunched together and tied with twine. Gesturing with her fingers to her mouth, the universal sign for food that Mary knew from back home, she took some loose raisins from her basket and held them out.

After a glance toward her mother, who nodded, the little one popped the raisins in her mouth, chewed, and smiled. She was a pretty child, with snapping brown eyes and hair neatly bound into two braids.

Here they were again, standing silently at the edge of the porch, looking hopeful. They must have watched her return to this house last week, after she left the storehouse. Gesturing that they come closer, Mary hurried inside to the kitchen and poured more raisins into parcel paper.

She opened the side door and gave the raisins to the child, receiving smiles in return, ample payment. Mary watched them walk toward the slaughter yard again. She noted the child's ragged dress and wondered if the poor women of Chicago were better off, even with half of their city burned. Mama had told her more than once that charity begins at home.

She walked around to the porch to see Sergeant Blade standing there, looking where she had looked.

"They don't have much, do they?" he commented. "The clerk in the storehouse told me last week that he was liberal with raisins, and you were, too."

"I hope that won't get me thrown in the guardhouse," Mary said, not certain if levity was the better part of valor, concerning a sergeant.

"No. I expect a lot of us would like to help," he said, and followed her onto the porch. "I know I would."

"Can't you?" she asked, curious.

"That's a problem with being a first sergeant, Miss Blue Eye. We're supposed to follow all regulations. Even stupid ones," he said. "I'll leave the charity to you."

What did one do with a sergeant on the porch? Mary knew she couldn't ask him inside; it wasn't her house, and no one was home. He solved her problem by indicating the rocking chair while he perched on the porch railing, somehow managing to look dignified while doing it. She decided this was not a man bothered much by inconvenience.

"I'm here to warn you," he began, with no preliminaries

other than a glance over his shoulder toward the parade ground. "You are going to Cheyenne for calico."

"Apparently your captain's wife told Mrs. Masterson that the trip was too dangerous for her, but not for me," Mary said. She wished she could hide the edge to her voice. "After all, we must have calico."

"You *will* be all right. I guarantee it. I'm leading the patrol. We are also to escort the paymaster, who is arriving tomorrow from Fort Fetterman, on his way to the railroad in Cheyenne."

He stood up and didn't disguise the edge to *his* voice. "He wants the ambulance to himself." She saw the discomfort on his face. "That's partly my doing. I asked if a lady could share it with him. He asked who she was, and I . . ."

". . . told him Miss Blue Eye, whereupon Major Pettifog decided it was a small ambulance and couldn't possibly accommodate another person," Mary finished.

"Bravo, Miss Blue Eye!" Sergeant Blade exclaimed. "Major Pettifog, indeed. Actually, his name is Pettigrew, so you were close."

"And he doesn't much care for Indians." Mary said what she knew he would not say. "I've heard it before."

"Even back East?"

"Not as much there. My skin is light, and I tend to blend in." She looked at the woman and child in the distance now. "Not so much out here."

"No, and more's the pity." He waved his hand. "Change of subject. Can you ride horseback?"

Mary couldn't help her smile. "I've been riding since I was young. I brought my riding skirt along, but I don't have a sidesaddle."

"I'll find you one. It'll be a fast trip. Major Pettigrew is eager to return to the comforts of Omaha. I am also informed by an unimpeachable source that there are many dresses for you to sew."

"Please don't tell me that Mrs. Masterson made a scene, with tears and demands," she blurted out.

"I won't, then," the sergeant said, amused. "Suffice it to say we all heard a convincing argument for calico."

Mary sighed.

"How did you get involved in this nonsense? It couldn't have been your idea."

She looked over his shoulder to see the Mastersons walking across the parade ground now. "Here they come. I will blame Mrs. O'Leary's cow back in Chicago. Think of the abuse that poor bovine will suffer in coming years."

The sergeant chuckled at that. "Tell me quick, because I want to know."

"Mrs. Masterson was put in charge of a calico ball because she is married to a second lieutenant who only outranks earthworms."

Aware the Mastersons were advancing, he laughed silently. "You are wise beyond your years, Miss Blue Eye. I suppose you can sew and she cannot, and you've suddenly become responsible for a lot of dressmaking because other ladies are equally helpless."

"Precisely, Sergeant."

"My name is Rowan."

"I'm Mary."

"Ready to ride the day after tomorrow?"

"As I'll ever be."

He gave her a small salute that made her smile. There was something in his eyes that reminded her of her own father, although they looked nothing alike. Maybe it was his genuine interest, which she knew she did not merit, because he barely knew her. She could probably tell him anything.

"Sergea... Rowan," she began.

He inclined his head in her direction, an invitation to continue.

"I think... I wish we could make dresses for that Indian woman and her little girl who are right here at Fort Laramie," she said. "I don't think they've rubbed up against much good luck lately if they're carrying buckets of guts."

"They haven't," Rowan agreed. "Over the Laramie beyond Suds Row, there's a whole camp of them that get by on handouts. Maybe her man died in a buffalo hunt. Maybe disease took him. They're on their own. Some people call them Laramie Loafers, but they work so hard to stay alive." He clapped his hands together, and she saw his frustration. "The West is changing, Mary Blue Eye. It's not a kind place for people who used to be the lords of the earth."

"I can understand that," she replied. "I'll be ready. Really early?"

"Really early."

· 5 ·

TWO DAYS LATER, with a pouch of money from ladies needing dresses, Mary found herself thrown into the saddle by a man who knew what he was doing. She smiled down at the sergeant, pleased to be riding with a well-organized, efficient troop, and not negotiating life, for a few days at least, with a childish employer and her increasingly baffled husband.

I am with an adult, she thought, relieved and not a little amused. "Just tell me what to do, and I will do it," she told Sergeant Blade. "I mean, I can stay out of the way however is most convenient."

"All you have to do is ride beside me. No eating dust on *this* trip. I'll take better care of you."

Why should that make her face go warm? The perpetual wind blowing cool across her face helped tamp down the pink. Thank goodness the sergeant had turned away to speak to Major Pettigrew, department paymaster who had finished his circuit of forts and was headed to headquarters in Omaha.

He turned back, and she noted that his face was red, too. Perhaps the wind was stronger than she thought. Or perhaps he wasn't any more practiced in female conversation than she was with talking to men not of her family. Mama had been scrupulous about her only daughter's deportment.

"Miss Blue Eye," he began more formally. She doubted the sergeant had mentioned to his troops that he was already calling her Mary.

"Yes, Sergeant?" she asked, not slow by any means.

She saw the appreciation in his eyes. "Major Pettigrew here has suggested you put the calico fabric money in the strongbox as we travel to the railroad."

She leaned over and handed the pouch to the major. "That way I won't be tempted to steal it, will I?"

"Miss Blue Eye, I didn't mean . . ."

"Sergeant, I know *you* didn't," she said, wondering where her nerve was coming from. "Major Pettigrew will feel safer if an Indian doesn't carry it."

"*You're* the Indian?" the paymaster said as he took the money.

"I am, sir," Mary said.

"I wouldn't have known," he replied. "I thought . . ."

"I know," she said, and started backing up her horse to get out of the conversation. "We Easterners of the Iroquois League do tend to look lighter, don't we? But I understand your reluctance." She couldn't help but notice admiration in Sergeant Blade's eyes. Whether it was the expert way she handled her mount or the fact that she stood up for herself, Mary had no idea. "I am Seneca, from Genesee, New York. My great-grandmother was Mary Jemison, whom you have perhaps heard of."

The major nodded. "Anyone who has read any history at all has heard of Mary Jemison."

What had gotten into her? "I am named for her. My great-grandfather was Hiakatoo, Mary's second husband.

And imagine this: my father is a graduate of Dartmouth College."

The major tried to return the pouch, but Mary backed her horse farther away. "No. It is safer with you, sir. I trust every man in this detail, but who knows who we will run into? I trust you, too," she added, feeling generous.

Mary sat a little straighter, overwhelmed by what she had just done. Up to this moment, she had spent much of her life hoping no one would notice that she was different from Victoria Masterson's other friends, or that she knew how to ride, or sit quietly in council in the longhouse. *I am Seneca*, she thought, *I am a Keeper of the Western Door*. She would have to write to Papa and let him know. It was a letter long overdue.

She sat quietly by herself as Sergeant Blade continued his work. When the detail had lined up, he motioned her closer, and she obliged.

They left the fort's corral area as the sun rose, fanning out soon so no one had to eat dust. Sergeant Blade set a brisk pace.

Mary knew she had said too much to Major Pettigrew. He probably meant well.

"Should I apologize to Major Pettigrew?" she asked her riding companion.

"Under no circumstances," Rowan said, with no hesitation. "I don't mind that he feels a little downtrodden." He looked around at his troopers. "You have a lot of allies here." He laughed, mostly to himself. "After all, they remember how you so selflessly leaped into the water to save Mrs. Masterson's china."

She shook her head at that one. "Sergeant Bl—"

"Rowan."

"Very well then, Rowan! You're fighting my battles, and I don't know why."

"It feels good," he said, after a lengthy pause worthy of a Seneca elder.

They rode in silence for some distance. It was enough to pound along on a good horse and breathe deep of autumn advancing and winter coming. There was something beguiling about the expanse of earth and sky here that appealed to her. No wonder the admittedly more primitive Sioux and Cheyenne were reluctant to give it up and submit tamely to a reservation. She understood. There were old Seneca who wore sad faces when they talked about land no longer theirs.

Mary watched the sergeant and saw his head on a nearly continuous swivel, watching, always watching. When they reached an area where the terrain became more gullied, he motioned to a rider on each end of the fan. When they rode ahead, the other soldiers pulled back into a double file.

"We're in an area where Sioux don't mind lying in wait to cause a bit of trouble," he told Mary. "If I see warriors, I'm plunking you in the ambulance."

She nodded and sidled her mount closer to his, an act that wasn't lost on the sergeant.

"You'll be fine, Mary," he said. "In fact, talk to me. Do you live on a reservation? I don't know anything about the Seneca."

Silently, she blessed the man beside her. She knew he was keeping her calm by letting her talk.

"My family lives on land that used to belong to Mary Jemison herself."

"The White Indian of the Genesee," Sergeant Blade said. "I'm from Connecticut, and I remember hearing the stories."

She thought she had heard a bit of New England in Rowan Blade's speech. "I am named after her: Mary Jemison Blue Eye." She couldn't help her sigh. "Everyone back home calls me Jemmy. Mrs. Masterson used to."

"What do you like to be called?"

No one had ever asked her that before. "I'm used to Jemmy."

"May I continue to call you Mary? *I* like it."

She wanted to tell the tall, careful man riding beside her that Mary would be a name for no one but him and her. Her practical nature reined in that thought. *He's just making conversation,* she told herself, but yes, she would be Mary now to this man.

"Certainly you may," she said, keeping her voice low. "I like it, too."

She wanted to say more, but the point rider on the west rode toward Sergeant Blade, who spurred his mount ahead. She looked around and noticed that all of the troopers watched intently, some leaning forward, ready to do immediate bidding. The corporal edged his horse closer to hers.

"Sarge's orders, ma'am," he said cheerfully. "If he's not beside you, I am."

"Is he this careful with all his hangers-on?" she joked, and the corporal surprised her.

"Nope. Just you."

"All because I tried to rescue a crate of china a few months ago?" she asked.

"He didn't mention any china, ma'am," the corporal replied, and there was no overlooking the twinkle in his eyes. "Here he is. Sarge?"

Rowan motioned his men to gather closer. When Mary started to back off, he reached for her reins and kept her there.

"Private Reilly saw a handful of chipper fellows in the next draw," he said. "No one's painted up, though. Be alert but not overly interested. Maybe they're just playing mumblety-peg."

The troopers chuckled at that. Mary saw no fear. "Where do you want me?" she asked.

"In the ambulance," Rowan said. He tightened his grip on her reins and led her back to the vehicle. "If any shooting starts, lie down on the floor."

She nodded and let him help her down. The sergeant spoke a few words to the major inside, and the door opened. "Major Pettigrew, here is Miss Blue Eye," he said. "Take care of her, sir."

The major ignored Mary, and she would have been fine with that, except that such a stance seemed almost cowardly. She took a deep breath and decided to make conversation. As they traveled that notorious part of the trail, Mary decided she had been hasty in thinking ill of the paymaster, who, she learned, had a wife back East he saw now and then and two grandchildren.

She was well on her way to telling him more about her father, a Dartmouth graduate who served as Judge Wilkins's secretary, and Mama, who cooked, when the driver set the brake and Sergeant Blade opened the door.

"I believe we'll arrive at Hunton's stage station with all our hair," he said. "Thank you, Major Pettigrew. I trust Miss Blue Eye wasn't unruly or demanding?"

"Not at all," the paymaster replied. "In fact, if she'd rather stay with me . . ."

"Your choice," Rowan said to her.

"The point is, I had a choice," she told the sergeant a few minutes later after she had thanked the major prettily and resumed her place atop a horse that didn't mind a sidesaddle or an Indian.

"That's all anyone wants," he said. "The major decided you weren't a fearsome creature?"

She knew he was teasing her, but Mary saw something

else in his firm expression. Funny that she had ever thought him formidable.

"I never was," she said.

He smiled at that. Maybe it was his turn to feel shy.

· 6 ·

HUNTON'S STAGE STATION was as noisy as Mary remembered it from her trip to Fort Laramie. With few travelers in late October, she had a curtained-off partition to herself, which was all the luxury anyone could expect. His eyes on some barely sober cowboys, Sergeant Blade posted a guard outside her curtain, which turned out to be him and then the corporal halfway through the night. Mary slept better than she thought she would.

They left at dawn, making a steady push that saw them to Cheyenne at dusk, just as the eastbound train pulled in to the Union Pacific depot. Sergeant Blade retrieved the calico money from the military strongbox and sent the paymaster on his way rejoicing.

Earlier that afternoon, another Indian scare meant the major heard the whole story of the calico ball when Mary joined him in the ambulance again.

At his request, she told the paymaster some favorite longhouse stories and answered his questions about life on the still-shrinking Seneca reservation. In turn he assured her that her relatives had almost nothing in common with western hostiles. She could have told him that earlier, when he chose not to share his ambulance. She decided the paymaster was better informed now, and she could be charitable.

Mary also arrived at an unexpected personal judgment. The only daughter with three older brothers, she had been raised by doting parents. Perhaps, just perhaps, she had been spoiled as much as Victoria Masterson. Perhaps it was time to grow up and face the fact that while she did not live in a perfect world, she could whine less about her own lot in life.

And so Major Pettigrew had given her a courtly bow at the depot and told Sergeant Blade to take care of "this charming little lady."

"You made a friend, charming lady," Rowan teased as they watched the train leave. He glanced at Mary. "I feared you would hop the train and head East yourself, and how could I ever explain that to my superiors?"

"I thought about it," she told him as they walked back to the troopers holding their horses. "I promised Mama I would weather out six months." She had to smile. "I find it singularly amusing that during a short jaunt to Cheyenne I became a 'charming little lady.'"

Sergeant Blade laughed at that as they rode along together. He sent the rest of the troop through to Fort Russell with the corporal. His face changed to the more serious expression she also knew. "I wish that all of us out here, white and Indian alike, had the luxury of such a discovery. Until that happens . . . Follow my lead here, if you will, and trust me not to be a scoundrel."

Mary mulled over his words as he dismounted in front of the Plainsmen Hotel and helped her down. Sergeant Blade escorted her into the lobby, calmly signed the register as Sergeant and Mrs. Rowan Blade, then handed her the single room key after the clerk finished and before her blushing confusion subsided.

"I didn't want to chance the clerk getting all huffy about Blue Eye and denying you a room," he said quietly. "It's a serviceable falsehood, and after all, unlike our major, he hasn't had the benefit of your company, has he? I'll meet you in the dining room over there at eight tomorrow morning, and we will scavenge the dry goods stores in town."

"I must pay you for the room," Mary said, and opened her purse.

"Captain Hayes already did," Rowan said. "He told me to make certain you had safe accommodations in Cheyenne. It was his contribution to this bit of female silliness, I believe was how he put it." He leaned toward her, a surprising conspirator. "Captain Hayes is, unlike his wife, not a foolish person." He put a forefinger to his forage cap. "Until tomorrow, Miss Blue Eye."

Sergeant Blade wasn't a man to argue with, so she didn't try. Maybe he was right in camouflaging her and protecting her behind his own name. The clerk appeared none the wiser, and must have thought they were married. She could think about Rowan's Gordian Knot way of solving a problem later, perhaps when she was riding home to New York on that eastbound train.

If that was still her plan. During a solitary dinner and then a peaceful evening in a pleasant room, Mary thought about Major Pettigrew. He hadn't apologized for his bigotry, but the major had changed. So had she. How much, she wasn't certain. As she drifted off to sleep, Mary Blue Eye considered that the answer to her question wouldn't be discovered if she ran back home when times were tough.

· 7 ·

MAMA HAD WARNED her that when it came to shopping, men were never the best companions. Mary made an exception for Sergeant Blade, who arrived promptly at eight o'clock in time for breakfast, which he admitted was his second one of the day, and better tasting than the first.

A waiter appeared when the sergeant sat down. After a brief negotiation, the man hurried away and returned promptly with two fried eggs, a mound of bacon, and toast.

"I could eat breakfast all day," he told Mary as he tucked in.

Mary smiled at him, thinking about this odd situation, sharing breakfast with an amiable man, who, if she gauged the admiring glances of female diners properly, was someone to look at once or twice.

Maybe it was the impeccable cut of his uniform, or possibly his excellent posture, acquired through years in the saddle. He had a satisfying tan just starting to fade with the changing of the season. Mary decided that it should be against the law for any man except a trooper to wear a moustache that drooped at the corners. She glanced around and saw no other man with shoulders so broad. She thought Rowan's face a little thin, but that seemed to be coin of the realm in the cavalry.

Knowing it was too much to hope he would go with her to pick out fabric, Mary felt generous enough to provide an exit, should he want one. "You needn't accompany me from store to store," she said cautiously. "Mama warned me about men and shopping."

That earned a hearty laugh from her dining companion. "Mary, I am made of sterner stuff than that," he assured her. "If you don't ask me to select a hat for you, or ask my opinion on something related to women's finery, we will manage."

"Very well, sir." She could laugh inside about that artless comment. Indians were good at laughing inside.

"Besides, I have commandeered the ambulance. How were *you* planning to haul enough fabric for fifteen dresses?"

She hadn't thought of that. "Did you commandeer a driver, too?"

"I did. He is in the ambulance, currently sleeping off a prodigious drunk."

"I probably should draw a curtain over this conversation, shouldn't I?"

"Perhaps. Let us say that when he wakes up and discovers he is not in the guardhouse, he will thank me." He touched her hand. "And *that* is the secret to leadership."

Cheyenne's Fifteenth Street featured more saloons than dry goods stores, but the sergeant shepherded his charge past still-shuttered bars to the quieter cross streets away from the depot. As if ready to spar with each other, the Cheyenne Mercantile Emporium and the less abundantly named Wyoming Dry Goods faced each other across a wide dirt street.

"Coin toss?" Rowan asked.

"Wyoming Dry Goods," Mary told him. "I have a good feeling about it."

Inside a cool interior featuring the tang of dried herring mixed with hair oil, the sergeant nodded approvingly. "I suppose ladies have an instinct about these things. I bow to your superior knowledge."

Her choice of stores was only the merest luck, but he didn't need to know that. They stood in front of a shelf boasting at least seven different fabric colors and designs. It was still a far cry from what she might have chosen from back home, but this was Wyoming Territory and not New York.

A dapper man in a white shirt and canvas apron, with a tape measure draped around his neck stood behind the counter. Mary felt herself leaning back as he looked her over, found her massively wanting, ignored her, and turned his attention to Sergeant Blade. Maybe she *didn't* have an instinct about Wyoming Dry Goods after all.

She knew what the sergeant would do before he did it, which nearly brought tears to her eyes. He casually put his arm around Mary's shoulders and drew her close to his side. "My wife and I have been sent to buy fabric for a calico ball at Fort Laramie," he said. "How many yards per dress, my dear?"

"Ten," she said calmly, as if Sergeant Blade spoke to her that way from dawn to dusk. Peace covered her right down to her soul. "The fabric is thirty-six inches wide?"

"Yes, ma'am," the clerk said promptly, after a quick look at the sergeant, who had leveled him with the same stare Mary had noticed Rowan use when leading particularly inept recruits through equitation on the parade ground.

Rowan released her and tapped his knuckles lightly on the counter, which seemed to unnerve the clerk. *You've made your point*, Mary thought, amused. "I can manage now, Rowan," she said. "We could probably use a sack or two of peppermints. I think your troopers have earned it, don't you?"

"Mary, you're a wonder," he said. "Good thing we brought you along." He tapped the counter again, once and hard. The clerk dropped the tape measure. "If you have any difficulty, my dear, just sing out." He walked toward the front of the store, looking back twice, which made the now totally unmanned clerk gulp audibly.

"He likes to make certain I have good service," she told the clerk. "Ten yards of each of these calicos, and then I'll need thread and boning."

Mary doubted any female patron in Wyoming Dry Goods had ever received such excellent service. They had similar luck across the street at the more grandiose Mercantile Emporium, once the sergeant established his connection with Mary Blue Eye in a way that no one would dream of questioning.

"I believe we are done," Mary said, after a lengthy time watching another terrified clerk measure and cut. "I imagine that will come as a relief to you."

"Not necessarily," Rowan said as he picked up the twine-tied bundle of fabric as if it weighed nothing, and counterbalanced it with the fabric he already carried from Wyoming Dry Goods. "Did you find some calico for yourself?"

"I never even considered that I would be dancing, too," Mary said when they stood on the street. She took a long look at all the fabric. "I wager I will be sewing dresses right up to the ball itself. No time."

He set down both heavy parcels. "That won't do. May I escort you to the ball?"

"*Me?*"

The sergeant looked around elaborately. "I don't know anyone else on this street."

"I never thought . . ."

He picked up the bundles, then set them down again, as

if he had arrived at some momentous decision. He put his hands on her shoulders. "I watched you on that first day of the trip to Fort Laramie. I saw the excitement in your eyes. In the last few months I have watched it diminish. What happened to that little lady?"

"You've been watching me?"

"I watch everyone connected in any way with G Troop," he said. "Soldiers and dependents alike." Astounded, Mary watched the lift and fall of his shoulders. "I watch you with those silly wives. I know you are being taken advantage of, and there isn't anything I can do about it."

Why did he have to say that? Tears welled in her eyes and spilled down her cheeks. He pulled her close right there and let her babble into his overcoat about her tiresome and childish friend and the huge gulf between them now. Keeping her voice low, she raged against the realization that the officers' wives saw her as someone biddable who would sew and do all that was expected of her because she was an Indian and a servant.

"It's not just the officers' wives," she said. "The corporal's wife who cooks for the Mastersons gets her digs in, too, that I am lazy and ignorant."

Mary thought about that a moment, until her innate honesty took over. "She might be right. I should know more about cooking."

"Are you the youngest in your family?" he asked.

She nodded. "Youngest and the only daughter. I might have been spoiled a little."

"Perhaps, but nothing prepared you for . . . this."

"No," she said, and felt her frustration dribble away. Maybe proximity to a man disinclined to judge her was soothing the wound no one could see. "They don't know anything about me," she concluded, embarrassed now. She backed away and he let her go. Maybe it was time for her own confession.

"And do you know something else? I see the Indians at Fort Laramie, the ones called Laramie Loafers. I watch the Indian mothers begging with their eyes. I see them in rags, and I feel superior to them. I am not, am I?"

Sergeant Blade picked up the fabric, his face serious. "None of us are. That's why I hate my job, at times."

She touched his arm and gestured at the calico bundles he carried. "This calico would make a lot of dresses, aprons, and children's shirts for the sad people hanging about the fort. I ask myself, why not start charity at home?"

"That, my dear, is a question for the ages," he replied. "Why not? Wait here. I'm going to put this fabric in the ambulance, check on my driver, and take you one more place."

· 8 ·

MARY WAS AMAZED that he wanted anything to do with her, after she had cried all over his greatcoat and made a spectacle of herself. She looked around cautiously, happy to see no one else on the street except two cowboys arguing in front of one of the saloons, and an old dog scratching himself and looking supremely indifferent.

"Where are we going?" she asked when he returned from the ambulance and offered his arm.

"There's a dressmaker I know . . ."

"You know a dressmaker?" Was this man always going to surprise her?

"Her brother was a corporal in the Tenth Cavalry, a Negro regiment," he said as they walked along. "I taught him to read, and he made sergeant. My Fifth and his Tenth were garrisoned at Fort Davis in Texas."

"He couldn't *read*?"

"Mary, he spent the first twenty years of his life as a slave on a Louisiana plantation. Reading was against the law."

"At least that never happened to Indians," she said.

"He came up to me one morning after guard mount and

asked me if I would teach him. Said his lieutenant told him he could make sergeant if he could read the manual of arms, call roll, and fill out reports."

"Why did he ask you?"

Mary watched the color rise from the sergeant's neck to bloom on his face. "It can't be that embarrassing, Rowan."

"Maybe not to you . . . He said I had a kind face, and there weren't too many of those at Fort Davis," Rowan said, after taking his turn to look around. "A sergeant with a kind face . . . I didn't know what to say. Well, except yes, of course I would help him. And I did. He's a first sergeant now. His sister used to live with him before she married a railroad man."

He appeared disinclined to say more, which suited Mary well enough. It was still before noon, and she had already examined her motives and character in light of the uncomfortable reality that she was probably as spoiled, in her own way, as Victoria Masterson, and also sadly lacking. Why Sergeant Blade continued to be so kind to her was a question for the ages.

One short block and one more took them nearly out of Cheyenne. Rowan stopped in front of a modest clapboard house with a sign in the front window: *Mrs. William Washington, Dressmaker.*

"Sukey told me that she wrote *Modiste* first, but no one in Cheyenne knew what that was," Sergeant Blade told Mary. "This is more of a dressmaker kind of town." He knocked on the door, listened, then opened it and ushered her inside.

Mary looked around in delight at the neat-as-a-pin parlor on one side and the business side with its cutting table, Singer, and mannequin wearing a dress she would happily commit a felony to own, if she thought she could get away with it.

"My goodness, but I want that dress," she told Rowan,

who laughed, then swept off his forage cap when a tall, supremely elegant black woman came into the room, tape measure around her neck, shears in her hand, and a smile of welcome on her face.

"Sukey Washington, are you ever going to look a day over twenty?" he asked, by way of greeting. "And where is that useless husband who should protect you from scoundrels like me?"

The dressmaker laughed. "Sergeant Blade, he's down at the railyard, and you know precisely how old I am!" she exclaimed. "My goodness, did you finally do the wise thing and marry?"

I won't look at him, I won't look at him, Mary told herself as her own face turned rosy enough for two people.

Sukey Washington glanced from Rowan to Mary and back. She rolled her eyes. "Forgive me, then, for assuming, but who is this lovely lady?"

That was all the impetus the sergeant needed to draw a deep breath and move right along. "This is Miss Mary Blue Eye. We have quite a story to tell, haven't we, Mary?"

If she lived to be eighty, Mary knew she would never forget the sweetness that was Sukey Washington. After enduring months now of wary looks and second glances as people wondered just who and what she was, this dark woman gazed at her with no guile and no hesitation.

"Blue Eye. What a beautiful name," she said.

"I have always thought so," Mary replied, then couldn't help herself. "At least until I came out West. It's kind of hard here." And then she horrified herself by bursting into tears again.

Feeling helpless and stupid, Mary turned for the door. She could wait outside while the sergeant visited with his friend. Why was she so foolish?

She got no farther than the thought.

"My goodness." Sukey Washington put her arms around Mary. "It's not easy, is it?"

"I don't mean to be a baby," Mary said when she could speak. Sukey was soft and comfortable, and she never wanted to move. "I'm tired of people looking at me. I really don't want to sew fifteen dresses, even though I have to." She stepped away. "Here I am telling you this when you already know how it is. I'm sorry. Forgive me."

Sukey pulled her close again. "A hurt is a hurt. I also wish people could see the me that I see."

Mary nodded. *The me that I see*, she thought. *Yes, that's it.*

She blew her nose and felt herself in control, even if too immature to be seen around grown-ups. "Let me wait outside while you visit with Sergeant Blade. I'm sorry I was so childish."

"Stay here," Rowan said. "I wanted to say hello, but also to ask Sukey if she has any calico."

"We already have what we need," Mary reminded him.

"But no fabric for you. I still want you to go to the calico ball with me."

Oh dear, he hadn't forgotten. "I have too many dresses to sew, Sergeant. Thank you, though, for the invitation."

"What do you have here?" he asked Sukey, obviously intending to ignore Mary.

"Follow me."

He did and motioned for Mary to come too. She shook her head, and he gave her what was probably a kinder version of The Stare.

"Very well, although I do not have time to sew." She might have been a cricket chirping on the hearth, for all the attention he paid.

Still, a lovely bolt of cloth caught her eye, one of five equally lovely ones stacked next to more expensive fabrics. She couldn't help her sigh of appreciation.

How strange that the sergeant pointed to the same bolt. Sukey pulled it out from between two others and carried it into the front room. She stretched out two yards, then looked from Mary to the material and back.

"I wouldn't have thought this, but dark blue with white polka dots is perfect for your complexion," Sukey said. She held up the fabric to Mary's face. "And black hair? My dear, you were born to wear this."

Sergeant Blade was reaching in his back pocket. Mary stopped him, her hand on his arm.

"You will not pay for this, Sergeant Blade," Mary said, and gave him what she hoped was an approximation of The Stare. "I will."

Their stare-down lasted a few seconds, and she won. He held his hands up.

Her eyes lively, Sukey named a price. Mary said, "Ten yards," and handed over her own money.

"I personally hope that was your train fare back East money," he whispered in Mary's ear while Sukey cut the fabric, humming to herself.

"I'm keeping my ticket money safe," Mary replied, flattered that it mattered to him.

"You know you'll miss me," he teased.

I believe I will, she thought.

"You'll let me carry your purchase, Miss Blue Eye?" the sergeant asked most formally, humor in his eyes, too, once they were on the street again, after tea with Sukey Washington and sandwiches to take along.

"Certainly you may," Mary replied. She took a deep breath. "And yes, I will go to the calico ball with you."

· 9 ·

THE AMBULANCE STAYED behind at Fort Russell and was replaced by a wagon containing mainly requisitioned supplies. Rowan wrapped the formidable mound of fabric for the calico ball in burlap and set it next to Mary's valise and bedroll, made from three of the pile of army blankets requisitioned for Fort Laramie.

Sergeant Blade tried to politely talk her out of riding sidesaddle, citing blustery weather and the hint of snow. She said it would take more than that to coop her up into a supply wagon with kegs of dried beef, red paint in tins, and surprisingly, even more dried raisins.

He finally shared news Mary didn't want to hear. "A patrol in this morning from Fort Fetterman crossed a big trail of Indian ponies headed north. I'd rather you stayed in the wagon."

Mary knew better than to argue. He added that the troopers had noticed the straight lines denoting travois, which usually meant women and children.

"It's no raiding party, Mary."

"Maybe we can give them some of the raisins," she joked.

"The logic here, Miss Smarty, is to cut a low profile and avoid what looks like a sizeable party, even if they aren't bent on raiding," he said. "The wagon for you."

"And if we surprise them by accident?"

"You're determined to worry, aren't you?"

"I like to know where I stand."

"If we surprise them, it won't be pretty," he admitted. "Trust me to keep you safe."

Maybe a joke would help. "You'd better, because I have fifteen dresses to make."

"Sixteen. Don't forget yours," Rowan reminded her.

Mary made herself comfortable by adding a few blankets to her stash in the wagon. Someone had put in a pile of newspapers, the *Chicago Tribune* among them, probably intended for enlisted men's day rooms and officers with subscriptions. She fished out the Tribs and settled in for a day reading about the Great Chicago Fire, as it was already being called, along with "One for the history books," and "A conflagration such as we have never seen, and we have seen a lot."

She spent the afternoon reading through pages of first-person accounts of the "raging inferno unequalled in all the annals of the United States," shaking her head over loss of life and stories of families searching for children unaccounted for and hotheads ready to lynch all Irishmen because of Mrs. O'Leary's cow. Sukey Washington's sandwiches went down with ease, and so did the handful of raisins Mary knew no sharp-eyed commissary clerk would miss.

She had just started an article detailing what the various churches were doing to relieve the suffering poor when she heard Sergeant Blade holler, "Close up, men, we're in for it."

The teamster turned to her. "Head down," he ordered. "Hang on."

From the time she was small, her parents had taught her

instant obedience. Her college-educated father had apologized for the lesson. "Nothing more will ever happen here to our Seneca Nation because it has all been done to us," he had told her. "Even then, my father so taught me, and his father before him, going back and back. When someone tells you to obey, you obey."

"Nëga:je:" Mary heard Papa speak to her from that corner of her mind called Seneca wisdom, the one she hadn't visited much. She sank to the wagon bed. "I will try," she repeated in English as she wedged herself between two kegs.

After trundling down and up through what she thought must be the Chugwater to the opposite bank, they headed on a run toward a higher point, then stopped with a lurch. She heard the teamster set the brake, then leap into the wagon bed with her. He rested his Sharps carbine against the wagon seat he had just vacated.

"Doing okay, missy?" he asked, his eyes forward on what, mercifully, she could not see.

"Doing okay," she echoed.

She heard horses close to the wagon and the creak of leather as men dismounted. "What is happening?" she asked the driver, hoping she didn't sound as frightened as she felt.

"There aren't enough of us to allow one in four to hold the horses while the rest of the troopers dismount and fight," he explained, then stopped to squeeze off a shot. "They've tied the horses to the wagon wheels. Glad I set the brake."

Another shot. A gasp. The murmur of voices. Sobbing and then silence. Her nerves tuned like fine wire, Mary heard someone fiddle with the canvas at the back of the wagon and flinched as the tailgate dropped.

"Help me, Casey."

She knew the sergeant's voice, marveling that he sounded so calm. "Can I help, too?" she asked.

"You can. We're handing in a wounded man. Casey will pull him toward you. Do what you can to stop the bleeding."

She waited for the teamster to crawl toward the bleeding trooper that Rowan pushed inside as gently as he could, considering.

"Degadënö:nyöh," she said.

"Come again?" Rowan asked.

"Just thanking my parents for teaching me things they thought I would never need," she told him.

"And I thank them, too," the sergeant said. "Keep your head down. We'll get through this." He slammed up the tailgate and jerked down the canvas.

The trooper stared at her with frightened eyes. Mary could not remember his name, or if she even knew it. "Your name?"

"Will Lemaster," he said. "Can you help me?"

"I will do my best."

Casey had returned to his crouch by the wagon seat. Will tugged himself closer to her, using his elbows because his left leg seemed useless. Mary saw the blood pooling under the fleshy part of his thigh, if troopers even had fleshy parts.

"Damn but I wish it had been an arrow. They don't bleed so much at first," he said. "Can you cut off my trousers above the shot hole?"

His question jolted her into motion. Mary opened her valise and took out her cutting shears. Thank goodness she had brought them along to Cheyenne. Like a typical Easterner, she hadn't trusted a town as raw and ungainly as Cheyenne to have any such thing.

She did her best not to cause him any pain, and Will did his best not to do more than suck in his breath when she did. Her fingers were soon slippery with the trooper's blood as she cut off the trouser leg and pulled it away.

"I don't think the ball went all the way through," she said.

The trooper grimaced. "A surgeon's going to need to probe around. Right now, stop the bleeding. I can only lose so much."

She looked with some longing at the pile of fabric that others had paid for, then returned to her valise, where she took out the beautiful dark-blue material with polka dots she had paid for a few hours ago.

She reminded herself she was leaving in January, and seriously, where would she have found the time to make that dress at all? Mary cut into the length of the material, moved the shears steadily up two yards, then cut across. Moving deliberately, her hands steady now, she folded the strip over and over until she had a respectable pad.

Another few snips and she cut more of the lovely fabric. She placed the pad over the wound weeping blood. "Hold it there," she ordered.

He did as she said, fear gone from his face. Heavens, the man must have thought she knew what she was doing.

"Hold it tight as I start the wrap," she said.

He did. After wiping her hands on her skirt, Mary wrapped the strip around the pad and his thigh until it was bound up neatly, with maximum pressure on the pad. If this didn't work, she couldn't think of anything else except a tourniquet, which even she knew would mean eventual amputation.

"Let's hope it works, Will," she said. "I've pretty well exhausted my skills."

Mary picked up the canteen Sergeant Blade must have left for her or Will and dipped another hunk of her material in it. She swabbed at the wagon bed until it was less bloody and set the brown paper down that had wrapped the fabric.

"If you can scoot onto this, it will tell us if the bandage is working," she said. "I'll help you."

She made him as comfortable as she could, with his head propped against a bag of cornmeal, then covered him with an army blanket. "It's the best I can do right now," she said. "I wish it were more."

The private leaned back with a sigh. "All things considered, Miss Blue Eye, I'm fine."

She smiled at that. "You're a liar, Will, but thank you."

"No, it's the truth," he insisted. "Just hold my hand now and then, and I'll be the envy of the entire Fifth Cavalry."

He honestly looked as though he meant it. Mary felt herself relaxing. There wouldn't have been time to make a dress for herself anyway, and this was more important. She poured a tin cup of water from the canteen and held it to his lips, because bravado aside, his hands shook. Hers were remarkably steady. Mama would be impressed. When he finished, he sighed again and closed his eyes. "Wake me up if you need any help," he joked.

She laughed, which made Casey, still kneeling by the wagon seat, look at her in surprise. He shook his head and turned his gaze outward again.

She sat beside the sleeping private and held his hand as the firing diminished and finally stopped. Obedient to the order from Sergeant Blade and from her own caution, she waited.

"Mary? Is he still alive? How're you?"

"We're fine."

Funny thing was, they were. A most pleasant feeling had shouldered aside her apprehension. For the first time in her admittedly cosseted and comfortable life, she felt useful and needed, with the sleeping trooper not remotely concerned that she was at least some part Indian and young. It was a pleasant sensation, and she wanted more of it.

Her euphoria disappeared when Sergeant Blade threw

back the canvas and dropped the tailgate again. He carried a young Sioux with his upper arm crooked at a strange angle.

"Ready to tackle another project?" Rowan asked, as casually as if he were commenting on the weather. "He fell off his horse. He's not too happy."

· 10 ·

"He says his name is Smooth Stone, or something like that," Rowan told her as he stood there. "Obviously he's having some trouble with sign language at the moment, what with one arm bent out of shape."

He peered into the wagon. "How's Private Lemaster doing?"

"Well enough, I think. I made a strong pad for the wound and bound it tight, but he needs a surgeon."

"We'll get him one. Help me with Mr. Smooth Stone, who I don't think is a day over twelve, if that." He sighed. "Bring along more of your fabric. We have some scrapes and nicks to bandage."

Will opened his eyes when she released his hand. She took a moment to lift the blanket and check the brown paper. No stains, which relieved her heart and mind. "I have to help someone else," she told him. "Go back to sleep."

"I'll watch Will." The teamster leaned his carbine against the wagon seat. "Don't think he'll want to hold my hand, though."

The rest of her own material in hand and holding the

shears, Mary let the corporal help her from the wagon. She leaned into the wagon for another blanket and spread it on the ground for the sergeant to deposit his burden, who looked none too pleased.

To call him twelve years old was generous. Mary would have thought closer to ten. "You're a little young to be doing this," she told him.

"Wasichu. Wasichu," Smooth Stone said.

Mary looked at Rowan and shrugged.

"I think he wants to know if you are white," Sergeant Blade said. He looked over his shoulder. "Private McIntyre, front and center."

Private McIntyre came forward, his hand against his head, blood on his fingers. "Thought I was just going to feel the whistle as the bullet passed, but it took a little detour, Sarge." He sounded apologetic that he hadn't leaped out of the way.

"How's your Sioux, Private?"

"Not bad, Sarge," McIntyre said cheerfully. "It'll get better once the little lady lets me have a strip of that material. Pretty stuff."

"Yes, isn't it?" Sergeant Blade said drily. "Sorry, Mary."

"At this point, I don't care," she said and ripped off a strip. "Sit down. I can do this better than you."

With a glance at Rowan, who nodded, Private McIntyre sat down. Practiced now in the art of medical improvisation, Mary dabbed the bullet furrow with water, then bandaged the private's head, with the knot over the wound for best pressure. "That should do until something better comes along," she said. She looked back at Smooth Stone, who waited more or less patiently because he didn't have much choice.

"Can you tell him that I am an Indian?"

"I'll show you how to sign it," McIntyre said. Despite

what she suspected was a massive headache, he seemed to be enjoying himself.

He showed her, rubbing the back of his left hand twice with his right hand. Smooth Stone added some commentary of his own.

"He wants to know what nation."

Her nation. *I have a nation, same as Smooth Stone*, she thought. *The Keepers have traveled the path of the white man longer than the Sioux. Whether that is good or bad, who can tell?*

"My nation," she said softly. "Private, tell him I am a Keeper of the Western Door." Pride filled her heart. "Tell him I live very far away from here, to the place where the sun rises."

"Your wish is my command," McIntyre said and signed her message. "Don't know what he understands, because I'm not so good."

"Better than I," she said. Once back home, she would improve her education. The Seneca let their women speak and make decisions. She could ask to learn more and not be ignored.

When Private McIntyre finished, Smooth Stone reached out his good hand and touched Mary's hand. He said something, and she looked at McIntyre.

"'Cure,' as near as I can translate it."

"Tell him I'll do my best."

"You tell him. It's like this."

She watched the trooper, then signed. The boy closed his eyes.

"Better tell him it might hurt," she added.

"He knows that."

"I'll help you, Mary," Rowan said. "Private, get Casey to find sticks about eighteen inches long. I signed a bill of lading for window shades, so he should find some slats inside those."

Rowan ran his hand along the odd-shaped upper arm as the boy steeled himself. Gently he manipulated the area where the bone digressed from its usual path. Mary pressed her hand against Smooth Stone's chest.

"It's bent for certain, but it's not snapped off completely," Rowan said. "I think I can realign it."

Mary touched the boy's face and looked deep into eyes much like her own. His stoicism vanished, but she saw no fear. "I want to be this brave someday."

"You already are," Rowan said. "Maybe you needed a reminder. Here goes."

It was over quickly. Smooth Stone tensed and gasped, and Mary tightened her grip. He lapsed into unconsciousness long enough for Sergeant Blade to probe a bit, then nod. Rowan cut Casey's window slats and held the boy's arm as Mary ripped off more strips of her beautiful calico and bound the arm and the improvised splint from shoulder to elbow.

Smooth Stone opened his eyes and looked at his arm. He raised it tentatively and nodded. Sergeant Blade signed, and he nodded again. Mary took another length of fabric and made a sling. Smooth Stone sat up so she could circle it around his neck and secure his forearm inside.

"We need to get him back to his people, and then I am riding for the surgeon," Rowan said. "We're much closer to Fort Russell than Laramie, and I want the surgeon to see to Private Lemaster."

"That sounds too dangerous," Mary said.

"I would have agreed, if Smooth Stone hadn't fallen off his horse and landed, so to speak, in your lap." He touched her shoulder. "Do you feel brave?" He leaned closer. "There's really only one answer, oh Keeper of the Western Door."

"Since you put it that way, yes, I feel brave," she told him, even though she didn't, not at all.

"We'll ride him back to his people. I doubt they've gone far."

"That sounds terrifying."

"Less than you think. I have no idea who Smooth Stone's parents are, but they'll be happy to see him."

"Certainly they will," Mary said. "Perhaps Private McIntyre could come along, too, if we need to say something. Would he mind?"

"You forget who he works for," Rowan said with a smile. "It'll be an order."

"Why doesn't this frighten you?" she asked.

"They weren't a war party. We surprised them, which I was afraid might happen. I believe they're Brulé, heading north to Spotted Tail's Whetstone Agency, because winter is coming."

Rowan clapped his arm around Mary's shoulder, then turned her toward the supply wagon. "Check on Private Lemaster, if you please, and pull on your riding boots." He gestured to Private McIntyre. "Tell Smooth Stone we are returning him to his people."

· 11 ·

MARY PULLED ON her riding boots, her eyes on Private Lemaster, who smiled faintly and returned to the half doze of a wounded man.

She stopped Casey before he swung her down from the wagon. "We should probably bring along gifts. If you don't think the army will be too upset with me, could you fill the pail with raisins? And please hand me the rest of my material and those shears."

She set the full pail beside the wagon and eyed the beautiful calico. She kept back three yards so she could change Private Lemaster's bandage, then folded the rest. Maybe Smooth Stone's mother could use it.

She let the sergeant throw her into the saddle again, then waited while he tied the fabric to the saddle.

He swung into the saddle and held out his arms for Smooth Stone, handed up by Private McIntyre, who mounted his own horse. The sergeant wrapped Smooth Stone in an army blanket, careful not to jostle him.

"How do you know where to go?" Mary asked.

"I don't. I'm following the direction where they last fired on us," he said. "I can't help but think they haven't gone far."

They rode west through terrain that the teamster had earlier told her was perfect for buffalo and Indians. "You might think it's all level ground, but see how it dips," he had pointed out. "The whole Sioux Nation could probably hide here and we'd be none the wiser."

Down in one dip, up another, rinse and repeat, and then there they were, a gathering of Indians that made Mary suck in her breath and hope Sergeant Blade hadn't heard.

As they rode up out of the gully, a line of horsemen turned and faced them, effectively barring passage. Behind them she could make out horses pulling travois, and women with babies on their backs. She remembered that Mama still kept the beaded cradleboard into which she had popped a much younger Mary.

"It will be yours someday," Mama had said. At the time, Mary had politely refrained from shaking her head over old-fashioned ways in modern times. As she watched Lakota babies in their cradleboards, she knew she wanted that pretty thing now. It was practical and lovely, and a woman could carry her baby and have hands free for housework.

Smooth Stone was leaning forward now, straining toward his people. "We'll get you there, buddy," Sergeant Blade said.

Rowan kneed his horse ahead, and Mary and the private fell in behind. She held her breath as the warriors moved into a *v* shape and effectively funneled them toward the main body of the travelers. She heard the horses and riders closing the gap once they passed through.

One warrior came close enough to strike Sergeant Blade on his shoulder, then cup that same hand against Smooth

Stone's cheek. He smiled, and Mary let out the breath she had been holding.

"Imagine that. He just counted coup on me," Rowan told her. "Here goes."

He pulled back the army blanket so Smooth Stone's father could see his son's splinted arm and sling. "He fell pretty hard," Rowan said.

Private McIntyre started to translate, but the warrior held up his hand. "I understand," he said slowly, as if he were trying out his English for the first time in a while. "He is too young, but he argues. His mother wanted to kill me."

Sergeant Blade laughed at that, and the warrior smiled. Between the father and the sergeant, they lowered the boy carefully to the ground.

Rowan dismounted next, then held his arms out for Mary, who lifted her leg over the upper pommel and let him help her down. She touched Smooth Stone's shoulder. "He was very brave and did not cry out once," she said.

The warrior made no comment to her but turned at another sound. A woman had dismounted and pushed her way through the warriors. Mary tried not to smile as she shook her finger at Smooth Stone, said something succinct that needed no translation, then carefully pulled him close.

Mary glanced at Rowan, who watched the whole scenario with appreciation all over his face, mingled with relief.

"We should probably go now," the sergeant said. "You know, while the going's good."

Mary nodded. It was enough to see Smooth Stone back where he belonged and to get her first up close glimpse of the power and might of the Sioux. She wondered if her own people had once looked this way. Now the Seneca were farmers and clerks like her own father, living different lives. Again she felt a strong urge to know more about her own.

"I have gifts," she said to Rowan. She unhooked the pail from the saddle and untied the fabric from its binding. Gifts in hand, she held out the raisins to Smooth Stone's mother.

Mary handed her the fabric next, which made her eyes widen in appreciation. The woman smoothed down the fabric, then put it to her cheek. She held it up against Mary's face and took a good look. She spoke to her husband, who cleared his throat against more English.

"Woman asks, who are your people?"

"I am a daughter of the Keepers of the Western Door," she said, pointing east. "We are of the Iroquois League, many, many sleeps that way. I am Mary Blue Eye."

He nodded and told his wife, who came closer, pressed her forehead against Mary's, and looked into her eyes. She spoke to her husband, who laughed and said, "No blue."

"It is an old family name," Mary said. "I am proud of my people."

"Good for you, Mary," Rowan said. He looked around. "Let us see if we can extricate ourselves gracefully. Personally, I think Smooth Stone should stand in a corner for a while, if tipis had corners."

"Oh, you!"

"We need to leave, and you need to be on your way," Rowan told the warrior.

The father held up his hand to stop them because his wife was whispering to him with some energy. He answered and she hurried away.

"Now we wait," he said.

Did nothing faze Sergeant Blade? Looking as casual as if the warrior sat in a parlor chatting about the weather, he asked, "Are you going toward Spotted Tail's camp?"

"We are. The winter moon comes soon." The warrior gestured overhead and made the obvious sign for birds. "In the moon of green leaves, we will return to seek buffalo."

"May you have good hunting," Sergeant Blade said. "Look, Mary."

Smooth Stone's mother had returned quietly. Shy, head down, she held out a small deerskin pouch on a leather cord. She gestured for Mary to bend down.

Mary did as she asked, and the woman put the pouch around her neck. Mary admired the quillwork on the small bag. "How do I sign 'thank you'?" she whispered to Rowan.

He showed her, and she made the sign. "What is it for?" she asked Smooth Stone's father.

"Good medicine," he said. "Thank you for my son." His voice hardened. "The Crow or Arikara would not have brought him back."

The warrior turned away and mounted his horse. His wife walked alongside him, her hand firmly on Smooth Stone's neck. The other warriors followed, and soon the three of them were alone again.

"They just vanish," Mary said.

Sergeant Blade helped her into the saddle. She breathed deep of the deerskin and touched the buttery softness of the pouch.

"What's my good medicine?" she asked Rowan.

"Whatever makes you happy," he replied and mounted.

They rode back to their makeshift bivouac in silence. Private McIntyre peeled off to join the other troopers standing by a fire. Mary smelled coffee.

"I'm taking two troopers with me to Fort Russell," he told her, after helping her down. "There might be cloth blown into Private Lemaster's wound. The surgeon will take him back to Russell and probe around a bit. He doesn't need an infection."

"But . . . but . . . you don't know that those Indians will not hang around here and try again," she said. He couldn't be seriously thinking of leaving them.

"They are not going to bother us," he said. "Don't worry, Mary. My corporal is in charge, and I have taught him everything I know."

"It's not me. What about *you*? Can't you send someone else for the surgeon?"

He seemed genuinely surprised at her concern. "What kind of a leader would that make me? Hey, don't worry."

He prepared to mount again, then stopped and looked down at his uniform. She had noticed earlier that one of his brass buttons was starting to dangle on its thread. As she watched, he worked the button loose, leaned close to open the pouch around her neck, and dropped it in.

"It's only twenty miles. Think of me, Keeper of the Western Door, and I'll be safe."

· 12 ·

Private Lemaster appeared to be sound asleep in the wagon, so Mary indulged in a bout of quiet tears as the three soldiers rode away. She touched the pouch, then rubbed it against her cheek and stowed it out of sight inside her shirtwaist.

"Miss Blue Eye, we have some hardtack and sow belly. Do you want to eat it in the wagon?"

"I'll be right out," she whispered to the corporal, so as not to wake the sleeping private. Lemaster startled her by opening his eyes.

He grinned at her and said, "Shhh."

She ate quickly by the fire, happy to warm her hands around a tin cup of mashed hardtack and bacon, with a sprinkle of salt. It tasted better than she thought it would.

She took a similar tin cup to Private Lemaster, who grimaced and rose up on one elbow to eat. He shook his head over more than three spoonfuls, wanting water instead. He drank with his eyes closed and her arm under his neck. "That'll do," he said finally. She laid his head back on the cornmeal sack, and he sighed. She didn't want to alarm him, so she said nothing about the flush on his cheeks and his warmth.

She moved slightly, mostly to make herself more comfortable, but he must have thought she was leaving. He put his hand out to stop her, and she held it. He *was* warm.

"I'm staying here," she said. "I wish I could make you some chicken soup. My mother calls it the white man's elixir."

He smiled at that, but just barely. "I've thought about reenlisting, because my five is almost up, but by golly, I miss Maine."

"Five years for one enlistment?"

"Yep."

"Sergeant Blade has two stripes on his sleeve. Does that mean ten years?" she asked, curious.

"Yep. He started pretty young in the war and stayed in. I think he's about due to reenlist." He closed his eyes. "Said he's been thinking about getting out."

"What would he do?"

He opened his eyes at her question. "My word, oh, wait, you haven't been here in the spring, have you?"

And I won't be, either, she thought. "What does he do in the spring?"

"Anytime there is an extra-duty detail that involves building or making cabinets, Sarge gets put in charge of the extra-duty men. Doesn't matter where we are—Fort Davis, Fort Abercrombie, Fort Shaw . . ." His voice trailed off, then came back. "He can build anything." His eyes closed and he slept this time.

Her worry grew as his fever mounted. The corporal brought her more water, and she continued to wipe Will Lemaster's face and neck. She wanted to check under his bandage but contented herself with touching the lovely calico she had wound around his thigh. It was dry, and there was no fresh blood on the brown paper underneath. She would have done more if she had known what to do, even as she admitted to herself she had nothing to do anything with. Rowan had been right to ride for the surgeon.

The one bright spot in the long afternoon came at dusk. She heard horses approaching and sat up, thinking that somehow the surgeon at Fort Russell had got the message through mental telepathy and rushed on ahead. That was stupid, but she indulged herself because she was Mary Blue Eye and never minded laughing at herself.

"Mary . . . Miss Blue Eye . . . come out now," she heard the corporal call.

She climbed out of the wagon and stared up at Smooth Stone's mother and father. "Hello," she said, not afraid.

"Hello you," the warrior said. "Shell gives this." His wife handed down a parfleche even more beautiful than the one Lieutenant Masterson wanted to hang on the wall in their quarters, though Victoria wouldn't allow it. "Take."

She took, and it was heavy. She opened it and saw a large hunk of meat wrapped in what looked like deerskin, so it would not drip on the parfleche.

"Good food," the warrior signed, hand straight out from his heart, then fingers to his lips.

He handed down the empty pail. "Wait," Mary said and climbed back in the wagon. She scooped out more raisins, all the while thinking how good that meat would taste and what nice broth there would be for Private Lemaster. She held up the full pail to Shell, who took it with a smile.

Mary stepped back, her heart full, wishing she could say something to them, or sign something. To her further surprise, Shell leaned down and handed her one elk tooth. She pantomimed for Mary to put it in her medicine pouch.

Mary pulled the pouch from her shirtwaist and dropped

in the elk tooth. On a whim, she took out Sergeant Blade's brass button and showed Shell, who put her hand to her mouth, her eyes lively. She spoke to her husband.

"Good man blue coat," he said. "Put your blanket around him."

She nodded, fully aware what he meant because she remembered a longhouse story told when Mama thought she slept. Mary stood beside the wagon until her benefactors were out of sight, then handed the meat to the corporal, who whistled and exclaimed, "No sow belly tonight, men!" He bowed elaborately. "With your permission, Miss Blue Eye."

"You have it," she said, her heart so full that the good feeling seeped into her soul, too, where she needed it even more. "Save some broth for Private Lemaster, if you please."

Will ate a little, then shook his head. One of the connoisseurs in G Troop told Mary it was elk meat, as good as any *he* ever ate. "You have some friends there, Miss Blue Eye," the private told her. She saw respect in his eyes and friendship, all she ever wanted.

After Casey saw to Private Lemaster's basic needs, Mary climbed back into the wagon and stayed the night by his side, holding his hand, praying, dozing when she could, and wiping his face. He never complained. When daybreak came and she heard what sounded like a wagon and a troop of horses, she closed her eyes in weariness and gratitude.

Mere minutes later, Captain Julius Patzki from Fort Russell introduced himself first like the Polish gentleman he was, then climbed into the wagon. He nodded to her, his eyes on his patient, lying as comfortable as Mary could make him. With her help, the surgeon peeled back the calico bandage.

"Lovely fabric, Miss Blue Eye," he said. "Sergeant Blade told me he picked it out. What talent in a sergeant."

Mary laughed. Why feel shy or reticent around a surgeon

as they crouched beside a grown man's bare leg? "It was intended for a calico ball," she said. "The ladies at Fort Laramie want to help the women rendered homeless by the Chicago Fire."

Maybe it was the way she said it. Papa had chided her once about her sly humor. Captain Patzki sat back on his heels and gave her his attention. "I sense some skepticism."

"Captain, people need help right here."

"They do. I wish you all success in trying to convince some officers' wives of that," he said. He looked down at Private Lemaster. "I'm taking you back to Russell. I think there is some cloth festering in the wound, and I need to get it out." He patted the private's shoulder. "You'll feel better when I'm done."

"I'd feel braver if you came along," Lemaster told Mary.

"I wish I could, but if I don't get back to Fort Laramie and start sewing, things will get ugly with the wives of your commanding officers," she joked.

"Take good care of Sarge."

Her traitor face felt warm. "I think he can take care of himself."

"Not really." Private Lemaster closed his eyes.

Come to think of it, where was the sergeant? Mary got out of the wagon so two troopers carrying the stretcher could climb in. She looked around. No sergeant.

"Please, sir, where is Sergeant Blade?" she asked the surgeon, hoping to sound offhand and casual.

"He said he had some paperwork at the fort and then something to do in town." The surgeon turned to the corporal. "He told me you are to start out and he will catch up."

"But . . . but we were set upon by Indians only yesterday," Mary said. "Surely it isn't safe to just . . . just . . . go off and leave him."

"He told me about the Sioux. Miss Blue Eye, you are quite the asset. He also told me you would worry."

Tears filled her eyes, which probably would have startled any man except a surgeon. He touched her shoulder. "He didn't mention you would worry *that* much. He has two privates with him."

Captain Patzki turned his attention to his patient. "I promise to take good care of Private Lemaster," he told her over his shoulder, and she had to be content with that.

But she wasn't. All her mental lectures about being a little braver did her no good, and it must have showed on her face. In the middle of the afternoon, the corporal rode back by the supply wagon and took a look at her.

"He'll be around by the time we get to Hunton's," he promised.

"He had better," Mary replied. "He has no idea that the Iroquois League, of which I am a member, raised scalping to an art form."

The teamster she sat beside laughed so loud that the troopers riding ahead turned around and joined in the laughter, even if they hadn't heard her joke. It *was* funny. Mary laughed along with him and considered it another lesson learned. She would grow up one way or another.

• • •

Looking both tired and dirty, Sergeant Blade and the two privates showed up at Hunton's as the proprietor was passing a platter of fried chicken down the table.

"I was about ready to start gnawing on my left leg," the sergeant said to the corporal, who grinned at him and made space on the bench. "How are you, gents?"

His men chuckled and continued with the weighty business of chicken, canned green beans, and biscuits in front of them. "And you, Miss Mary Blue Eye?" he added. "I passed Captain Patzki, and he had nothing but compliments for your nursing and the calico bandage."

She wanted to smile and toss off a joke like the others, but there was no stopping the tears of relief that slid down her face. She bowed her head and let them fall quietly, another lesson learned from Mama. No Seneca ever made any noisy tears. Her tears dropped on the oilcloth in a suddenly silent room.

"I'm sorry. I was worried," she said simply, as she stared at the plate in front of her.

"Oh, Mary," was all the sergeant said.

· 13 ·

THE ROOM WAS too small. Mary excused herself and made a beeline for the back door. *You never have to leave New York again, once you get home,* she reminded herself. *Someone else can keep that western door.*

What a relief it was to step outside and take a deep breath of . . . corral. Mary shook her head at her own folly and walked around to the bench by the front entrance. She toed the spittoon out of sight under the bench and sat down, trying to pretend she was on her own front porch, snapping green beans with Mama.

Sergeant Blade was so quiet. She started when he sat down beside her, then turned her head away, embarrassed. "I really was worried for you," she said finally.

"I was, too," he admitted, "right up until Mrs. Shell gave you that medicine pouch."

She had to smile at that. Who wouldn't?

"Let me fill you in on Shell," Rowan said. "After I routed out Captain Patzki, I went to the barracks where I knew another troop of the Fifth was quartered. When I told Thad Mueller—he's another sergeant—about the whole experience and mentioned Smooth Stone and Shell, his eyes nearly bugged out."

"Why?"

"She's the favorite wife of His Pony, quite the warrior among the Brulé." He moved closer to her on the bench. "Rest assured that no one in that jolly band would have dreamed of bothering us further, not with Mr. and Mrs. His Pony on our side."

Mary produced a smile from somewhere, wondering if she could lean against his shoulder a little. She was tired of feeling alone and useful for nothing except for a minor talent in dressmaking.

She took a grand chance and leaned, which had the remarkable reflex of causing his arm to go around her shoulder as he pulled her closer. She took another chance and tipped her head against a suddenly available chest. It was just a small lean. He didn't have to think anything of it.

"I don't belong here," she said. "I'm tired of officers' wives convinced I am just another Indian in a dress and shoes, who maybe thinks she is higher in station than is legally allowed."

He chuckled at that. "Mary, they've never met anyone like you. I'll give them that, but just barely." He hesitated, as if he had his own doubts. "But you don't mind being here on this porch?"

She took another chance. "Not a bit."

He must have taken one, too, because Rowan Blade kissed her. She took another chance and kissed him back, wondering how it was that a body could feel so miserable a mere twenty seconds earlier and then feel *this* way.

The kiss came to a natural conclusion. He kept his face close to hers, which meant he was out of focus, blurry but reassuring. She knew down to her marrow that this was not a man to kiss and tease.

He sat back. "I haven't kissed a lady in ten years," he said. "My goodness, Mary Blue Eye. It's nice to feel human again."

"I've never kissed anyone before."

"Then you have a natural talent." He leaned against the bench but kept his arm around her. "I've complicated things, haven't I?"

She thought about his comment, thinking of the many times she had blurted out words that fell with a thud, and her father's patient reminder to think once, think twice, and then speak or don't. She was leaving Fort Laramie when her six months were up; she had fifteen dresses to make in two weeks; army life was never going to be to her taste. On the other hand, there was this man seated beside her.

"That remains to be seen, Rowan."

"Fair enough."

• • •

They pushed hard and arrived at Fort Laramie the next evening, just as a snowstorm of daunting proportions rolled in. Sergeant Blade helped her from her horse and walked her to the Mastersons' quarters, two troopers carrying the fabric and her valise.

Victoria Masterson opened the door, her face wreathed in smiles to see the fabric. She told the privates to set the fabric in the dining room. When they looked around, she frowned and jabbed her forefinger at that portion of the meager sitting room designated as the dining room.

Aren't we pretentious, Mary thought, and felt like a servant once more.

Sergeant Blade must have noticed how her face fell. He

moved closer and even stepped slightly in front of her, as if to shield her. The gesture was instinctive; she knew it.

"We had quite a return trip, Mrs. Masterson," he said. "Indians attacked, Mary tended a wounded man, and she gave away enough commissary raisins to placate a whole bunch of Brulé Sioux."

Victoria rolled her eyes. "As long as the fabric came through! No wonder Captain Hayes's wife said I should not go! Mary, we'll set up the sewing machine in the kitchen lean-to. I'm having a card party here tonight, and you would be in the way."

Humiliated, Mary walked Sergeant Blade to the porch as quickly as she could, because she saw the slow burn rising north from his uniform collar. "At least I don't have to sew outside," she joked. "Two weeks and I'll be done with those blasted dresses for a calico ball no one needs."

"I'd like to wring her neck," he said.

"That would land you in the guardhouse and then off to Fort . . . Fort somewhere."

"Leavenworth. I'm throwing you to the wolves, and I don't like it."

He stood on the porch, which meant she had to stand there, too, feeling more cheerful than he did, because she had realized something: Victoria Masterson had never been her friend. There was no point in thinking otherwise, so she needn't waste any more energy on the matter. Over and done.

"Rowan, let me tell you a longhouse story that my great-grandfather told me once when I was impatient about something I can't even remember now."

"A longhouse? You told me you live in a regular house."

"I do, but every year we travel to the longhouse, eat too much, laugh a lot, and listen to our elders tell stories. I have one for you: There was Spider, who spun a beautiful web. She would get it nearly completed, and bad-tempered Badger would break it and stomp away laughing. She began again, and the same thing happened. Over and over, she worked on her web, each part more lovely than the time before." She folded her hands in front of her. "That is the end of the story."

"That's no ending," the sergeant argued.

"It is if you are an Indian. She persisted, and so must I."

He squeezed her hand. "I'll think about that story."

Mary watched him cross the parade ground, head down against the snow, with that purposeful stride she had become accustomed to. He stood still a moment on the other side by the guardhouse, then turned and walked toward the stables. Still she watched, and smiled when he waved to her and made ushering motions, as if doing more than suggest she go inside. He was a sergeant, after all, and used to obedience.

She watched until Rowan was out of sight in the swirling snow. She thought of Shell, Smooth Stone, and His Pony and hoped they were at least close to Spotted Tail's agency.

As tired as she was, she knew she would lie in bed and think about Sergeant Blade, and getting kissed, and helping Smooth Stone, and worrying and maybe, perhaps, falling in love. Sleep could wait.

· 14 ·

THE FIRST THING she did in the morning was select the light-blue and yellow calico—the one for Victoria—and put the others out of sight.

Hers was a simple plan: she would make one dress at a time and not muddy up her sewing area with other calicos. When each dress was done, she would reward herself by choosing her next favorite color. She was Spider, spinning her web over and over, despite silly interruptions from Badger, also known as Victoria.

She yearned to see Sergeant Blade again, just see him. She contented herself with sewing in the lean-to and remembering his features. She had seen handsomer men, to be sure, many among her own people. What she had not noticed in those otherwise excellent men was anyone with so much capability. True, his nose was probably too long, and his lips almost but not quite chiseled enough to make any other girl take notice. His cheekbones weren't as high as hers, but not everyone could look as fine as an Indian; she was willing to make allowances.

His eyes were distinctly blue, which amused Mary no

end, considering that she was the one with the Blue Eye name. He had long legs and a pleasant walk, better seen from the rear, although she would never admit that to a soul.

Mostly he was kind, not a trait his men probably saw too often, considering that he had to be a firm leader. He was kind to her, and that was what mattered.

And so Mary passed a pleasant time. When the dress-to-be turned onerous—knife pleats, boning in the basque—she let her lively mind venture deeper, to whether Sergeant Blade liked children, and whether he had much experience with women. She worked in silence and no one knew her thoughts.

Between her other duties, the first dress took her two days. At this rate, Mary knew she would still be basting pieces together while the ladies danced in petticoats and shimmies. This would never do.

How was it that Sergeant Blade seemed to know precisely when her web had been trampled by too many badgers?

She had laid out the next fabric on the parlor floor over Victoria's strenuous objections that it wasn't proper and should be done somewhere else.

"Suppose one of the other wives comes to call?" Victoria wanted to know.

Mary asked herself what Shell would do, when faced with a ninny of startling proportions, and acted. She set down her shears. "Victoria Masterson, you want these dresses. If you will not let me do it my way, I will go into my room and close the door. I never agreed to any of this. There is a Thirteenth Amendment now, and I am not your slave."

She wasn't certain which of the recent amendments had abolished slavery, but she was equally positive Victoria Masterson had no idea. She narrowed her eyes and tried to look ferocious like His Pony.

"If you must," Victoria said, after a long pause.

"I must. I have to spread out the material to cut it."

"This will go in a letter to my mother, after this wretched business is finished and I have done my duty," Victoria said with something of a flourish, as in, *So there.*

"I will take that letter to your mother when I leave here in January," Mary said, equally firm.

Oh, the panic! Oh, the sudden consternation! Victoria Masterson turned pale. "You're . . . you're . . . *leaving?*" She suddenly sounded like a child who has thrown away her favorite old doll and realizes she misses it.

"I only promised you six months."

Victoria's lips quivered. "Very well," she said, and reached for her coat. "Do what you want."

Mary sighed. Now the dratted woman was off to terrorize the captain's wife, who would carry the news of Mary's impertinence to her husband, who would do who-knew-what to placate tearful females. If that was the price of getting to use the floor to do her work, so be it.

When there came a knock on the door a half hour later, Mary looked up from her position on her hands and knees on the floor, cutting fabric. "Come in," she said, ready for the worst.

The door opened, and there stood Sergeant Blade. She sat up, her face red.

"Miss Blue Eye, you have fair terrified *your* employer. She's sobbing all over *my* employer's desk."

"Good! Maybe she will leave me alone so I can cut out material on the floor."

He shook his head. "I'm to escort you to the guardhouse."

Mary gasped. He grinned at her. She threw the tape measure at him, which he caught, strung around his neck, and lolled there, as if hanged. She laughed until tears ran. He helped her to her feet and grabbed her in a bear hug.

"Resistance is futile! I know all the moves to subjugate nearly anyone except, well, probably you. There you go. Laugh some more, and then seriously, come with me to the guardhouse. I think I can solve your problem."

"Seriously. I get on my coat and follow you to the guardhouse?"

"I never lie about duty, Miss Blue Eye."

He helped her into her coat and waited while she debated a hat. "Too windy," he said. He unwound his yellow muffler and draped it over her hair. "This is better."

The force of the wind made her gasp. He pulled her arm through his so she couldn't blow away, and they struggled across the parade ground to the small stone building on the banks of the Laramie River.

"No one is going to live in Wyoming Territory for long, and it will never become a state," she announced, when she stood, shivering, inside the guardhouse, where the sergeant of the day grinned at her.

"Shall I bring up the prisoner, Sergeant Blade?" the man asked.

"Absolutely."

She gave Rowan such a look that he backed away and held up his hands in a defensive posture. "Miss Blue Eye, whether you believe me or not—and I have never and will never lie to you—Private München is the answer to . . . to . . . Captain Hayes's prayers."

He was right. Enter one Private Heinrich München, a thin, furtive-looking fellow with worried eyes, probably as worried as hers.

"Make a bow to Miss Blue Eye, Private München," Sergeant Blade said.

The little German obliged, clicking his heels together like a Prussian, and nearly toppled from the effort. While the duty sergeant leaned against his desk and tried not to laugh, Sergeant Blade introduced Mary to a drunkard, a scoundrel, and a tailor. "This is Private München. He drinks too much, and this guardhouse is his second home. He is also a tailor of some renown."

"My goodness," Mary said. "*Really?*"

"*Jawohl,* fräulein. You ask. I do."

"Could you cut out pattern pieces for me?"

"Nothing simpler," Private München said. "I do all button holes. My specialty." He bunched his fingertips to his lips and kissed them.

"That will save me hours," Mary said.

"He'll be able to stay up here and work. With proper supervision, of course," Rowan said.

"Of course," she repeated, amazed at her sudden good fortune. She eyed the tailor. "We'll need another pair of shears and dressmaker pins."

"In my locker for foots in the infantry barrack," he said promptly, which made Rowan grin.

Mary looked around the room, which, with four people in it, was hardly spacious enough for cutting out fabric. "Somehow we can make this work, but ..."

Rowan indicated the closed door, which he opened. "Take a look, Miss Blue Eye, and tell me what you think."

She followed him into the adjoining room, which contained a long, wooden shelf about knee high and wide, and a potbellied stove. "What in the world?"

"The perfect place to cut fabric, although Private München will have a backache from bending over. This sleeping platform can hold four soldiers on guard duty. It will become Private München's cutting board tomorrow."

No one else was in the room. Mary stood on tiptoe and kissed Sergeant Blade's cheek.

He smiled at her. "No bumbling badgers to disturb that industrious little spider, eh?"

"Not one. She can make those dresses." Mary looked out the little window to the parade ground, wishing she still had fabric for her own dress.

"A penny for your thoughts."

"With Private München helping me now, I would have had time to make my own dress, if I still had the material. I would need a miracle."

"Oh, you never know."

· 15 ·

PRIVATE MÜNCHEN WAS as good as his word, cutting out each newspaper pattern, giving her tailoring tips, and demonstrating a superior way to make knife pleats. Mary moved the sewing machine into the room adjacent to the duty sergeant's office and sewed in there. When the German tailor tired of cutting fabric, they traded duties.

Beyond the blessing of working with a talented tailor for longer hours, Mary hoped that Sergeant Blade would feel at liberty to drop by, something that could never happen in the Mastersons' quarters, because he had no business there.

To her delight, Rowan stopped in several times a day. He never seemed to mind holding out a skirt to make certain the pleats were even, although he wouldn't wrap it around himself. When she made a mistake and had to rip out a seam, he obligingly did that for her so she could move quickly to another task.

"Did you help your mother sew when you were a boy?" she asked, on the third day of dress production.

"My parents died of typhoid, and I was raised in an

orphanage," he told her as he concentrated on the seam. "No brothers or sisters. Just me."

When she was silent, he didn't even look up. "Mary, if your eyes get blurry with tears, you'll run over your fingers when you sew."

"How do you know I'm crying?" she asked, as she sniffed back tears.

He did look up then. "I know you pretty well. You have a soft heart."

"It's no crime," she said and blew her nose.

"Hardly. I think it's charming."

What could she say to that?

Then he stopped coming. Two days passed, and she found herself looking out the window so often that she sewed the wrong side of the material to one of the skirt panels.

Sobered up, Private München was a true Prussian taskmaster. "Fräulein Blue Eye, focus the mind."

She gave him a tragic look, which allowed the man to relax his standards, as far as fabric was concerned.

"Fräulein, he'll be back."

"I don't know who you're talking about," she assured him.

Sergeant Blade returned the following day. Private München was ironing pleats in the duty sergeant's office next door.

Rowan came in quietly and sat in München's chair. There was no overlooking the sorrow in his eyes. Mary stopped treadling and gave him her attention.

"What has happened?" she asked, wondering if she was prying or if he had come to her—whether he knew it or not—for sympathy.

"It's a bad business. The wife of one of my Ree scouts is dying." He hitched the chair closer. "The surgeon doesn't know what to do, but she's losing weight and in pain nearly all the time now. I like Bill Curly and Mathilde, and I've been sitting with them."

"Is there anything I can do?" Mary asked.

"Not really. I guess I don't care much to be sad by myself."

She thought of the longhouse back home, when families used to all live together and bear one another's burdens. She remembered sitting with other cousins, aunts, and uncles, bored and tired, but aware even as a child that families drew together in times of grief.

The sergeant seemed to take heart as Mary told him about the longhouses and the smokes, sweats, chants, and tears. "I used to think it was alien somehow, since we lived in a modern house with wood floors and hinged doors," she said.

"You don't think it is alien now?"

She shook her head.

"What changed?"

"I did." She said it softly, as if trying out the words. She found them to her liking and repeated them. "I did. I want to go home."

He sighed at that, which told her heart more than words could have. She glanced at the locket watch pinned to her shirtwaist. Her back ached from doing close work, and the afternoon light was fading fast. She knew she should be heading back to the Masterson quarters soon to hear Victoria's complaints about everything, but she didn't want to.

"Let me go with you to your scout's house. Maybe I can help."

"It's pretty humble," he said.

"Why would that bother me?"

"Let me get your coat."

He insisted on holding her hand as they crossed the footbridge over the Laramie that separated Suds Row from the main garrison. "It's icy," he said, although she couldn't see any ice.

Her arm crooked through his now, he took her past the attached quarters for the families of sergeants and corporals down a trail that led to another attached row, this one for scouts. Beyond that, she saw ragged tipis and wondered if the Laramie Loafers existed there.

"I don't even know what a Ree is," she said to Rowan as they hurried along, night coming fast.

"Arikara. They hate the Sioux with a great loathing and make excellent scouts, among those Bill Curly. His wife is Mathilde, the daughter of a French trapper and—I think you'll like this—an eastern Indian."

"Oh, I do," she said. "Children?"

"Three girls."

He tapped on the door of the house on the end, then opened it and ushered her in.

To feel shy would have been a waste of time, as three little girls, all tidy with hair in neat braids, swarmed over the sergeant. He picked up the smallest and tickled her, which made her giggle and lean into his chest.

I love this man, Mary thought suddenly as she watched him. *I do not want to live without him.* She looked around, hoping she hadn't spoken out loud, and found herself regarded by a thin woman propped up with pillows. The woman gestured to her, and Mary sat beside her bed.

She introduced herself, remembering how her papa taught her. "I am Mary Blue Eye of the Genesee Valley Seneca, Keepers of the Western Door."

To her surprise, the woman nodded. "Sarge has told us about you. I am Mathilde Frere of the Oneida."

"My goodness, we are nearly neighbors!" Mary exclaimed.

"Years have passed since I have been in the land of Ontario," Mathilde said. Her tired eyes took on a wistful look. "Is it as beautiful as ever? Not so much wind? Green in summer?"

"Yes, yes, and yes," Mary said, which made Mathilde laugh and hold her stomach. Mary leaned closer. "People here have no idea, do they?"

Mathilde's eyes brightened. "*We* know. May I call you sister?"

Mary nodded. She understood Indian relationships.

"Hold my hand, and I will close my eyes."

Mary did as Mathilde asked. She looked around the single room, with three small rolls of bedding against one wall, a dish cabinet made of what looked like an apple crate, and a table and stools. Everything was in its place.

"Lean closer."

Mary obeyed.

"My man is going to ask your man to build me a coffin. Sarge will find it hard."

How calm she was. Mary felt tears gather and spill onto her cheeks, quietly, quietly, because that was the Seneca way. She looked at Mathilde and knew it was the Oneida way, too.

"You are far from home, Mathilde," she managed, after monumental effort.

The dying woman shook her head. "Home is here with my man and my children," she whispered. "You will understand someday. You are still young."

Not as young as I was, Mary thought, touched to the depths of her soul. She glanced at the little girls, who sat close together on the floor while the oldest one handed around what looked like jerky. Beyond them sat the scout and the sergeant, the scout's hand on the sergeant's back. As she watched, Rowan nodded, then leaned back, as if trying to distance himself from what she knew he must have just agreed to do.

She returned her gaze to Mathilde, then wiped the woman's face with the damp cloth on the nearby table. She wiped around Indian eyes much like hers and hair wispy now but probably once as full and dark as her own. Disease was exacting a cruel toll, but Mary saw no complaint. She thought of uncomplaining, patient Spider, undefeated by Badger.

"Your mother trained you, too," she whispered and received a tiny smile in answer. *So did mine*, Mary thought. *I must thank her when I see her in a few months.*

The men stood up. "Go now," Mathilde said.

Mary rose, but Mathilde did not release her hand. "One thing."

She sat again and leaned close.

"If you have a picture of your valley, could I borrow it?"

"Sergeant Blade will bring it back tonight."

They left the house hand in hand, with no pretense about ice or snow. "I'm going to build a coffin," Rowan said after they crossed the footbridge. "God help me, but life is hard."

His arm went around her. She hesitated, then put her arm around his waist.

"Walk me home," she said. "I don't want to go there because the lieutenant and Victoria are either really silent or they are carping at each other. It's not a good place now, and I don't like it."

"I wish you had a choice."

"Come inside with me, please. I promised Mathilde a picture of home."

The lieutenant and Victoria were sitting on opposite sides of the postage-stamp parlor in stony silence. Sergeant

Blade saluted, and his superior raised a languid finger to his forehead in return.

"I'll only be here a moment, sir," he said.

Mary felt her stomach ache. They must have interrupted them in mid-quarrel. She hurriedly took her favorite painting of the Genesee Valley off the wall in her room. Mama had insisted she take it with her. "So you don't forget us," Mama had said.

She thought of Mathilde so far from her green heaven in Ontario above the border, the white man's line that separated one country from another, when every Indian in the area knew that drawing a line meant nothing. Ah, well.

She handed the small painting to Rowan, who ushered her out the door with him.

The porch was cold and windy, but far better than the parlor, where Mary suspected a brand-new marriage was coming apart.

"Tell Mathilde she can keep it as long as she needs it," Mary said. "What will you line the coffin with?"

"The quartermaster clerk said there is plenty of bed ticking. I'll try to stop by to see you at the guardhouse, but I fear I must hurry with a coffin."

"I'm on schedule now, thanks to your German tailor," she said, walking him down the porch steps, loath for him to leave her.

"I would like to have taken you to the calico ball," he said.

She nearly said, *There will be other dances*, but there wouldn't be, not if she was returning to New York. She gave the darkness overhead a quick glance, looking for wisdom or courage or maybe both, but there were only stars and a rising moon.

"I would have gone gladly," she said, "even in this work dress."

He started to say something, then closed his mouth. She touched his arm and hurried inside, only because her feet were cold and there was more web to spin.

· 16 ·

THERE WAS NO question now that Mary would finish the dresses on time. Private München mentioned that he could do more if she needed to be about her duties in the Masterson household. She assured him that Victoria Masterson could manage well enough.

It really wasn't true. Victoria complained when Mary returned from the guardhouse that she wasn't paying her to neglect her duties. Mary finally took a page from Sergeant Blade's book and gave her employer the Sergeant Stare.

"You bullied me into making fifteen calico dresses for this stupid ball," she snapped. "The ball is in two days, and after that I will do whatever you need, at least until I leave."

Her former friend burst into ready tears and spilled out her own misery at having to decorate that barn of a commissary warehouse for the ball and round up glass dishes and cups for the desserts, which would probably include pounds and pounds of raisins, and what could they do about that? Snow had stopped any wagon trains from Fort Russell north. At least the hostiles were hunkered down on their reservation to the northeast and no one was going to lose any hair, and she didn't think she and the lieutenant were going to be together much longer.

That last bit of misery popped out before Victoria could close her mouth in time. She put her hand to her mouth, her eyes wide and tearful.

Mary's head ached. She wanted to rush to her tiny room and flop on the bed, yearning for solitude to untangle her own thoughts. At least she was leaving Wyoming without the baggage of a marriage gone wrong, or at least at cross purposes, since one or both of the parties were too childish to apologize and try again. Instead, she held out her arms to Victoria, because under all her own turmoil, Mary was kind.

They cried together, Victoria sobbing because she was still a spoiled, pouty thing with her prettiest years probably already behind her, and Mary because she suddenly did not want to leave without her man, who probably thought, when she came right down to it, that *she* was too childish or maybe even too Seneca. How could she know? He was busy with his usual duties, plus making a coffin, which had to render a man melancholy, at the least. There was no time to talk.

She soldiered on in the morning, because Indians did that as well as troopers. She marched herself to the commissary storehouse and used her own money to buy raisins, which she wrapped in fabric scraps. She watched for the child she had first seen weeks ago, trudging behind her mother to the killing floor for scraps. She gave away her raisins.

The word must have got out, because other dark-haired children came for raisins, which meant more trips to the commissary. She handed out raisins, and sewed dratted dresses, and wished for money to buy better food for little friends cast adrift in that uncertain land where the truly poor existed.

Whether he knew it or not, Private München turned the

guardhouse duty room into her haven. On the day when only one dress remained, the rest having been handed over to delighted owners, he produced a doll made of white ticking and stuffed with lint from the hospital steward, who was also German and who liked to share a drink now and then with a fellow German.

"Fräulein, with these scraps, think of the dresses we can make." He set the doll beside her sewing machine. "Do you have yarn for hair?"

She did. Mama had sent her with a skein of black yarn to knit herself some mittens. "I do. I'll get it when I go home for luncheon." She held the doll and imagined other dolls with black yarn hair. She knew three little girls about to lose their mother who might need a small distraction. Four girls, counting the hungry one with raisins on her mind.

Her mistake was mentioning the matter to Victoria when she hurried home for a quick sandwich of nothing much beyond army bread and canned meat of mysterious origin. "We'll have the last dress done at the end of the day. After that, Private München and I are going into the doll business."

Victoria clapped her hands, looking more cheerful than Mary had seen her in a week. "What a delightful notion! We can send all the dolls you can make along with the dresses to poor children in Chicago. Mary, this is wonderful."

She tried to set Victoria straight. "These dolls are staying here. There are Indian children *here* who need our attention."

Victoria wouldn't have it. "All our efforts are for the women and children rendered homeless by the Chicago fire. You promised."

"I promised no such thing," Mary fired back. "I have nearly done my task for you. We are using the scraps for another purpose." She left the house before Victoria had time to finish her next sentence, angry and certain she would get a visit soon from Captain Hayes's wife.

Head down against the wind and snow, Mary crossed the parade ground, desperate to see Sergeant Blade, who had plenty of his own worries and no time for hers. The badgers were starting to circle her lovely web, and she wanted to fight back this time, patience be hanged.

Private München heard her out in silence, shaking his head. "When this last one is done," he said, indicating the half-finished dress, "it's back to the cells for me." He brightened. "Can you drag out this dress while I make more doll bodies?"

"I can and will," she said and started picking out a perfectly straight seam in the skirt.

It was worse than she thought. Exactly one half hour later, Captain and Mrs. Hayes arrived in the duty room. Her heart in her throat, Mary looked up from the next seam she was picking out.

"She is making dolls and doll clothes now for the Indian children here and refuses to consider sending them to Chicago, along with the dresses and money we will raise," Gertrude Hayes said, pointing an accusing finger in a most theatrical gesture, as if there were many seamstresses in the tiny room and Mary needed to be singled out.

Mary swallowed. She had never needed to stand up for herself at home, not with big brothers and a respected father who clerked for a judge. She had coasted through her life, pampered, well fed, and happy. She also remembered lessons about silence and quiet tears and standing her ground, if need be. She knew those lessons would never apply to her, until finally, at a fort far west of her ancestral home, they did.

Mrs. Hayes was looking at her husband, a captain with the brevet of major, a Medal of Honor recipient for some remarkable bit of military daring at Antietam, a man used to obedience, respected. "William, what are you going to do?"

Private München slipped next door to the duty sergeant's

office, abandoning her, or maybe not. He came back into the duty room at the same time she heard someone else running from the other office.

Captain Hayes cleared his throat. "Miss Blue Eye, the dolls should go to Chicago and the worthy poor."

The little spider prepared to defend her web. "There are worthy poor right here, Captain, if you please," she said. "Mathilde, the wife of your Arikara scout, is dying. Sergeant Blade is making her a coffin, as I am certain you know."

He nodded. "Bill Curly is a good and faithful scout."

"Bill and Mathilde have three daughters. I want to give them comfort with dolls and dresses to play with, something to distract them from the sorrow coming their way soon. There is another little girl who follows her mother to the killing floor for meat scraps and offal. I doubt she has ever had a doll of her own. I am making a doll for her, too. I know there are others."

Mary spoke simply, ignoring Mrs. Hayes. She knew enough about women to know that Mrs. Hayes could easily make her husband's life miserable. He was the leader of his troop, she reasoned, and maybe that would be enough to sway her argument. If not, she would not surrender the dolls without a struggle.

"We're dealing in scraps, sir," she said. "Some ticking and some lint. The yarn is mine. Please, sir."

The outside door to the duty room opened, and Sergeant Blade stood there, breathing hard. He must have run from the quartermaster warehouse where she knew he was making the coffin. He was out of uniform, and his sleeves were rolled up to expose muscled forearms covered with sawdust. Mrs. Hayes sniffed and stepped aside, as much as she could in a small room with too many people and far too much anger.

Captain Hayes looked like a man who had just seen the

coming of the Lord. "Sergeant Blade, kindly reason with Miss Blue Eye and let me get to work." That last bit was directed at his wife, who glared back.

Rowan shook his head. "She's in the right, Captain. She was asked—no, told—to make dresses, and she has fulfilled that task. Scraps are scraps. That's all Indians get, so what's the harm done? You and I both know that matters out here will only worsen. I say we leave her alone to her work of charity. Real charity."

Mrs. Hayes narrowed her eyes. "I never thought a sergeant in the US Army would side with . . . with . . ."

"An Indian?" Rowan asked. "Yes, I am on Mary's side. She has done what you demanded, ma'am. Don't ask more than she is willing to give."

"What will she do?" Mrs. Hayes demanded.

"I have no idea," Rowan said with a smile, "but I lay odds on Mary to see that four little ones get dolls with fantastic calico wardrobes."

Apparently Captain Hayes agreed. "There you have it, Gertie," he said. "I am figuring out next year's budget. Unless you want to help me with that, I suggest you go home and leave the tailors to their work."

The door slammed. Captain Hayes grinned at Mary and rubbed his hands together. "It'll be cold as can be in my quarters for a few nights, but what the hell? As you were, Miss Mary Blue Eye. Make those doll clothes. Sergeant, back to work."

He left the room, chuckling to himself, and obviously a husband who knew his wife pretty well. Mary couldn't help but think of Shell and His Pony.

Private München went into the adjoining office, muttering something about checking the flat irons, which gave Sergeant Blade perfect leave to gather Mary close. She wasted not a moment and practically leaped into his arms, shivering with the effort of standing up for herself.

"I hope Captain Hayes won't give you a difficult time, Rowan," she said into the sawdust on his shirt. "Thank you. I was afraid of what I was going to do to that dreadful woman."

"I recall you mentioning something once about the Iroquois League and scalping techniques," he said into her hair.

"Oh, you! I would never do such a nasty deed."

"Kiss me, then, and send me back to work."

She kissed him, pulling him close and pressing her lips softly against his, despite the sawdust. He did smell nicely of pine, and that was no liability. He took the liberty of patting her hip, then apologized, his face red.

"Go to work," she said. "We can settle up later."

"That's one way to put it," he told her. He started whistling before he even closed the door, and the little spider sat down to continue the unbroken web.

· 17 ·

THE LAST DRESS found its way to a grateful sergeant's wife by midmorning the next day. By then, Private München had finished three more doll bodies, down to the black yarn hair, which he neatly sewed into black braids. He left the faces blank because neither of them knew how Sioux, Arikara, and Crow felt about personification. They cut out little dresses until after dark, then plotted tomorrow's strategy.

They decided on simple dresses, held together by two hooks and eyes and a ribbon sash. Mary dashed back to the Mastersons' and returned with four of the lieutenant's handkerchiefs, begged for and given to her by a surprisingly cooperative Victoria. Perhaps word had gotten around that Sergeant Blade was even more formidable than anyone had previously imagined and Mary should be helped, for the good of the garrison. Mary was far too wise to question anyone's motive.

The lawn handkerchiefs turned into nightgowns, on which Mrs. Hayes herself obligingly crocheted scalloped edges. The surgeon's wife found scraps of blue wool uniform fabric and hand sewed cloaks herself, to Mary's amazement.

"Hats would have been nice," Mary told Private München when night came on, "but I promised to help Sergeant Blade."

She went to the quartermaster warehouse to sew the blue-and-white mattress ticking into lining for Mathilde Frere's coffin.

Rowan had scrounged a mattress pad from the post surgeon's supply. He helped her tack the lining down and sat back, his eyes tired, to watch her sew it in place. She glanced over at him a time or two and watched him sleep sitting up.

She finished at midnight. Sergeant Blade walked around the coffin, running his hand over the sanded pine, then making sure the hinges didn't squeak. "I'll paint it early in the morning, and then we'll wait," he said.

She would have gone directly home, but as Rowan walked her by the guardhouse, Mary heard the sound of the treadle louder than usual, which meant someone was pushing down extra hard through stiff fabric. Curious, she dragged herself up the few steps and peeked in the window.

She opened the door to see Private München finishing the last of four bags made of canvas, just the right size for dolls with wardrobes. He looked up with a guilty expression, so she knew better than to ask where or how he had acquired canvas.

"You've been working so hard for me," she said.

"It's cold in the cell," he told her. "This is better."

"I wish I could pay you."

"You have, fräulein."

Rowan walked her home. "Tomorrow's the big day?"

"Yes. Since Mrs. Masterson and Mrs. Hayes have been surprisingly helpful today, I told them I would assist with finishing touches on what I will laughingly call the ballroom."

"They've been stringing Fourth of July bunting today, and the band has been practicing. A person could almost dance to their music now." He chuckled. "The commissary clerk has developed a tic in his eye, but he'll recover."

"I think refreshments will be limited, at best," Mary added. "I wish a supply wagon had been able to get through."

"No one wishes that more than I do."

"You were expecting something?"

"I was, but there might be an advantage to this isolation currently foisted upon us," he said as they walked up the front steps. He put his hands on her shoulders. "It might mean you can't leave as soon as you want to."

Mary looked into his tired eyes and knew they mirrored her own. She rested her cheek against his chest, and his arms went around her.

"Don't be in such a hurry to leave, Mary," he said.

•••

The day of the calico ball was like the day before, but with less wind and snow. Mary looked out her small window that was growing increasingly iced over, longing for a place where spring came when it was supposed to, then ushered in a mild, humid summer, the kind that left her cheeks smooth and soft and not peeling and tough from high plains wind.

She missed the little picture she had loaned to Mathilde Frere. Rowan had told her that Bill Curly had hung it right by her bed. He said she looked at it all the time now.

Mary lay in bed, steeling herself to throw back the warm covers and rush into her clothes. Lately she had started dreaming of dresses and dolls and charitable women who chased her around the guardhouse duty room, demanding this and that. And what could she do about that, since she was a spider? Oh, enough. She made the leap from bed, dressed quickly, and laid a fire in the kitchen range.

The little house was starting to smell fragrant with coffee

when someone knocked. She hurried to the front door to see Sergeant Blade. She took his arm to pull him inside. He shook his head and pulled back.

"Mathilde died this morning, while I was painting her coffin."

"I'm so sorry," she said, and meant it. Who would take care of her three daughters? She thought Bill Curly was a good man, but what happened when a good man went on detached detail with his troop? What then? So many questions.

"Rowan, take the three dolls. Maybe the girls will want them right now. Leave me the one doll for my own particular urchin."

He smiled at that. "She'll be by for more raisins any day." He touched his hand to his hat brim. "No dance for us tonight?"

"No dress," she reminded him. "I'm truly sorry, because it would have been fun."

The sergeant seemed to take the disappointment in good cheer, which left Mary a little irked, because she was still Mary, after all, and wanted a few more years to mature and improve her character, or so she reasoned.

"A person can plan and plan, and everything still changes," he said. He tugged the collar higher on his overcoat. "On the bright side, a supply wagon from Fort Russell is stuck at Hunton's stage station. With any luck at all, it might be here tomorrow or by the Fourth of July, depending."

"Alas, too late," she said with a laugh. "Mrs. Masterson told me the ladies were wishing for those canned oysters to arrive in time for stew tonight."

She waved him into the cold again, wondering if there would be a funeral, wondering how the little girls would manage without their mother, and wondering why she wasn't so overjoyed at the prospect of leaving. She wanted to go home. Didn't she?

The day passed quickly. As promised, Mary swept the commissary warehouse floor over and over, looking each time for some improvement and seeing little. She quickly hemmed the last remaining yards of her pretty, dark-blue fabric on the Singer still in the duty room. By the time she finished, the hospital steward had drafted two nearly healthy patients to return the sewing machine to the post surgeon's quarters.

She asked the duty sergeant if she could say goodbye to the tailor, only to be informed that Private München had been released to D Company again. He had left behind four doll hats woven of broom straw and lined with calico. She took the little dainties with a smile. She would wait a few days, then drop the hats off to their new owners, because every lady needs a hat.

She took her ironed material to the commissary warehouse and let Victoria arrange it on the white bedsheet loaned by the medical department. Her employer set the punch bowl on top and pronounced it successful.

"I'd like the fabric square back when the evening is over. I'll take it back to New York as a souvenir of the dress that wasn't and the dance where I didn't," she joked, and Victoria laughed.

Mary strolled home in the gathering twilight. The wind had died down, and the sun was setting in a fury of vivid pinks and purples that softened into lavender before it turned ordinary again. She heard laughter behind her and saw Victoria and her lieutenant walking arm in arm. Maybe there was hope for the Mastersons. It couldn't be easy for a spoiled girl to turn into an army wife overnight. Perhaps things would work out, and fifty years from now in 1921, when the lieutenant was a general and Victoria terrorizing servants in

Washington, DC, the Mastersons would look back on their time at Fort Laramie with fondness. Stranger things had likely happened.

· 18 ·

THAT EVENING AFTER a supper of hash and stewed tomatoes, Mary helped Victoria into the light-blue calico dress with the pale-yellow squares, smoothing down the boned basque and admiring Private München's knife pleats and well-turned buttonholes.

"Here is the plan," Victoria said as she put her gold earbobs in place. "At midnight we will retire to a back room and take off our calico dresses, then put on our ball gowns. Everything will be packed away and ready to mail to the First Congregational Church on Hamlin Avenue. Mrs. Stanley says we have already collected seventy-five dollars for the deserving poor."

Mary nodded. Maybe in a few days or weeks, or until she left, she could suggest that Victoria and the other officers' wives consider the deserving poor closer to Fort Laramie, across the footbridge and down a draw behind Suds Row.

After the Mastersons left, Mary stood at the window and watched the snow. She hoped that His Pony, Shell, and Smooth Stone were at the Whetstone Creek Agency with Spotted Tail. Rowan had said the newly formed agencies near the Black Hills were protected.

"Let's just hope no one discovers gold in the Black Hills. I hate to think what will happen then," the sergeant had told her last night, when she was tacking down the coffin lining.

"I can tell you what will happen, if someone wants Indian land," she told her reflection in the window glass. "Take care of your family, His Pony."

She had gone to her room to find some stationery for a long letter home to Mama when she heard footsteps on the porch, Rowan Blade footsteps. She knew them by now. Heavens, but the man was persistent. She didn't have a dress.

She opened the door with a smile to see a man with a heavy heart. He carried a pasteboard box, which looked remarkably like something a dressmaker would use. She ushered him inside, and he set the box on the dining room table. *Sukey's Dresses* was stenciled on the box in a flowery script. She looked at the sergeant in surprise.

"The supply train got through a half hour ago. Open it."

She lifted the lid and gasped. It was the dark-blue calico with the white pinpoint dots that Sergeant Blade had picked out for her in Cheyenne, done up with lovely mother-of-pearl buttons and row on row of tucks on the bodice, the work of hours. The shirt had a knee-deep flounce that would look magical on a dance floor.

She ran her hand over the fabric. "Rowan, my goodness." She felt brave and put her arms around his neck. "You did this when you went back to Fort Russell, didn't you?"

"Guilty as charged. I did have paperwork at the fort, and there was time. Sukey didn't mind getting up early to help me out."

He hugged her close, then held her off so he could look into her eyes. "There's something else, Mary, and it's more important. Sit down."

He didn't look like a man ready to take a lady to a calico

ball, even though he wore his uniform. She could almost smell the sorrow under a layer of bay rum. This was a sergeant whose first concern would always be his men. "What's the matter?" she asked.

"I don't even know how to ask this," he said simply. "I wanted to surprise you with this dress."

"You certainly did," she assured him. "But that's not what is bothering you."

"No. I finished painting Mathilde's coffin by noon. We took it down to Bill Curly an hour ago." He swallowed and shook his head.

He couldn't talk. Mary understood this sort of silence. She thought of her one visit to the Curly quarters, tidy and clean but absolutely bare bones. The girls were dressed neatly, but she doubted they had anything more. She thought of their mother. Her heart went out to this lovely man because she knew what he was asking for without the strength to ask.

She took the dress out and held it against her body. It was complete and utter perfection, the work of a talented dressmaker. She knew it would fit her. She also knew it would fit Mathilde Frere.

Mary held the dress a moment longer, then arranged it back in the box. She put on the lid. "Take it to Mathilde."

He clung to her and cried, and she held him close, smoothing his hair, knowing this man could never do enough for those he led. If by some miracle he asked her to marry him, she would probably have to make allowances for his strong sense of duty. A wife could get used to that, if she loved her husband enough.

He pulled back finally and opened his mouth. She put her fingers to his lips. "Don't you dare apologize to me," she told him, startled at how fierce she sounded, almost like Grandmama Jane in the longhouse when she spoke of soldiers, and longhouses on fire, and retreat.

"Thank you from the bottom of my heart." Rowan picked up the box and left as quietly as he had come.

She sat at the table and stared at her hands, thinking of all the sorrow in the hut behind Suds Row. Maybe the dolls would help Mathilde's daughters. She knew she would go there tomorrow and take raisins and her love. Maybe the Arikara sat in silence by coffins. She had done that before, impatient and bored. Now she would do it quietly, her heart invested in lives closer to hers than she could have imagined only weeks ago.

How odd to realize that this six-month exile to the Wild West she had undertaken so grudgingly had come full circle and taught her lessons she could have learned nowhere else. She could write Mama about that.

She was still staring at the blank sheet of paper in front of her when she heard Rowan on the porch again, stamping snow off his boots. She rose to open the door, but he opened it before she stood completely on her feet.

He carried a pasteboard box with *Sukey's Dresses* stenciled on the top. She wondered why he hadn't just left the box at the Curly house. Boxes always had their uses.

He set the box on the table and took off his overcoat this time, as if he planned to stay awhile. She went to take his coat from him as a good hostess would, but he tossed it onto the settee.

"Open it."

She smiled at him. "I did, remember? I do hope Bill Curly was all right with what we did."

"He was so appreciative. So were the other scouts' wives. Open it."

"You're a knothead."

He put cold hands on her neck, and she swatted him. "Mary Blue Eye, open it."

She did as he commanded, then stepped back in amazement.

"I asked Sukey to make another dress for you. I picked out this material too. I know wedding dresses aren't supposed to be wool and deep pink, but it's cold here, and I like it."

Mary reminded herself to breathe. The wool was cashmere, softer to the touch than a rose petal and about the same shade. More mother-of-pearl buttons marched down the nicely boned bodice that came to a vee. There was a flounce on this skirt, too.

She picked it up as she had picked up Mathilde's calico dress, holding it to her, smoothing around her curves, which made her smile when the sergeant sighed. Her shoes barely peeked out from below the flounce. She would be the most beautiful bride in this entire godforsaken territory.

"What do you think?"

What did she think? "Do you mean about the dress, or what might have been a proposal, or about needing wool because it's cold outside? Explain yourself, Sergeant Blade."

He took the dress from her and set it carefully on the table. "I've never proposed before. I know that I love you. That's the first thing. I think you will be a lovely mother to our children. Heavens, don't cry about that! They'll probably drive you to distraction on a regular basis."

"I like children," she wailed, and he gave her his handkerchief. "I love you."

"This is encouraging," he teased, more sure of himself now. "If you think the army won't do, I'm one step ahead. That paperwork at Fort Russell was to inform my regimental commanding officer that I will not pursue another enlistment."

"My goodness."

Somehow she was sitting on his lap now, her head tucked against his chest. She wondered what her parents would think of all this. They had always been such careful parents, warning her, teaching her, training her, whether she knew it or not. And here she was sitting on a man's lap and enjoying every second of it.

"How do you plan to support me and all our children?" she asked, which made him laugh and run his hand down her sleeve.

"I build things. Cheyenne needs builders. Maybe your Genesee Valley needs builders. There are any number of pretty towns in Nebraska that need builders, because this country is growing. We can reconnoiter the terrain when we go to New York in a month to get married."

"We're getting married here before we take that trip," she informed this man who might or might not have proposed yet. "Imagine how much fun a Pullman compartment will be if we're married. Um, *have* you proposed yet?"

When he stopped laughing, Sergeant Blade held her off so he could see her face. "Miss Blue Eye, I love you. The thought of continuing on this arduous journey through life without you is distressing in the extreme. Please marry me. There. Will that do?"

"I will marry you, Sergeant Blade," she said, and kissed him. "You would even move to the Genesee Valley if I wanted you to?"

"The matter is open for consideration. I will live where you are happiest."

She thought of something Mathilde Frere had said. "I will be happiest where you are."

He reached into an inside pocket and took out a blue bead. His fingers were warm now, and she didn't mind them on her neck this time as he tugged out the medicine bag that Shell had given her. He opened the pouch and dropped in the bead next to the brass button and the elk tooth.

"Bill Curly gave me this bead for you." He reached in his pocket again and pulled out a wedding ring. "This is from me. Let's keep it here until we do the deed. I was a busy boy in Cheyenne that morning."

She gasped and hugged him close. "Rowan, what time do stores open in Cheyenne?"

"Anytime you want, if you bang on the door hard enough." He held her in a loose embrace and fingered her sleeve. "We can go to that blamed calico ball, you know. They're still dancing in the storehouse."

"I'd rather sit here with you," she said, then sat up. "Hmm. There's no church here, and no pastor."

"True." He kissed her cheek, then found her lips. After a lengthy pause he resumed his commentary, out of breath now, but game. "I happen to know of a corporal in D Company, Ninth Infantry, who is an ordained Methodist minister."

"What is he doing in the army?"

Rowan shrugged. "You'd be surprised why men enlist. I don't prod too much, and you shouldn't either."

She digested that. "I'm still a Keeper of the Western Door. I would die if people slighted you because of me."

"That will never happen, Mary Blue Eye. If you haven't already noticed, I'm very good at taking care of my own."

Mary rested her head against his chest. She thought of packing dresses for shipment to the General Relief Committee in Chicago, attending a funeral, finding that little girl who needed more raisins and a doll of her own, and assuring Victoria Masterson that she could manage without a servant.

"I am, too, Sergeant Blade."

About Carla Kelly

What to say about Carla? The old girl's been in the writing game for mumble-mumble years. She started out with short stories that got longer and longer until— poof!— one of them turned into a novel. (It wasn't quite that simple.) She still enjoys writing short stories, one of which is before you now. Carla writes for Harlequin Historical, Camel Press, and Cedar Fort. Her books are found in at least fourteen languages.

Along the way, Carla's books and stories have earned a couple of Spur Awards from Western Writers of America for Short Fiction, a couple of Rita Awards from Romance Writers of America for Best Regency, and a couple of Whitney Awards. Carla lives in Idaho Falls, Idaho, and continues to write, because her gig is historical fiction, and that never gets old.

Follow Carla on Facebook: Carla Kelly
Carla's Website: www.CarlaKellyAuthor.com

A Convenient Arrangement

Sarah M. Eden

· 1 ·

Wyoming Territory
September 1880

BEFORE LEAVING FOR the annual cattle drive, Patrick Quinn sent telegrams to several Topeka establishments, placing orders for a whet stone, a cast-iron stove, four pairs of heavy work trousers, and a wife. He was really only particular about the trousers.

The train carrying his bride-to-be arrived on a clear day in late September. Thornwood wasn't a busting town, but they had a fair amount of coming and going. A handful of women stepped off the train.

Quinn eyed the new arrivals and couldn't say any quite matched the description. All the bachelors 'round about had come to the station. Women were so few and far between in their corner of Wyoming that the arrival of any as-yet-unwed ladies was reason for a regular town gathering. More than once, a woman had been claimed by someone other than her intended, having changed her mind at the last moment.

That would *not* happen to him.

He pulled from his coat pocket the telegram he'd received describing his intended.

Hair, light brown, with curl. Eyes, blue. Of a smaller build.

He surveyed each woman as he passed. Quinn was tall for a man and used to towering over the womenfolk. How, then, did he know what the telegram meant by "smaller build?" Most everyone had a smaller build than he did.

He eyed a woman with black hair pulled in a tight bun. *Black hair*, thus not his bride. Another had light brown hair, but ample proportions. Still, it didn't hurt to ask.

"Mirabelle Smith?" he asked.

Her eyes grew wide as she surveyed his height. She shook her head. Quinn didn't waste time discussing things further. He had a woman to track down.

"Mirabelle Smith?" he asked a brunette, just in case the telegram had things a little wrong.

But she wasn't Miss Smith.

Quinn stood apart from the others on the platform, eyeing them all with growing uncertainty. He didn't think any of the women were his Miss Smith. Had she missed her train? Or had she changed her mind? That'd be something of a kick in the chops.

Another woman stepped off the train. He only knew she was a woman and not a child because she wasn't built like a twelve-year-old, despite being about the same height as one. *Smaller build*, the telegram had said. This woman was smaller than everyone.

She had light brown hair that clearly curled, though she'd pulled it back in a very proper bun. *Hair, light brown, with curl.* She had blue eyes, as well.

"Mirabelle Smith?" he asked when she came close enough to hear him.

Her gaze slowly shifted upward. Her neck craned by the time her eyes reached his face. "My, but you don't ever seem to stop," she said.

"You're Mirabelle Smith?" He phrased it as a question, though he no longer doubted he was right.

"I am. And that, I'm guessing, would make you Patrick Quinn."

He gave a quick nod. "I'm called Quinn. Just Quinn."

"Well, then, Quinn, I'm pleased to meet you." She stuck her hand out for him to shake, not seeming the least bit intimidated by a strange man who must have seemed like Goliath to her. One she was about to marry, no less. He'd give her credit for having a touch of steel to her. That would serve her well in this life she'd agreed to.

Quinn shook her hand, though very carefully. Something that tiny would probably break easily. Still, her grip was firm. The porter set a traveling trunk down beside Miss Smith before moving on to other duties. Quinn let her hand go and took the trunk up instead.

"Best come along," he said. "We'll stop at the preacher's on our way out of town."

She didn't blanch. Didn't hesitate. Either she was tough as leather or too naive to know she ought to be at least a little unnerved by the whole thing. *He* was, heaven knew. If a man did the thing right, he only got married once. He and Miss Smith would spend the rest of their lives together. She didn't seem the least concerned about that.

Why am I dithering about the whole thing? It's for the best. It's needed.

A wife would help see to the house, help him run the place. She, according to the information he'd been sent, had no family and no future. It wasn't a terrible arrangement for either of them.

It's needed.

He carried her trunk away from the depot, only just remembering to keep his strides a little shorter so she wouldn't have to run to keep up with him. He glanced at her more than once, struggling to reconcile the woman at his side with the adult-sized version of her he'd anticipated.

What am I to do with such a tiny little thing? I might accidentally step on her.

The preacher lived near enough the depot that they reached it quickly. They weren't, however, the first to get there. More than one bride had arrived on the train. Quinn set Miss Smith's trunk down on the wood-plank sidewalk beside them.

"Seems a few people had the same idea we did." Miss Smith's gaze took in the couples waiting their turn. "They certainly wasted no time seeing to the business of things."

Quinn nodded. "A few of these men have two-hour drives ahead of them. They don't have any time to doddle or fuss."

"You've a strange way of doing things around here."

Quinn eyed her sidelong. "You ain't backing out, are you?" If she meant to toss him over, he was enough of a gentleman to accept it, but that sure wasn't what he'd prefer. The business of finding himself a wife had been a hassle.

"Not at all." She smiled reassuringly at him. "I'm only saying that meeting a woman for the first time at a train station, hopping in a line to marry her, and then heading off home, all in a single afternoon, is different from how this is done in most places."

Quinn had lived in Wyoming from the time he was ten years old. He didn't really know anything different. "I don't imagine we do *many* things here the way they're done anywhere else."

Her eyes wandered back to the street. That put an end to conversation between them for the next quarter of an hour. Quinn stood with his hands in his coat pockets, unable to think of anything to say to the woman he was about to marry. He knew little enough about her. She seemed perfectly content to watch the comings and goings out in the street and the couples in line in front of them. She only occasionally looked up at him. And she most definitely had to look *up*.

I didn't even know adults came that size. Can the woman reach anything? I'll constantly need to fetch things off shelves for her.

"How tall you are, Miss Smith?" The question jumped right out of his mouth.

"You can call me Mirabelle," she answered quick as anything. "And I'm four feet and eleven inches."

Not even five feet tall? No wonder he felt like he'd ordered a horse and received a pony instead. He stood six feet three inches with his boots off. They had to be the most mismatched pair in all of Wyoming.

Two couples had left the parsonage by that time, and only two more waited ahead of Quinn and Mirabelle. Still, they'd likely be waiting another half hour for their turn.

"Would you like to sit, Miss—Mirabelle?" he asked. "The trunk's probably not the most comfortable seat, but it'd be better than being on your feet another thirty minutes."

"Thank you, but no." The smile hadn't left her face. Quinn didn't know what to make of a person who smiled all the time. "I've spent a great deal of time sitting on a train. My feet could use the reminder of what they're there for."

Sensible. "Are you hungry or thirsty?" The mercantile was not far off. He could go get her something if she needed it.

But she shook her head. "Thank you, though."

She wasn't uncomfortable, hungry, or thirsty. Her light jacket and sensible footwear were a good match for the mild weather, so she likely wasn't cold. Quinn couldn't think of anything else she might need just then. He took the seat she didn't want and waited.

In another few minutes, he'd be a married man. He'd planned for it all summer, yet the idea still knotted up a bit inside him. He watched Mirabelle as he sat there. She certainly wasn't a bundle of nerves or a wilting flower or any of the other ways he'd heard soon-to-be brides described. She stood up straight, if not tall. She didn't fidget or pace or wring her hands. Her expression was light and almost eager as she looked out over the small town.

And she's so tiny. The wind often blew fiercely in Wyoming. One good gust was likely to blow her clear across the territory.

And more worrisome still, she had Da to deal with. Quinn's father was a difficult man, with the very obstinacy for which the Irish were famous. Someone as small and fragile as she didn't stand much of a chance if Da took a disliking to her.

The last couple in line ahead of them came out of the preacher's home, having completed their business there.

"Our turn." Quinn offered the words as a final warning. He'd let her beg off if she wanted.

She nodded and stepped inside. Quinn brought her traveling trunk inside and set it just on the other side of the door. Reverend Howell met them at the door to the parlor.

"Quinn," he greeted. "And this must be—" His eyes pulled wide, darting from Mirabelle back to Quinn. He stepped closer and lowered his voice. "Quinn, there are laws about age in a marriage, you know. You—"

"I am twenty-one," Mirabelle jumped in, "not twelve. So, you can go right on ahead without worrying about laws or any such thing."

Reverend Howell sputtered a moment but found his voice. "I hope I didn't offend you, miss," he said with all sincerity. "Upon closer look, I can see you're not so young as you at first seemed."

Mirabelle waved off the apology. "A woman as short as I am is quite used to being mistaken for a child."

She stepped into the parlor, leaving Quinn and the preacher in surprised silence. Reverend Howell shot Quinn a questioning look. All he could do was shrug. He himself didn't know quite what to make of Mirabelle Smith. For such a small thing, she had gumption and plenty of it. And for a woman about to be married to a perfect stranger, she didn't seem to have any obvious misgivings.

Mrs. Howell wore an expression of barely withheld surprise when Quinn and her husband came inside.

In a whisper of concern, she said to Quinn, "She's so tiny."

"That she is." What else could he say?

"And you're so . . . *not* tiny."

"That I am." He eyed his miniature bride-to-be. "Still, she didn't run off in terror. I think we'll do just fine."

"Mail-order marriages are always something of a risk," Mrs. Howell said with a nod.

Every sort of marriage was "something of a risk." His da had married for love, and he'd suffered greatly for it these past years.

The register was signed and the ceremony completed in a matter of a few minutes. Mirabelle Smith became Mirabelle Quinn, and Quinn the bachelor became Quinn the married man. He had a wife—a tiny, seemingly unflappable wife—and he'd managed the thing without any of the complications a man usually encountered.

That was easier than I expected.

An omen of a simple and uncomplicated life to come. He hoped.

· 2 ·

I AM MARRIED to a giant. A sure-enough giant.

Mirabelle was quite accustomed to people seeming large, but Quinn took the cake. The information she'd received from the William's Matrimonial Bureau in Topeka had painted a picture of a decent sort of man with land and the ability to see she didn't go cold or hungry. The bureau insisted their clients provide references. Mr. Patrick Quinn was described as hardworking, dependable, respectful of his neighbors and associates. The bureau had said nothing about him being enormous.

What if the man had a terrible, raging temper? He could flatten her with the smallest swat of his hand. She was like a mouse dropped into a lion's cage.

She'd do well to find out what she could about her new surroundings and her new husband. Though her history wasn't one to inspire bouts of optimism, she'd long ago decided that rosy was her preferred hue for viewing of the world. Something better was always just around the corner, she was certain of that.

"How far from town do you live, Quinn?"

"A half hour when driving at a sight-seeing pace."

"Like we are now?"

He gave a quick nod. Was he driving slow for her benefit, so she could see the area? She didn't expect him to act like he was courting her—her grasp of the situation was far too firm for such fanciful thinking—but she liked that he was being considerate. That was a promising beginning.

"How long have you lived here?" she asked.

"Since I was a lad of ten," he said. "My parents homesteaded the land."

She'd noticed from the first words he spoke to her that he had a hint of an accent. She couldn't place it though. He sounded almost as if he'd once lived somewhere else—Scotland or Ireland, perhaps—but had been away for decades and decades, enough to erase all but a hint of that far away place. The surname Quinn made her think Ireland, but she couldn't be certain.

Rather pathetic, Mirabelle. You are married to a man and you don't have any idea where he was born or grew up.

"Do you farm or ranch?" she asked.

"Ranch."

"Do you drive your cattle all the way to Kansas?" She knew there were several depots in Kansas of significance to the cattlemen.

"Cheyenne." He guided the horses off the road onto a narrower path.

She searched her mind for something he couldn't answer in a single word or gesture. "What would you like to have for dinner tonight?"

So help me, if he answers 'food' and nothing else...

"There's beef in the root cellar," he said. "And vegetables. We've flour, most baking things."

So was he not particular about his meals or did he simply

not want to be bothered with the menus? A wife needed to know these things when she was married to a man as enormous as Quinn.

"I think I'll make a beef roast. And, if you have cornmeal, some johnny cakes to go with it."

"That'll do," he said.

"And your father? Will he approve of stew and johnny cakes?" The bureau had mentioned Quinn's father lived with him. Most new brides would probably have objected to the arrangement. Mirabelle, who had never known her father, was excited. She had no family. This new life she'd embarked on came with one already assembled.

"Da'll not object to the meal." Quinn was not a man of many words.

They drove around a bend in the path and past a small cluster of trees, behind which sat a meadow. In the midst of the meadow was the loveliest and quaintest cottage-like house. Mirabelle fell instantly and irrevocably in love with the place.

"Is this your home, Quinn?"

"It is."

Her gaze took in every inch of the home, from its deep-green shutters and trim to the diamond-paned windows along the front to the tall rock chimney reaching toward the sky. There was space under the windows that would be perfect for planting flowers when the spring came.

This is to be my new home. She'd hoped for something pleasant and had been handed something perfect. For one who'd only ever lived in orphanages and boarding houses, the realization was breathtaking.

"It is a lovely house."

"It keeps the rain out. And it's warm in the winter." He shrugged the smallest bit and guided the team down the path toward the barn, just coming in to view. He pulled the team to a stop. "I'll bring your trunk after I unhitch the team."

She managed the climb down with a bit of ingenuity and blatant disregard for grace and dignity. When a person is hardly taller than a wagon wheel, climbing down one is a bit of a challenge. Still, her feet reached the ground without incident.

She set herself on a direct path for the house, walking quickly around toward the front when she didn't find a door facing the barn.

"It really is lovely," she said to herself, eyeing the place once more. She pulled off her glove and ran her fingers along the horizontal wood planks that made up the front facade. She paused long enough to trace a diamond-shaped pane in the front window. The house wasn't large, by any means, but it was sweet and quietly elegant. And it was hers to call home.

She turned the knob and opened the front door, half expecting to find a fairy-tale cottage inside. What she saw very nearly matched her expectations. The door opened directly onto a parlor of sorts, with lovely furniture—two chairs near the fireplace, two end tables, a rocking chair in one corner—small trinkets and keepsakes throughout the room. It was clean, which was a pleasant surprise. New curtains at the windows, a little rearranging, a good polish of the end tables and the room would be simply lovely.

"With any luck, my giant of a husband will be generous with the household budget," she said.

"He's no closefisted miser, if that's what's gotten into your head."

Mirabelle nearly jumped out of her skin at the unexpected and unfamiliar voice, with its gruff tone and heavily Irish inflection. She'd had no idea anyone was in the room. She spotted the speaker in the next moment.

He sat in a chair by the low-burning fire, watching her with a look of complete distrust. His eyes were narrowed and his shoulders a little hunched. His unkempt hair was heavily silvered, his face lined by passing years.

"Hello." Her greeting sounded more like a question.

"You're the woman Quinn ordered?" the man asked.

The woman Quinn ordered? That was a fine *how do you do*. "I'm Mirabelle, and this is my new home. I assume you're Quinn's father."

"That I am." His gaze narrowed on her. "You don't have the look of Ireland about you. Where're your people from?"

A truthful answer seemed best. "I don't rightly know. I grew up in an orphanage with no knowledge of my parents."

"Life's difficult for everyone," Mr. Quinn said.

It wasn't exactly an empathetic response, but neither was it pitying. She appreciated that. Pity, she found, quickly grew tiresome.

Mr. Quinn turned his attention fully to the embers in the fireplace. No hint of a smile touched his face. He sat bent over, his lips turned down, his eyes heavy. Perhaps he was crippled or in pain, though she could see no obvious injuries or disfigurements. Whatever his affliction, he was clearly unhappy.

Hmm.

Her eyes settled on the two doors and a hallway along the back wall. Through one of the doorframes, she spotted a dining room—something she hadn't expected out in the uncivilized West. She'd heard the houses were too simple for such things, that the dining table was generally set up right in the parlor, along with the stove and everything else. Sometimes, she'd been told, the house was nothing but one large room, with sleeping areas divided off by a hanging blanket, if that.

When a woman married a man strictly as a matter of

mutual convenience—and theirs, it was fully understood, was little more than a business arrangement—and the man's father lived with him, that woman very much needed a space of her own. Mirabelle couldn't imagine living tossed together in the same room with both men every minute of their lives.

This arrangement gets better and better. For the first time in her life, Mirabelle could imagine a future that didn't involve a constant struggle to stay cheerful and optimistic.

She crossed closer to the dining room and peeked inside. The table was a fine piece of furniture. The chairs pulled around it appeared to be part of a matched set. It seemed well cared for, needing only a good polish and perhaps a vase of flowers set in the middle for some color.

Through another open doorway sat the kitchen. Knowing she'd likely spend most of her days in that room, Mirabelle took extra time perusing it. The stove appeared new. The cupboards were not bare. Better and better.

She heard the door open and heavy footfalls draw closer. A man as large as her husband likely made a great deal of noise wherever he went.

"I'm in the kitchen," she called out.

He joined her there in the next moment, holding her trunk. It wasn't light by anyone's estimation, yet he carried it as easily as he might an autumn leaf. He showed no signs of strain or struggle. Giants, it seemed, were not only large but strong.

"I haven't yet discovered the whereabouts of my bedroom," Mirabelle said. "If you could just point me in the right direction." She was excited to settle in, to make her space her own.

"It's just off the parlor, like the other rooms." He twitched his chin in that direction.

Mirabelle stepped around him and back through the

doorway. She heard Quinn's footsteps as he came up behind her. She glanced back at him and couldn't help but be amazed all over again at how tall he was. And broad. And generally enormous. Mirabelle had only ever known life from the opposite perspective.

"This is the empty room." He pointed at the last door on the far side of the room. "It hasn't any linens in it, but there are some in the tallboy in the kitchen."

She stepped inside the bedroom. "The view through the window is lovely."

"I suppose." Quinn offered nothing more than that. He set her trunk down.

She watched him leave, unsure yet what to make of the grumpy giant she'd married or his equally grumpy father. "Grumpy" didn't at all fit in the vision she'd had for her new home and family.

But she had never been one to give up easily. She didn't mean to start now.

· 3 ·

Quinn pulled a pair of wire snips from a nail on the wall of his barn and handed them to Sam Carpenter. They were neighbors and regularly lent each other tools or helped make repairs to each other's houses, barns, or fences.

"Did your woman arrive yesterday?" Sam asked.

"Mm-hmm."

Sam nodded. "Must not have given you over for someone else. Otherwise you'd be mad as a nest of hornets."

"She didn't."

Sam chewed on a bit of straw. He leaned against a post, the hand holding the wire cutters hanging at his side.

"How is she working out?" Sam asked.

There was no good answer for that question. Mirabelle wasn't at all what he'd expected. It was more than the initial shock of her size. She had dictated the course of nearly everything since arriving. The dinner hour was moved, as was the furniture in the parlor. She'd declared her intention to hang new curtains and replace the tablecloth. She'd turned their lives topsy-turvy with an unwavering smile on her face. He'd never met a more cheerful despot in all his life.

His silence must have said something. Sam gave him a commiserating look. "She's platter-faced or something?"

Quinn shook his head. Mirabelle was a fine-looking woman, more so than he'd expected, in fact.

"A nag, then?" Sam tried again.

Quinn suspected she might be, but he didn't mean to say as much to someone who hadn't yet met her. He hardly knew her himself, but he'd vowed just the day before to care for her. Insulting her in front of the neighbors felt like breaking that promise.

"How is Tiernan taking to her?" Sam asked.

Da hadn't said a word. He'd come to the table the night before, ate his meal in silence, then left without a word to his new daughter-in-law. When she'd set to moving things about in the parlor, Da had held firm in his chair, glaring at her as if challenging the newcomer to move his chair from its spot.

"We're adjusting," Quinn said.

Sam worked his jaw so the sprig of straw in his teeth fluttered in the air. "That, my friend, is why you ain't gonna see a woman at my house. Too much fuss and folderol."

Quinn felt a smile tug at his mouth. "Face it, friend. That's not the reason at all. No woman would have you."

Sam laughed. "Not even a mail-order bride, I'd guess."

"Aye, there's not one among even that lot who's desperate enough to marry you." Quinn sat on a tall stool near the cow stall.

Sam's gap-toothed grin grew. "I swear, for a man who never set foot in Ireland, you sure sound like it sometimes."

"Blame my da and ma for that," Quinn tossed back. They'd been near about his only companions for much of his growing up years. He was well into his teens before he realized most people in America didn't sound like his parents.

"I knew your mother, Quinn. I'll not let even you say anything unflattering about that fine woman."

Sweet, darling Ma. Everyone who knew her had loved her. Saints, he missed her.

Mirabelle stepped inside the barn the very next moment. Quinn was on his feet in an instant, watching her approach with wariness. Was her whirlwind of upheaval expanding from the house now? She was a tiny wisp of a thing who hadn't even been there an entire day, yet she seemed destined to take over the running of everything.

"You didn't return for lunch," she said. She held in her hand what looked like a plate with a kitchen towel draped over it. "So I've brought your meal out to you."

Without the slightest wobble of the plate, she set it on the stool Quinn had been sitting on and pulled the kitchen towel off with a bit of flourish.

Sam eyed Mirabelle. "Tiny thing, ain't she?"

Mirabelle looked Sam up and down before declaring, "Mouthy thing, ain't he?"

Her quick and candid response clearly caught Sam off guard. Though Quinn had known his bride not quite twenty-four hours, he wasn't at all surprised by her take-charge manner.

"Mirabelle"—he took up the introductions—"this is Sam Carpenter, our nearest neighbor. Sam, this is my wife." The last two words felt horribly awkward, but he managed them.

She held her hand out to Sam exactly the way she had to Quinn when they first met. Though women out West were often just as straightforward and imposing as the menfolk, he'd never before seen such a tiny, delicate-looking woman be so completely unintimidated.

"Pleased to meet you, Mr. Carpenter," she said as she firmly shook Sam's hand.

"Call me Sam." He looked very unsure of her.

"I suppose that's better than what I had planned to call

you." She dropped Sam's hand and turned to Quinn. "Your father says he doesn't care for cold beef sandwiches, but when I asked if he preferred the beef hot, he told me to quit being cheeky."

Da had likely said exactly that. Would Quinn have to play peacemaker between the two?

"So which is it?" Mirabelle asked.

"Which is *what*?"

"Does your father not care for beef sandwiches or does he not care for *cold* beef sandwiches?"

Before he could answer, Sam spoke up. "I'll just be on my way back to my place," he said. "Thanks for the loan." He held up the wire snips.

Quinn nodded his acknowledgment. Sam left with only one backward glance.

Mirabelle kept her expectant gaze on Quinn. He took a moment to remind himself what question she'd asked.

"Uh . . ." She'd asked about beef versus cold beef. "Da likes beef." They were cattle ranchers. Of course he liked beef.

"He wouldn't eat it." Mirabelle leveled him a pointed look.

What could Quinn say to that? "Perhaps he didn't want beef today."

"He also didn't eat the greens or the bread the beef was on. The only thing he accepted from me was water."

Quinn took the plate off the stool and sat, setting the plate on his lap. "Da's just getting used to you. Don't let him fret you."

"I don't want him to starve." There was just enough laughter in her eyes to convince him she didn't actually think Da was going to die of hunger.

Quinn tucked in to the meal she'd brought him. If he ate quickly, maybe Mirabelle would be on her way and he could get back to work. He didn't have time, or the desire, to sit around talking to a woman. Winter was coming. His list of chores was long.

She climbed up one of the stall walls and sat on the top rail, facing him. How she managed the feat in a dress and as small as she was, he didn't know.

"I can't tell if I'm preventing your father from doing whatever he usually does or if he simply doesn't usually do anything." Mirabelle leaned against the post next to her. The curl in her hair was a touch riotous just then, at odds with the calm of her expression and the casualness of her posture.

Quinn swallowed a large bite of the sandwich. If Da really had refused Mirabelle's lunch, he'd missed out. The beef was sliced thin; the bread was sliced thick.

"Da's an old man," Quinn explained. "His days are quieter than they used to be."

"Your father can't be much more than fifty years old," Mirabelle said. "He doesn't exactly have one foot in the grave."

Da was only fifty-five, in fact. But in a lot of ways, he was older than that. The past four years had aged him. "Just leave him to his own self. Everyone'll be happier that way."

"Do you know you sound a little Irish?" Mirabelle seemed to settle in. Apparently, she intended to have a cozy chat right there in the barn.

"Likely because I *am* Irish."

"I like it." Mirabelle nodded firmly. "There is something about an Irish accent that makes words sound musical."

Was he supposed to thank her? Quinn had no idea.

He'd already finished his entire lunch. He discovered, between dinner the night before and breakfast that morning, that Mirabelle didn't truly understand just how much food a man his size, who worked as long and hard as he did, actually required each day. Never mind Da; she'd starve *him* to death.

"Is there a local ladies' society?" Mirabelle asked.

"I don't know." He slid off the stool and set the plate on it.

"A quilting circle, maybe?"

Quinn held his hands out in a show of ignorance. What did he know of quilting circles?

"Is there at least a watering hole where the local wildlife gather?"

He could match her dry tone. "Of course there is. It's called The Golden Cup Saloon."

She smiled all the way to her eyes. That was intriguing. He liked that she understood his humor. That boded well for eventually finding a comfortable peace together.

"Do you go to church on Sundays?" Mirabelle asked.

"No." He had nothing against church; it just didn't particularly appeal to him. He went now and then if it struck his fancy. He realized in that moment he didn't know anything about his new wife's religious leanings. "Are you a regular Sunday worshipper?"

"I think I'd better be," she answered in all seriousness.

She *had better be*? "Why's that?"

"Otherwise, how will I ever find out about ladies' societies and quilting bees and all those things you don't know anything about? It's either church or The Golden Cup Saloon." The smallest twinkle of mischief shone in her eyes. She was joking with him still? He didn't quite know what to make of that. "I'm afraid I never learned to drive a team. Is it a long walk to town?" she asked.

"Too far to walk, especially on your own. If you ever need to go into town, I'll drive you."

She gave a firm nod and offered a straightforward, "Thank you."

"I'd best get back to my work." He hoped the hint was enough to send her back to the house.

She started forward, but didn't move more than an inch at the most. She copied the motion a couple of times, glancing behind her repeatedly. Her eyes settled on him.

"I'm stuck."

"Stuck?"

She nodded. "My dress is caught on something, but I can't tell what. A splinter, maybe. Or a nail." She looked down at the slat. "I don't know what it is, but I can't get down."

He crossed to where she sat, eyeing the skirt of her dress. He didn't see any snags, nothing to indicate where her dress was caught.

"If you didn't go climbing about like a monkey, these things wouldn't happen." He leaned around her, trying to see if anything was snagged from behind.

"If you weren't three times as tall as I am," she tossed back, "I wouldn't need to climb up the walls in order to look you in the eye."

He set his hands on the rail on either side of her. "Is that why you sat up here, so you'd be as tall I am?"

It had done the trick, actually. They were more or less the same height now. They were eye to eye, something that hadn't happened since they'd met. Her eyes weren't simply blue. He saw flecks of green and golden brown. He discovered something else standing there so close to her. He'd been right when talking with Sam earlier that day; Mirabelle *was* pretty.

"Will you help me get down?" she asked. "I hadn't planned to spend the rest of forever perched here like a bird."

Pull your thoughts together. No time for pointless wonderings.

"I'd guess you're sitting on whatever it is that's caught hold of your dress," he said. "If you lean one direction or the other, I'll see if I can spot it."

A little of the color drained from her face. "If I lean too

far, I might fall," she said, her voice quieter than it had been. Was she afraid? She, who had scaled up there without hesitation, who had agilely climbed down from the wagon the evening before, was afraid of falling?

"Lean that direction." He motioned with his right thumb. He curled his arm around her waist, so she'd have something holding her there.

She leaned against his arm, but only just.

"I can't see anything unless you lean further," he told her.

"I'll fall," she little more than whispered.

She really was afraid. That surprised him. Greatly.

"I won't let you fall," he promised.

He held her gaze for a drawn-out moment. She was clearly trying to decide if she could trust him. Quinn knew he had shortcomings, faults like anyone else, but no one had ever found him undeserving of their trust. Not ever.

"Lean further," he repeated.

Whether she found him trustworthy in that moment or simply gave in to the inevitable, he didn't know. But she leaned as he instructed, putting her weight on his arm. He was struck again by just how small she was. His arm wrapped easily all the way around her. He could probably carry her around in one hand, perhaps in a pocket.

He used his free hand to carefully move the flowing fabric of her skirt, searching for the snag. He found it: a long, nasty-looking splinter shoved clear through her skirt. She was fortunate it hadn't pierced all the way through to her leg.

"Just give me a minute," he said. "I'll have you free."

"You found it, then?" Her voice had regained some of its fortitude.

"A splintered bit of wood," he said.

"Please be careful not to tear the dress—it's the only one I have."

That stopped his efforts and brought his gaze back to her face. "You only have one dress?" He himself had four new pairs of trousers and a half-dozen shirts, even a couple jackets to choose from. A second thought occurred to him. "What do you wear on wash day?"

"I do the wash in my underclothes."

His eyes pulled wide, and he felt heat rise immediately to his face. He'd inherited enough ginger coloring from his Irish parents to flush when he was embarrassed. He hated it.

Mirabelle laughed, the sound bouncing off the walls of the barn. "Don't fret, Quinn. I'll not scandalize the neighbors. I have a wrapper I found in a rag pile that I wear on wash days. It's absolutely hideous, but it lets me get my dress clean."

She wears something she found in a rag pile? Just how desperate was her situation before coming here?

"So am I destined to sit here for the rest of forever, or do you think you can unsnag me?" Mirabelle looked down at her stuck dress but hadn't let go of his arm.

He carefully inched the fabric back over the splinter. He had her free in a moment's time. "It left a little hole," he said.

One hand still clutching his arm, she held up the side of her dress for closer inspection. "Well, a hole's easily mended if it's seen to right away. I'll sew it up tonight after I've changed into my nightdress." She shrugged and gave him an amusedly resigned smile. "Will you help me down? If I try, I'll probably snag somewhere else, and I'll walk away with a dress no better than a slice of Swiss cheese."

Helping her to the ground took no effort whatsoever. He set his hands on either side of her waist and lifted her up from the railing and down to the ground. She couldn't have weighed much more than a sparrow.

A tiny, tiny thing.

"What does that look mean?" She eyed him with uncertainty.

He shook his head. He might not have known much about women, but he felt certain telling her he was pondering how shockingly little she was would be a mistake. He broke off the splinter she'd caught herself on, telling himself to add sanding the wood to his list of jobs.

That brought to mind the list of chores he had for her. He reached into his shirt pocket and pulled out the folded paper he'd jotted her jobs down on. "Here are the things that need seeing to before winter arrives."

He held the list out to her. She eyed it a moment before taking the paper with obvious hesitation. She unfolded it. Her eyes darted back and forth as she read. She looked up at him briefly before flipping if over and reading the rest.

"This is a long list," she said, turning it over again.

"There's a lot of work to be done."

He wasn't asking so much of her out of spite or orneriness. Life in Wyoming required preparation against the long, bitter winters. He'd done the work by himself for years but never managed to get to it all. Part of the reason he'd sent for a wife was to help him with these things.

"Some of these I've never done before." She looked at him over the paper. "Sealing up drafts around the windows? I don't know how to do that. I probably can't even reach all of the windows."

"I'll show you how. And you can use the ladder if you need it."

Mirabelle swallowed audibly. "I don't care for heights."

He'd sorted out that much during her battle with the splinter. "I'll see to the drafts if need be, but you'll have to sort out the rest. I simply haven't time enough, but it has to be done. Life here is unforgiving. That's why I needed a wife. I'll do my work and you do yours. That arrangement will mean we'll survive the coming winter."

She looked over the list again. "Is there a preferred order in which these ought to be finished?"

"The heavier snows will keep us from town," he said. "So start with inventorying the food and supplies."

"I'll begin today." Mirabelle nodded firmly.

With that, she walked out of the barn, taking the empty plate with her. *I'll begin today.* She wasn't going to complain or insist on doing things her way without regard to his thoughts on the matter. He'd debated for years whether or not to send for a wife. They'd employed a good number of maids over the past years, but none stayed long. An unwed woman in the wilds of Wyoming was generally snatched up in a matter of weeks, months at the most.

He needed someone who wasn't simply going to turn around and leave, but he didn't want the complications usually associated with courtship and marriage.

This was going to work. This was going to work just fine.

· 4 ·

QUINN NODDED TO a few men he knew as he walked down the street toward the mercantile. He tipped his hat to the preacher's wife and returned the preacher's brief wave. He wove through the crowd just inside the mercantile door—not an easy thing for a man his size.

Mirabelle was not the only one in the mercantile ordering supplies for the coming winter. She was, however, the only one getting exactly what she insisted on. Mirabelle had her list in hand and was pointing and verbally directing the merchant and his son toward the things she wanted.

"That broom looks as though it has already gone through a few years of use. If I'm to pay for a new one, I'd like to *get* a new one." Mirabelle sent the young Mr. Carlton back for another broom. She caught the elder Mr. Carlton in the next moment. "I believe my husband prefers the coffee in the red tin." And with that declaration, the tins of blue coffee were carried back to the shelves.

At least a dozen people stood in the building waiting their turn while Mirabelle more or less ran the place. She somehow even managed to get a few of the customers to grab things for her and set them on the counter. Quinn watched it all with equal parts approval and uncertainty.

He'd married a bundle of energy. That was a promising thing. But he'd never known a woman quite like her and didn't know what to expect.

Mirabelle spotted him after a moment. "The heavier items are being put in the wagon," she said. "I'm just arranging for the final things on the list." Without batting an eyelash, she shifted her attention to Mr. Carlton Sr., thanking him for gathering the coffee she'd ordered and directing him to the proper amount of marmalade.

Quinn had fully expected to need to step in and help complete the order, but his tiny wife didn't need his assistance at all. "I'll meet you out in the wagon," he told her.

She gave him a quick nod and immediately returned to her task. She accomplished her work with efficiency, not expecting him to hover around or bemoaning the workload. She undertook unfamiliar jobs with confidence and determination. He seemed to have gotten exactly what he'd needed.

His wagon was quickly filled with precisely the things they needed for the winter. Mirabelle followed a few minutes later, her plain brown bonnet tied securely under her chin once more. She climbed into the wagon and settled herself on the bench beside him.

"I believe that's enough, along with what's already at the house, to see us through the next six months," Mirabelle said.

"Good."

She dug around in her small drawstring bag. "And"—she pulled out a roll of paper money—"there is even a little left over."

Quinn counted out the bills. "This is nearly ten dollars, Mirabelle. How can you possibly have this much left over?"

"Mr. Carlton agreed that, seeing as you were placing a

large order, he could give you a discount on a few of the smaller items."

He watched her a moment, stunned into silence. "You haggled with Closefisted Carlton?"

Her eyes widened. "Is he really called that?"

Quinn set the horses to a trot. "Yes. And for good reason." No one, as far as Quinn knew, had ever talked Carlton down on a price.

"Well, I found him perfectly reasonable," Mirabelle said. "He could see the wisdom in allowing some flexibility in pricing when his molasses and extracts were clearly on the old side—not spoiled, mind you, simply not as fresh as they might have been."

"You told Mr. Carlton his goods were second rate?" Saints above, she might have made an enemy of their shopkeeper. He was something of a hard man.

"Of course not." Mirabelle sat with her usual confident posture. "I simply asked him what fraction of the price he would charge if I took a few of the older items as opposed to the newer ones. I let him know how clear it was that he prided himself in the quality of his goods and would surely be removing those things from his shelves shortly, costing himself the money he'd invested in them. He saw the wisdom in getting *some* money for those things as opposed to none at all. And, of course, I only made the deal on items that wouldn't lose much quality simply by being on the shelf a little longer. What we paid for, paid *less* for, really isn't fundamentally different from what we might have bought at full price."

Quinn allowed an inward smile but found it wouldn't stop there. His lips twitched upward, first one side and then the other. Before he knew it, he was grinning. His tiny Mirabelle had out-bargained one of the shrewdest businessmen Quinn had ever known. The farther they drove, the broader he smiled.

"Am I to assume, then," Mirabelle asked, "you don't mind mustard powder that's the tiniest bit stale and molasses that will need a little warming to be soft again?"

With the money she'd saved him, he wouldn't mind molasses that required a hammer and chisel. "I've never known Mr. Carlton to be talked down on price. Not by anyone."

"Well, Quinn, I think you should know I am not just 'anyone.'"

He looked at her for a long moment as that declaration sunk in. "Do you know, Mirabelle, I'm beginning to think that's true."

"Are you saying you struck an even more cunning bargain with the William's Bureau than I did with Mr. Carlton?"

"That depends," he answered. Glancing away from the road and toward her, he could see she'd set her gaze firmly on him.

"Depends on what?"

"On whether or not you're the tiniest bit stale."

She smiled at him. Mirabelle was a fine-looking woman, especially with her expression light and amused.

"I saw two of the women I met on the train ride here," she said. "I invited them over this next week for a sewing circle. You don't have any objections, do you?"

Quinn was seized with a clear and sudden memory of his mother and her friends sitting in the parlor sewing. They'd filled the house with laughter and the smell of rose water. Da would stand in the kitchen doorway with a smitten smile on his face, his eyes never leaving Ma, never wandering to anyone else.

". . . and I'll still have plenty of time to get dinner on the table." Mirabelle was finishing a sentence Quinn hadn't heard but could guess at. She was explaining all the reasons he shouldn't be bothered by her sewing circle engagement.

Did he object to her having some of her friends over? He didn't. But he wouldn't be hovering around like an adoring puppy the way his father always had. Being that lovesick had caused Da no end of pain. It was the reason he'd amassed so much debt, the reason he'd often neglected his work, the reason he was now so utterly broken by Ma's death.

"So would you mind?" she asked again.

"I don't mind," he said.

But would Da mind? Quinn couldn't rightly say. Having ladies in the house again, doing some of the same things Ma had done, might help pull Da from the dark place he'd been in the past four years. Quinn had hoped as much when he decided to send for a wife. But it might just as easily make things worse.

"This is what I hoped for all the way here on the train," Mirabelle said. "I wanted friends, even just one. But then I didn't meet anyone after I arrived—except you, of course, and your father—and I started to wonder if I would make any friends at all."

Quinn set his sights on the road, guiding the horses down the familiar path. The day Mirabelle had stepped off the train, Quinn had congratulated himself on finding a quiet wife. He'd discovered in the days since then that, once she got to talking, Mirabelle was more than capable of chattering on.

Quite without warning, he could sense Mirabelle looking at him again. How was it he could *feel* her gaze? It didn't make any sense. He let his eyes drift from his horses to his wife. She was, in fact, watching him.

"Are you certain you don't mind?" she asked.

How many times did she mean to ask? "I not only don't mind, I don't particularly care one way or the other."

Until that moment, he hadn't really understood what seeing a face "fall" looked like. Mirabelle looked away from him, as if watching the scenery, but her eyes didn't seem to focus on anything in particular. Her smile disappeared. The amusement in her face was gone.

He was likely expected to say something, to make amends. But if he hadn't done anything wrong, what was he supposed to apologize for?

"Will your father mind if I have two ladies visit me?" Mirabelle asked the question quietly, but with the firmness of purpose he'd seen in her every moment of their acquaintance.

Da might very well mind. He might mind a great deal. But getting Da to return to the world of the living was high on Quinn's list of priorities. Having two of the local ladies come around was a step in that direction.

"I'll talk to Da," Quinn said. "But I don't think he'll have any objections."

Mirabelle didn't look convinced. And she'd lost some of the fire she'd had before.

"Is something the matter?" he asked, guiding the horses down the lane leading home.

"I'm fine." She punctuated the declaration with a firm nod of her head.

But she clearly wasn't. Why was it women clammed up when they were upset instead of just talking things out? Well, if she didn't want to talk, he wasn't going to make her. They'd accomplished their list of chores in town. They'd be busy with their chores at home soon enough. Work was always a good distraction.

· 5 ·

By Wednesday morning, Mirabelle began to question the wisdom of inviting Jane and Caroline to visit with only two days to prepare for their arrival. In those two days, she'd been charged with getting the winter supplies organized in the root cellar and pantry, something that had taken the remainder of Monday and all of Tuesday. She had hoped to give the parlor a good cleaning, polish the furniture, perhaps find fabric to make curtains. She hadn't had time to even wash the floor, for heaven's sake.

"For years I've been dreaming of entertaining guests in my own home," she mumbled to herself in the kitchen. "Now that my chance has come, I have dirty floors and faded drapes."

She stood in the doorway between the kitchen and the parlor, looking out over the room in which she'd be hostessing her new friends. She set her hands on her hips, thinking through her dilemma. Ought she to spend the remainder of the morning getting the parlor as close to sparkling as she could manage, or ought she to spend that time baking something for her guests to eat?

She didn't have time nor the materials to replace the curtains. And she couldn't very well have people over to visit and not offer them anything to eat.

If that weren't a convincing enough argument, her father-in-law's presence in the parlor rather convinced her to avoid that room as much as possible. She hoped he would leave when her visitors arrived. He was a quiet presence in the room, but a trying one. He tended to glare, watching every move she made as though searching for something to criticize. When he did speak, it was never a thank-you or a compliment or any recognition of all the work she did. He was unhappy, and he nudged her uncomfortably close to being unhappy herself, something she worked very hard not to be.

Mirabelle slipped back into the kitchen and set herself to the task of preparing something to serve her guests. She eyed the supplies in the pantry, grateful it was well-stocked. She had pearl ash, enough to make a simple, but enjoyable, tea cake. Her baking skills wouldn't win her any accolades, but she could make a respectable cake. And she had tea to serve with it. A well-brewed cup of tea or coffee, she'd learned during her year serving meals at a train station, could make up for a multitude of shortcomings in the kitchen.

She glanced at the clock. If she worked without a break, she could manage to get the cake in the oven with enough time to make Quinn and Tiernan their lunch. Baking the batter in cups rather than a full-sized cake pan would save her time as well. She could straighten the parlor while the cakes cooled. The timing would be close, but she might manage it.

Mirabelle had a great many moments during the next quarter of an hour in which she could almost imagine herself back in the bustling kitchen of the railway restaurant. Speed was essential when trying to serve meals during the short

A Convenient Arrangement

duration of a train stop. She was calling upon those hard-learned skills again.

She had the cakes divided up and in the oven with barely enough time to spare. She pulled down two deep plates from the cupboards and set two thick slices of bread in each. A slightly thickened gravy was hot and ready in a matter of minutes. She put the pot off the heat.

With the efficiency that came of experience, she sliced two apples, setting each in a small bowl, lightly sprinkling the fruit with cinnamon. Mirabelle poured gravy over each of the double-slices of bread and placed the plates on a large serving platter with two pairs of forks and butter knives. The apple bowls went on the platter next, then two cups set upside down, stacked inside one another. She pumped water from the sink into a pitcher and placed it at the center of the tray.

Mirabelle lifted the tray, not nearly as heavy as many platters she'd carried around the restaurant, and made her way with hardly a wobble to the dining room. She had the men's places set and their meal set out just as Quinn arrived.

He gave her a single nod of acknowledgment, which she returned. That constituted a drawn-out conversation with him. Only on the rarest occasions did he actually speak. The longest they'd spoken was in his barn the previous week and during the ride back from town two days earlier. This was part of her motivation for inviting Jane and Caroline over for a visit; she needed someone to talk to.

She stepped to the back of the sofa and addressed Tiernan, still sitting near the fireplace. "Lunch is on the table."

She made her way back to the kitchen without waiting for a reply of any kind. Tiernan, while not nearly as taciturn as his son, wasn't likely to respond to her. He only spoke when he had complaints.

The cakes were nearly done. Mirabelle set herself to

tidying up the kitchen while she waited. She would move on to the parlor in just a moment. Everything she'd pulled out and dirtied making the men's lunch was cleaned and put away just in time to pull the small tea cakes out of the oven. She set them on the windowsill to cool and took her brand new broom and a few dust rags into the parlor.

With the desperation that can only be understood by a woman about to entertain other women in her unkempt home, Mirabelle set to the task of making the room as presentable as she could. Windows were wiped, surfaces dusted, the floor swept. Though she couldn't replace the curtains, she did straighten them, making them as even on either side of the window as she could.

The bits of ash that managed to sprinkle themselves along the hearth were swept and dumped into the ash can. The portrait above the mantel hung the tiniest bit crooked. Mirabelle pulled over a footstool and carefully adjusted the portrait frame until it hung straight once more.

She'd been intrigued by the woman in the portrait from her first day in Quinn's home. The woman was lovely, strikingly so. She had the daintiest of noses and a perfect rosebud mouth. Her brown hair held the same hint of red that Quinn's did. But it was her eyes that first told Mirabelle that this beauty was her late mother-in-law. Those piercing gray eyes were the same shape and had the same quality as Quinn's, though his eyes were blue.

This was the previous mistress of the house Mirabelle now ran. Could they have been more different? The late Mrs. Quinn was lovely and obviously graceful. The dress she wore had inspired instant envy in Mirabelle. Even more than a decade out of date, that dress was finer than anything Mirabelle had ever worn, precisely the sort of dress she had often daydreamed about wearing to a ball or dance or fine social. The fabric looked luxurious. The lace ruffling at the collar and front of the gown was stunning. She would never have been able to afford even a small bit of that lace. Perhaps her late mother-in-law's fine apparel meant she herself would be permitted a reasonable clothing budget. She had but the one dress, and it had seen far better days. How she would love to own something pretty and new.

Enough of your woolgathering, Mirabelle. You have guests arriving soon.

She gathered up her cleaning supplies and returned to the kitchen. The men hadn't yet brought their plates back from the dining room. She crossed to the windowsill. If her cakes had cooled enough, she would sprinkle them with a bit of sugar.

But the cakes were gone.

She looked around, although unsure where she expected them to be. They weren't on the countertop or the work table. *Perhaps the cakes fell out.* Mirabelle stretched up onto her toes, peering out the open window. But she was too short to see.

They wouldn't have fallen out. The sill was deep, and the cakes had been farther inside the window than out. *Where in heaven's name?* The cakes were nowhere to be seen. She would have to check outside after all. She'd have nothing to offer her guests if the cakes were lying out there in the dirt.

Her first time as a hostess. What if it was a disaster? A lump started in her throat, but she pushed it down again. There was no reason to believe the cakes were ruined. She simply had to find them and finish her preparations.

She could ponder the puzzle while she washed the men's lunch dishes. She moved into the dining room. Not even one step inside, she froze.

"My cakes." The words came out as a gasp.

Tiernan sat there, his lunch plate untouched, with one of her small cakes in his hand and the crumbly remains of at least one other on the table in front of him. Another cake sat awaiting its fate. How many had he eaten?

"My cakes." There was more force behind the words that time, more accusation. "You ate my cakes."

"Didn't know they were yours." Tiernan took another bite, finishing off the cake he held.

Mirabelle looked at Quinn, but he seemed as unconcerned as his father.

"Those were for the ladies who are coming today for my sewing circle. I made them special." A horrible thought hit her without warning. "Did you eat them all?"

Tiernan picked up the uneaten cake. Mirabelle moved to his side in two large strides and snatched it from his hand.

"These were *mine*."

"I am not a child," he said. "I don't have to ask permission in my own home to eat a cake."

How could she argue with that? And, yet, he ought to have asked. And, yet again, she hadn't warned them the cakes were special. This *was* Tiernan's home, his and Quinn's. But it was hers as well. At least it was supposed to be.

"They were special for my guests." The protest sounded weak even to her ears.

She looked to Quinn for some support. He kept as quiet as ever, not offering any excuses or apologies. Would neither of them show the slightest remorse?

"What am I to serve them?" She looked from one man to the other.

Tiernan nudged his untouched plate in her direction. "Give 'em this lot." He scrunched his nose up. "Best of luck to you getting them to eat it."

First, he ate all her tea cakes, then he insulted the meal

she'd made for him? Quinn had finished his lunch, so it couldn't be as terrible as Tiernan made it out to be. Again, her husband made no effort to defend her.

Mirabelle let her frustration firm her resolve. She hadn't crumbled under indifference before; she certainly wouldn't do so now. "If you two are finished, I'll just clear the table."

Without looking at either of them more than was necessary, she set their dishes on the platter she'd left in the dining room for just that purpose. She'd learned well how to disappear while clearing tables. A good waitress was unobtrusive.

But I'm not supposed to be merely an employee anymore.

The men stood from the table and made their way from the room, not bidding her farewell or thanking her for the meal.

"I do my work and you do yours," Quinn had said. But surely he intended her to be more than a worker. Surely.

"It will get better," she whispered to herself when the room was empty. "It will. It has to."

In the meantime, she had a more immediate difficulty to solve. What was she going to serve Jane and Caroline?

She lifted the tray in her hand and carried it into the kitchen.

I can't offer them buttered bread. That would be too humiliating.

She could tell by looking that Tiernan hadn't even tasted the lunch she'd made. None of his utensils were the slightest bit dirtied. The gravy had a thin skin from sitting undisturbed as it cooled.

Mirabelle pushed out a breath. She was about to eat leftover lunch because she hadn't the luxury of making herself a meal. This wasn't quite what she'd imagined when she'd pictured a home and family of her own. She'd never been invited to eat with Quinn or his father during their morning or noontime meals. She ate her dinner in the dining room, mostly so she could sit for a few minutes, but neither of the men talked to her.

She took a fresh fork from the utensil drawer and returned to the cold plate of bread and gravy on the counter. She stood there, alone, eating her hand-me-down meal.

She'd known this wasn't a marriage of love, that she was there to work and help around the house. She hadn't expected immediate tenderness or affection, but she had anticipated being appreciated and shown a little kindness. She needed at least that.

"Pull yourself together, Mirabelle. This melancholy mood is not like you."

She was nervous was all—nervous and a little overwhelmed.

Heavy footsteps announced Quinn's arrival without the necessity of looking back to see him.

"Da didn't know about the cakes," he said.

But once he did know, he didn't care. Neither of these men did. Heavens, she was struggling to shake this gloom. She took another bite of the cold, now-unappetizing meal.

"He is an old man," Quinn continued. "He hasn't a lot of pleasures in life. The cakes are a small thing, really."

Except it wasn't about the cakes. Reaching out to these would-be friends was the only thing she had done for herself in the week she'd been in Wyoming. It was her first chance for connection and companionship, an opportunity to find people she could matter to. It was a bit of hope she'd offered herself, and it was slipping away.

"I haven't a lot of pleasures in my life either, Quinn.

Having friends over for tea and cakes was meant to be one of them."

"What time are the ladies arriving?" Quinn didn't sound overjoyed at the prospect. But he'd agreed to it, and she had lost enough battles that day.

She took a breath and firmly grasped her optimism once more. All would go well. She was determined it would. "They'll be here at one o'clock."

"It is one o'clock now."

For the first time since he arrived, she looked back in his direction, but her gaze slid past him, through the doorway, to the clock just visible on the mantel in the parlor. It was, indeed, one o'clock. She hadn't even smoothed out her hair or brushed her dress.

So much for lunch. Mirabelle moved quickly to the scrap bucket and scraped the remainder of her meal into it. She had her apron off and hanging on its peg in a trice. Quinn all but blocked the doorway. She was forced to pause in front of him.

"Da really didn't know about the cakes," he said.

Find a reason to feel encouraged. Search out a silver lining. "I appreciate that he didn't do it intentionally. Next time, I'll be certain to warn him so we'll not have this difficulty again."

Quinn gave one of his quick nods. That, she'd discovered, could mean anything from "hello" to "I agree" to "I'm sure you just said something, but I wasn't really listening."

In that moment, she needed more than that from him. She needed a kind word, a bit of appreciation, someone to lean on while she regained her own strength.

She needed to not feel so alone.

· 6 ·

MIRABELLE'S GUESTS HAD arrived a half hour earlier or so. That had been Quinn's cue to do some work away from the house. He didn't begrudge her the company. He simply wasn't keen on having visitors himself. She could have her bit of socializing; he would stick to his work.

"'Tis a regular hen party in there, it is."

Da had obviously come into the barn, though Quinn hadn't heard him enter. Quinn hadn't his father's knack for moving about quietly.

Da pulled up a tall stool and sat nearby. "So much chatter in the house just now. You'd think a colony of magpies had nested in the chimney."

"Women do like to talk." Quinn kept at his work. Da didn't come out to the barn often, and Quinn was glad to see him there, but he'd learned over the past four years that if he made much of a fuss over Da's doing anything other than his usual quiet contemplation, the man got himself into a huff and retreated ever further.

"That woman of yours sure beats all, she does. Either talking a body's ear off or silent as the grave. Never anything in between."

That was a fair description of Mirabelle. Quinn still wasn't sure what to make of her.

"I haven't asked you since you kindly informed me of her existence the morning she was due to arrive," Da said, "but I mean to ask m' question now."

Quinn looked up from his saddle and directly into Da's piercing and determined gaze.

"Why'd you do it?" Da asked.

"Do what?"

Da came noticeably close to rolling his eyes. "Don't act like I've no more brains than a rock. You know perfectly well what I'm asking you."

"I married for the same reason any man does," Quinn said. "I needed a woman around the house. The place's been falling to bits with just the two of us."

"That, son, is why a man hires a maid. It's not reason enough to marry."

Quinn looked over at Da. "How quickly you've forgotten what's happened every time we've hired a maid up to the house. Just as soon as we get one accustomed to our ways and preferences, some bloke swoops in and marries her. That's how it is around here. So few women, so many men in need of one. This was a better solution."

"'Tis a fool's solution, lad. You don't marry a woman because you need someone to clean your house and cook your meals, but because you love her, because she's everything in the world to you."

Quinn shook his head in exasperation. "And where was I to find this love of my life, Da? In town? You can count on your own fingers the number of unwed women within fifty miles of here, and there's not a one of them I could live under the same roof with and not want to throttle her within a week."

Da folded his arms across his chest. "How do you know you won't end up at daggers drawn with this woman just as you would with those others?"

Quinn couldn't know that, not for sure. "A marriage arranged by telegram is less complicated." It was the explanation he'd given himself many times over. "Neither of us have any expectations of affection or attentiveness. Any woman I courted into a marriage would expect both of those things."

Da didn't express any relief or agreement with Quinn's logic. Did he really need to be even more specific?

"All I expect from Mirabelle is a clean house, food on the table, and help with the work around here. All she expects from me is a roof over her head, shoes on her feet, and food to eat. We understand each other. This way is less complicated."

"I suspect neither of you will be satisfied with your 'less-complicated' arrangement for long. 'Tis a painful thing, realizing you'll never have what you truly want."

Da could have been talking about himself as much as anyone. He'd courted and married a woman he loved to distraction, and now he was left without the person he truly wanted. He'd been rendered old beyond his years, alone and broken, spending his days lost in memories. No. Quinn's way was best.

The sound of approaching hooves and the turning of wagon wheels brought an end to their discussion. They moved to the barn doors in time to identify the arrival. Horace Franklin.

"Here to collect his woman, no doubt," Da said.

Horace's new wife had arrived on the same train as Mirabelle and was one of her guests. Quinn crossed to his wagon just as he climbed down. They shook hands and exchanged the usual brief greeting, followed by comments on the herds and conditions as they walked toward the house.

Quinn opened the door, and Da and Horace stepped inside. The women were sitting around the parlor, sewing, but looked up as the men came in. The black-haired woman's eyes settled immediately on Horace, and her lips turned up in an almost besotted smile. Quinn glanced at his neighbor to find a nearly identical look on his face.

They'd not known each other any longer than Quinn and Mirabelle had, and their marriage had been arranged in the same way. Why, then, did the two of them look so lovey-dovey?

"Are you ready to come home, Jane?" Horace asked, his tone solicitous and gentle in a way Quinn was not accustomed to hearing. Horace wasn't an ornery sort by any means, but he was usually as unsentimental as Quinn himself.

"Oh, yes, of course." Jane gathered her sewing. Horace moved to where she sat and helped her put the fabric scraps into her basket. The two of them repeatedly glanced at each other, smiling a little, lingering over the moments when their eyes met.

Horace Franklin has gone and lost his wits.

With her sewing basket arranged and packed, Jane rose from her chair. Horace seemed to remember himself and turned to address Mirabelle's other guest.

"Marcus asked me to fetch you home as well," he said.

Mirabelle helped gather that lady's things. Horace and Jane were too busy whispering something to each other. Quinn leaned against the rock fireplace, oddly fascinated by the whole thing. He'd seen men act lovesick before—heaven knew his da had invented that state of being—but he'd never before seen a man lose his head in a matter of days over a mail-order wife.

Mirabelle walked out with her new friends to the waiting wagon, though Jane hardly needed the company. Horace hadn't moved so much as an inch from her side. The man was lost on her. Quinn inwardly shook his head. If Horace didn't keep his wits about him, he'd end up a broken man, just like Da.

Quinn watched the women bid farewell to one another. They hugged a great deal and waved as Horace's wagon rolled around the bend and out of sight. Mirabelle returned to the house, though with a look of regret.

Her disappointment pricked at him. "Did your visit not go well?"

"It was very pleasant," she said. "They said there's to be a calico ball. They both seemed to know what that was, but I've never heard the term before."

He folded his arms across his chest, leaning against the fireplace. "It's a tradition hereabouts—a town social where the menfolk wear their working clothes instead of their finest and the womenfolk make themselves ordinary dresses from plain fabrics instead of silks and satins and the fancier togs a lady might usually wear to a dance."

"A dance?" Her face lit at the word. The eagerness he'd seen in her expression that first day as she'd surveyed the town returned in full force. "There'll be dancing?"

"There's always dancing. Will, who works here, and Sam, who you've met, play the fiddle and guitar. Another man plays the accordion. The three of them keep the calico ball lively."

"With dancing?" The answer seemed to matter to her.

"A whole evening of it."

She sighed, the sound one of pure joy. "Dancing. I've always wanted to—" She stopped abruptly, her thoughts seemed to have gone elsewhere very quickly.

Quinn had no trouble filling in the gap. She'd always wanted to go to a dance . . . to dance with someone. "Have you never danced before?"

"Not ever," she admitted.

He'd danced now and then at the calico balls over the years and at other sociables. He couldn't say he was particularly adept; his size alone made his attempts at anything graceful extremely awkward.

"I'm something of a lumbering buffalo when I dance. I prefer leaving the doing of it to others."

Her smile slipped. "Do you not mean to attend the calico ball?"

"I'll take you, if you're wanting to go." He'd no objections to that.

Her brow pulled ever lower. "But you won't dance?"

"Believe me, you'd rather I didn't."

A hesitant little smile tugged at her mouth. "I don't know how to dance at all. You can't possibly be worse than I am."

"Is that a challenge?"

Her amusement grew. "One I look forward to."

He felt an odd tug as he watched her move into the kitchen, an unexpected urge to follow her, no matter that he had chores aplenty waiting for him.

She did her work and he did his; that was their arrangement. Yet he found, in that moment, he was tempted to remain with her and try to make her smile again.

· 7 ·

Mirabelle hadn't broached the topic of dancing in the days since laughing with Quinn about it, but the hope of attending her first dance had grown in the silence. She "practiced" in her room at night, though she had only a vague idea what she was doing. While going about her work during the day, she let herself imagine dancing at the calico ball. Despite his protestations of gracelessness, despite theirs being an arrangement of convenience rather than affection, it was Quinn who quite specifically filled her imaginings.

So preoccupied were her thoughts that she nearly plowed into the mountain of a man early one morning as she made her way to the chicken coop.

"Your thoughts seem miles away," he said.

"Miles and miles." That wasn't exactly true. Her thoughts had been on him, and he was standing right next to her. "What're you seeing to this morning?"

"Snow's early this year. I have to make sure the coop'll hold up if the winter's long."

He stood with a thumb hooked through his tool belt, hat sitting a little crooked on his head. The picture he made standing there set her heart fluttering. Quinn was a fine-looking man. She'd thought so from the very first. He also showed no interest in anything more personal between them than they currently had. She'd do well to remember that.

"Halloo!"

Mirabelle turned at the unfamiliar voice. A man, not much older than she was, with dark, wavy hair and a day's worth of stubble, sauntered toward them. Even in the dim light of sunset, Mirabelle could see he was exactly the devastatingly handsome kind of man that women couldn't help noticing.

The newcomer's eyes settled on her, and he slipped off his hat, holding it in his hands as he nodded in acknowledgment. "Ma'am," he greeted respectfully.

She smiled back at him but found her tongue a little tied. She'd never been shy before. Why was it a ridiculously handsome face could do that to an otherwise intelligent woman?

"Mirabelle," Quinn said, "this is Trevor Clark, one of the ranch hands. Trev, this is my wife, Mirabelle."

The tiniest hint of emphasis he placed on the word *wife* pulled her eyes to him. Had he issued a warning or a reminder? And was it meant for her or Trevor? She didn't see any signs of jealousy or concern. She'd likely heard more in his tone than had been there.

"I'm pleased to make your acquaintance, Mrs. Quinn," Trevor said.

Mirabelle held out her hand to shake. "And you, Mr. Clark."

"Trevor," he corrected. He glanced at Quinn. Something passed between them, and Trevor finally shook her outstretched hand.

"What brings you around?" Quinn asked.

"Sam's got a leak in the roof of his place. Are you free to come help with the patching and some repairs in the barn?"

Quinn gave a firm and immediate nod.

Trevor turned his Adonis smile on Mirabelle. "This might put your supper off schedule."

Mirabelle was so unaccustomed to being taken into consideration that, for a moment, she could do nothing but stare at him. She managed to recover her voice and thanked him for his concern but assured him she didn't begrudge the havoc to her schedule.

"After all the repairs are finished, you and Will and Mr. Carpenter can come back here for dinner." Mirabelle made the invitation casually, though she truly hoped it was accepted. The one thing she'd enjoyed about working at the railway station was the chance to talk to people. She'd had almost none of that since coming to live here.

Trevor smiled warmly. "I shouldn't speak for Will or Sam, but I will anyway. We'll none of us turn down an offer of a well-cooked meal."

"How do you know it'll be well cooked?" she asked with a laugh.

"You could burn it to a crisp, and I'll still enjoy it."

She pretended to be relieved. "I *was* planning to char it pretty thoroughly."

He laughed deep from the belly, the kind of laugh that shook a person's shoulders.

"Off with you, Trev," Quinn said. "Tell Sam I'll be by in a spell."

Trevor tipped his head to her, then to Quinn, and turned and walked away.

"He seems like a nice, sociable sort of fellow," Mirabelle said.

"Yeah, Trev's just dandy." That was a dry tone if ever

Mirabelle heard one. Quinn was making a thorough examination of the coop's roof.

"Don't you like him?"

"Do you?" he asked.

A strange question. "Well, based on the thirty seconds I've known him, he seems friendly."

Quinn muttered, "Too friendly."

Well, if he meant to be a grump, she'd let him, but she wasn't going to stand around listening to it. She had a meal to plan and company to prepare for. He joined her a few minutes later in the kitchen.

"Was there something you needed?" she asked.

"Why did you invite Trevor over for dinner?" He didn't look angry, but he appeared to want an answer.

"I invited them because Will and Trevor work for you and Sam's your neighbor, and—" She stopped, not ready to admit more.

"And *what*?" he pressed.

"And we've not had any visitors since Jane and Caroline. I've been a little lonely. It will be nice having someone talk to me."

Beneath his confusion she saw the earliest hint of pity. *That* she couldn't bear.

She turned away and pulled a chair over to the cupboard. The pan she needed for dinner was on a high shelf. She climbed onto the chair, her heart thudding a little—even such a small height as this made her a bit nervous. Keeping her focus on the pan, she reached into the cupboard.

Quinn crossed the room to her. Standing on a chair like she was made her a little taller than he was—a decidedly odd position.

"I can set that down for you." He indicated the pan in her hand.

"Thank you." She gave it to him. He set it on the work table with a stretch of his arm, then turned back to her. He held his arms out to her. She accepted the offer and set her hands on his shoulders just as he set his hands on either side of her waist.

But he didn't lift her down. He stood precisely where he was, hands holding her, looking up into her face. Heat crept into her cheeks. No man had ever looked at her that long and lingeringly. She couldn't say quite what it was he was seeing nor what had so captured his attention.

She felt his thumbs move the tiniest bit along her waist. The light movement sent a shiver straight through her. He still hadn't looked away. She simply couldn't tear her gaze from him.

"Quit standing there like a simpleton, lad." Tiernan had wandered into the kitchen. "I'm sure you have plenty of work to do."

The spell was broken. Without so much as a word of warning, Quinn lifted her from the chair and set her on the floor. He gave a single nod of acknowledgment and walked out of the room.

Mirabelle stood where he'd left her, watching him go, confused. What had just happened?

· 8 ·

"SMELLS GOOD," QUINN said, stepping into the kitchen.

"It does, though I say so myself." Mirabelle flipped over the steaks. If she kept her focus on her work, his arrival might not overset her. She'd not entirely recovered from the way he'd held her in the kitchen that morning. It had been fleeting and confusing and, though she fought the inclination, hopeful.

"Is that a chocolate cake?"

"It is."

He brought his gaze back to her. "Are you always going to make sweets when you have company?"

She smiled at that. "Probably."

"Well, then, I'm glad Trev got himself invited over."

"So am I." She did enjoy company. "I think I have everything ready. The potatoes can come out of the oven in another minute or so. These steaks are ready now. If you'll have the men sit down in the dining room, I'll bring it all in."

Quinn left, presumably to do exactly that. Mirabelle dished the steaks onto a serving plate and set the plate on the large platter she always used to carry food into the dining room. The potatoes went in another dish, placed beside the steaks. She had snap peas and applesauce to round out the meal.

The men's eyes didn't stay on her long when she stepped into the dining room. All five men immediately focused on the food. Trevor eyed each dish as she set it out. "I can't remember the last time I saw a meal like this. You're an angel from heaven, Mrs. Quinn."

"Worth busting my thumb," Will added. His thumb was, indeed, wrapped in bandaging.

"What happened?" She placed the bowl of peas on the table. "Did you miss the nail?"

He hung his head a little and nodded.

Mirabelle gave him an empathetic look. "I suppose you'll need an extra large slice of chocolate cake then, to help you through your suffering."

Her eyes met Quinn's as she laid out the last of the food. His was a look of gratitude. That meant more to her than nearly anything else she might have seen in his face. In that moment, she felt appreciated.

She cut a generous slice of chocolate cake, set it on a small plate, and walked to the head of the table where Tiernan sat. The older man looked as surprised as all the others.

She set the plate of cake beside his dinner plate. Voice lowered, she said, "I have not always remembered to have enough cake for you to have as much as you wish. I will make certain of it going forward."

His eyes raised slowly from the plate to Mirabelle. His surprise had only grown, but with an added hint of approval. She knew he'd not appreciated the scolding she'd given him over the tea cakes. Whether or not the scolding had been deserved, she didn't wish to have that disagreement coming between them forever. If providing him with cake would ease their tension, she would make certain he always had some.

"Thank you," he said.

"I can make most any kind of cake or sweet roll. Please tell me if there is something in particular you're wanting."

He nodded, enthusiasm beneath his hesitancy, then pulled his plate of cake closer.

Mirabelle did her best not to show how significant that moment had been. Tiernan had never been happy about her being in his home. He seldom spoke to her, and when he did, it was generally to lodge complaints. But he had just thanked her. He had accepted her offering without disapproval. Perhaps she had begun to strike a tentative peace with one of the two men in this house.

Now, if only she could find the key to Quinn's elusive affection.

· 9 ·

"I suppose I ought to learn to drive the team," Mirabelle said as they rode toward Thornwood. "You wouldn't have to take time from your work to take me to town."

Quinn just shook his head. Driving his wife to town wasn't the enormous inconvenience she made it out to be. He wasn't such a shabby husband as all that.

"I don't know how you'll entertain yourself while I thumb through the bolts of fabric," Mirabelle said. "You don't have any sewing of your own to see to, do you?"

His lips tugged upward at her quip. "I do have a bit of fancy stitching I've been meaning to finish."

"You have a talent for needlepoint, do you?" Mirabelle matched his teasing tone.

She had a fine sense of humor. He liked that about her. "Aye," Quinn replied. "Learned it from m' da, I did."

She shook her head in amused disbelief. "You two are full of surprises."

"You seem to be getting on better with Da," he said.

"We're beginning to, and I'm certain it'll get better and better."

There was the hopeful positivity he'd seen in her from the moment she'd stepped off the train. It had confused him at first, but he'd grown increasingly grateful for it. She lightened their home and eased many of his worries. She'd changed things for the better since she'd come, and he appreciated that.

"I've discovered a bit of cake or sweet bread puts him in a good mood," she said. "I've also learned, through difficult experience, that touching anything that once belonged to your mother, especially the trunk of her clothes, puts him in a sour mood—sometimes for days."

"He doesn't even let *me* touch Ma's things. He carries a lot of pain there." As deeply as he'd loved Ma, Da now ached for her. "Thank you for being patient with him."

"I know what it is to be lonely," she said. "I can be patient with that."

She'd been lonely. Was she still?

"How will you pass the time while I do my shopping?" Mirabelle asked.

"You don't believe I'll be taking up my embroidery?" He gave her a dramatically overdone look of shock.

Mirabelle laughed lightly. He liked the sound of her laugh; he had from the very first. She simply didn't laugh often. Why was that? She was a decidedly happy person. She ought to laugh more.

"Are you the kind to spend the day at the saloon, or shall I look for you napping under an obliging tree?" Her smile told Quinn she wasn't making any accusations.

"As an Irishman, I do have a taste for whiskey, but having seen far too many of my countrymen grow needy for it, I hardly ever touch the stuff."

"Meaning I ought to look for you asleep under a tree somewhere." Mirabelle's smile lit her entire face. "I'll keep that in mind."

Quinn found it something of a struggle to keep his focus on the road and not on her. Her smile hadn't disappeared by the time they reached the edge of town. He liked knowing he could bring happiness to her eyes as easily as Trev had. That had been weighing on him. It wasn't jealousy, not entirely. It simply pricked at him when she looked sad or worried. He wanted her to be happy.

Maybe I'm more like Da than I realize.

Surely there was a balance between being kind and caring about his wife and losing himself the way Da had.

"Here we are." He pulled the team to a stop in front of the mercantile. He hopped down from the wagon and circled around, reaching the other side just as Mirabelle slid to the end of the bench. She could climb down on her own; he'd seen her manage it more than once. But he'd also seen that she appreciated a bit of help navigating to the ground.

He set his hands on either side of her waist, lifting her easily from the wagon. *Such a tiny thing.* Why was it her size continually surprised him? Perhaps it was simply that she didn't seem little. She took on tasks without fear or concession to her size.

"Would you fetch my basket?"

Until she made the request, Quinn didn't realize he'd stopped, hands holding her, standing as still as could be, right in front of the mercantile. The familiar warmth of a blush spread over his face. How he hated that about his coloring. The slightest embarrassment sent him flushing like a schoolgirl.

Quinn dropped his arms immediately, reaching for her basket without looking at her or in the direction of the whispers he heard just behind them. Likely, other townsfolk were in the mercantile, witnessing him standing about, red as a turnip.

"I'll come back in a half hour or so," he told her. "So, take your time. Pick something you like."

Mirabelle hooked her arm through the handle of her basket. She turned back at the door and gave him a wave and a smile. He returned the silent farewell. She slipped inside and out of sight. Quinn remained rooted to the spot for a moment, fighting the oddest urge to follow her. She'd been away for mere seconds, and he missed her. He missed her.

He missed her.

This convenient arrangement of theirs was turning worryingly complicated.

• • •

Mirabelle was deeply grateful that the calico ball specified plain and inexpensive fabrics. Quinn was not a wealthy man, despite having a successful cattle ranch. He had vaguely mentioned some debts he needed to pay off. She didn't wish to add to his financial burden.

The mercantile had several shelves of calicos and muslins. An ivory fabric with tiny, multicolored flowers caught her eye. It was lovely and delicate. It was not, however, practical. She would struggle to keep it clean, being so light in color. Perhaps if she only wore it now and then . . . but that would defeat the purpose of having another dress to wear.

A bolt in a solid shade of dark green pulled her interest for a moment. She did like green, and it seemed a good color for her complexion, but she'd like something a little prettier. And she really wanted something blue.

When she was a child at the orphanage, one of the other little girls had been adopted by a family who brought her a blue dress to replace the gray they all wore. Mirabelle had dreamed of a blue dress ever since. She'd briefly had a dress in a shade of dark blue while working for a seamstress in St.

Louis, but it had been so dark it might as well have been black. She wanted a happy blue, a cheerful blue.

Why, then, was she looking at any fabrics that weren't blue? The mercantile had several options. White with little blue flowers. Blue with gray stripes. A solid, muted blue. She pulled from the shelf a blue gingham. It was not so light that she would struggle with staining, but not so dark that it lost the cheerfulness she wished for. The blue had a hint of green in it, rendering it almost gem-like.

She ran her fingers over the fabric. It wasn't soft—calico seldom was—but it was smooth and would be comfortable. The weave was tight enough that it wouldn't wear out quickly. And it was blue.

She pushed back a smile, not wishing to appear ridiculous growing giddy over such a plain fabric. She held it carefully to her, not wishing the fabric to be taken by someone else before she could obtain her bit of it. A spool of blue thread and a few pins and needles rounded out her purchase. The house had all the foodstuffs and other supplies they needed. This trip had been made exclusively for her to choose fabric for her calico ball dress.

Quinn might not have been desperately in love with her, but he was kind and thoughtful. That was what she had hoped for. Why, then, did it no longer feel like enough?

Jane and Horace stood at the counter, making a purchase of their own. Mirabelle had been so engrossed in making her selection she hadn't even seen them there. She stayed back, allowing them a chance to finish their business.

Horace's arm slipped around Jane, pulling her close to him. He pressed a kiss to her cheek. She rested her head on his shoulder. Horace grabbed the paper-wrapped bundle of purchases and tucked it under his arm, keeping his other arm around his wife.

"I love you, my sweet Jane," he whispered as they passed.

Jane had been married as long as Mirabelle had. They were both mail-order brides, both married to men they hadn't known before their arrival. Mirabelle had been happy about receiving a simple look of gratitude. Jane was receiving declarations of love.

Mirabelle pushed the thought away. Love was not a given when one agreed to marry a stranger. She had no right to feel cheated.

She made her purchase quickly and with minimal comment. Two women came inside while Mr. Carlton wrapped her fabric and notions in brown paper.

"Thomas proposed to Bernadette last night," one of the ladies said to the other. "We are so pleased for them."

"Of course you are; they are so happy and in love."

Happy and in love.

Mirabelle took up her purchase and slipped from the mercantile, trying hard not to think about Jane and Horace and their tender expressions of love or the fortunate Bernadette and her loving happiness.

I knew what I was accepting when I agreed to an arranged match. I knew. I cannot complain now. And yet, she couldn't ignore the ache in her heart. It had begun small and easily overlooked, but had grown of late. She longed to be cared about, to be loved a little. Though she saw Quinn every day, she was lonely.

Quinn's wagon was not sitting outside the mercantile. Mirabelle hadn't taken as long as they'd guessed. She never had found out what he meant to do to pass the time while she made her selections, so there she stood, alone.

She took a deep breath, attempting to dispel her heavy mood. Logic told her she was being ridiculous, but her heart simply wouldn't listen. Seeing and hearing of others who had the love she longed for stung. She didn't know how to make that wish less important to her.

Concentrate on finding Quinn. He'll likely not mind heading home early.

She made her way up the street. She'd learned at a young age that appearing as though nothing in the world was weighing on her helped her pretend she was carefree.

She passed the bathing emporium and the barber shop. Though Quinn might easily have been in either location, she didn't feel comfortable searching for him there. The saloon was across the street, not many buildings down. But that establishment also held a firm place on her list of locations she didn't mean to step inside.

Her eyes fell on a wagon and team that, if she wasn't mistaken, belonged to Quinn. They were stopped across the street near the preacher's house. Indeed, it seemed to be not far from the church. Mirabelle carefully made her way across the street and walked in that direction. The closer she came, the more certain she was. But what had brought Quinn to the church on a Tuesday morning? He'd admitted himself that he was not a particularly religious man.

The wagon sat just a pace beyond the building. She didn't stop until she reached it.

The churchyard. She spotted Quinn quickly, sitting beneath a tree amongst the gravestones. He held a book in his hand, his hat on the ground beside him. He leaned back against the trunk, reading.

An odd place to spend an afternoon. For a moment, she started to turn around, feeling uncomfortable interrupting his quiet moment. She knew how hard he worked, and how constantly. He deserved a respite from all that.

But where would she go?

She clutched her basket more tightly and fixed her

expression into one of ease. She made her way slowly around the grave markers to where he sat. He looked up a moment before she reached him. A question filled his eyes, one he asked the moment she was within speaking distance.

"Finished already, are you?"

She nodded. *Heavens, why does this hurt so much? I knew what to expect when I accepted this arrangement.*

Quinn's brows pulled in. He watched her, as if searching for some explanation he knew she wasn't giving him. He would think her ridiculous if he knew she was sulking because of people's happiness. She felt rather pathetic, in fact. She sat on the grass beside him, pretending to be extremely interested in the book lying open on his lap.

"Did something happen, Mirabelle?" he asked. "You look so unhappy."

Mirabelle didn't lift her gaze. She didn't trust herself to keep her heavy heart hidden. She simply shook her head. "I am usually a happy person. I certainly haven't given that impression since arriving in Thornwood those weeks ago."

"Sure you have. You're a little overwhelmed is all, yeah?"

"More than I wish I was." She wanted to be more capable, less beaten down. "I know you're depending on me to do the work required of me."

"And you've done it," he said. "Every bit of it. I've no complaints."

No complaints. There was a stark difference between her husband having no complaints about her work and the words of tenderness Jane had received from her husband. When she'd agreed to this mail-order marriage, she'd convinced herself "no complaints" would be enough for her. What was she going to do now that she knew she was wrong?

"Did you find everything you came for?" he asked.

She knew he referred to her errand at the mercantile that

day, but her thoughts were on far more than that. Had she found what she'd been expecting in this marriage and this life she'd accepted? "I found what I'd expected to find."

Quinn slipped one of his hands around hers, holding it gently. The gesture was entirely unexpected, but utterly welcome. She needed the reassurance that, though there was not love between them, he didn't entirely overlook her—that for at least that one moment, she wasn't completely alone.

She leaned forward, allowing her forehead to rest against his shoulder. "I'm so very tired." Her voice broke a bit as she spoke.

"We've time before needing to head back. Rest a spell."

"I'd be keeping you from your work," she reminded him.

His arm wrapped around her and tucked her close, allowing her to sit in the reassurance of his embrace. "Rest, Mirabelle. I think you need it."

She closed her eyes, holding back a surge of emotion.

Oh, Quinn. I need so much more than that.

· 10 ·

"Something's weighing on her," Quinn told Da that evening. "She said she was tired, but I know it's more than that."

They sat on either side of the fireplace. Mirabelle was in the kitchen preparing dinner.

"Was she angry?" Da asked.

"She seemed more sad than anything else." Quinn had fully expected to return to the mercantile and find her as cheerful and bantering as she'd been when he'd dropped her there. "I'd only just paid my respects to Ma and sat down with my book when Mirabelle came walking up. She had such a look on her face, like her whole world was crumbling."

"That doesn't sound like Mirabelle. She's about as likely to crumble as the mountains themselves."

For precisely that reason, Quinn couldn't shake the impact of seeing her so heartbroken. She'd made a valiant effort to hide her feelings, but the pain had been there in her eyes and in the quiver he'd heard in her voice.

Quinn scratched the back of his head. "What am I supposed to do?"

"Considering you brought her here as a worker, I'd say

you're 'supposed to' not be bothered by her unhappiness." Da's tone emerged drier than dust. "Less complicated, remember?"

"I ain't heartless, Da. She's hurting. What can I do?" His mind had grown heavy as she'd sat in his embrace. The comfort he'd offered hadn't seemed sufficient. "What did you do when Ma was upset?"

"'Twas different between your ma and me. We knew each other well, deeply. There was seldom need for guessing what she needed and why she was hurting." As always, speaking of Ma brought a sadness to Da's expression that nothing else did.

"I don't have that with Mirabelle."

"Then I'd say you have the answer to your question." Da skewered him with such a look. "You care enough to want to comfort her, so care enough to let her into your life and your heart as well. It'll be complicated, but it'll be worth it."

"Considering your half decade of agony, I've a difficult time viewing things that way."

"You think a life spent loving your ma wasn't enough for me, that I'd rather give that up than grieve?" Da sounded almost offended.

"You've far more than grieved. You've disappeared, faded to nothing. If that's what love does to a man—"

"No matter the pain I've felt, I'd not trade a single moment I had with her. I'd love her fully and deeply, even if it meant hurting more now. You'd understand that if you allowed yourself to care even a little about the woman you've made your wife."

The sharp rebuke raised Quinn's hackles. "I do care about her. More than just 'a little.' I care that she's unhappy. I care that she's lonely. I care that she's desperate for people to come over because she feels like no one here ever talks to her." His bluster quickly ebbed. "I do care."

"But maybe not enough," Da said quietly. "Maybe that's why she's grown more unhappy."

I'm lonely.

I'd have someone to talk to.

I found what I'd expected to find.

Mirabelle's words that afternoon repeated in his mind but with new meaning. He assumed she'd been saying that she wanted to have company over or that she had a successful bit of shopping. What if Da was right, though? What if she had, instead, been telling him why she was so sorrowful lately?

"Dinner is on the table, if the two of you are ready to eat."

There was something odd in thinking about someone only to have them speak without warning. Da seemed to have no such moment of surprise. He simply nodded and rose from his chair, heading for the dining room.

Quinn pulled himself together and followed the same path. He slowed a bit as he approached the spot where Mirabelle stood, just outside the dining room doorway. She smiled, but it didn't reach her eyes. Whatever had been weighing on her hadn't entirely lifted.

"Are you feeling any better?" he asked.

"That nap in the churchyard was just what I needed."

Perhaps he had helped her more than he'd realized.

Da stepped out of the dining room and passed them, holding a dinner plate heavy with food. "I want to eat by the fireplace. You two don't need to join me."

His "don't need to" held a heavy hint of "better not." Quinn met his eye. Da motioned with his head back toward the dining room.

"Talk to her," Da mouthed silently.

Talk to her. Da had told Quinn to build something more between himself and Mirabelle than was currently there; he was providing the opportunity to begin.

I can work on a friendship. There needn't be more risk than that.

"Let's eat, shall we?" Quinn indicated she should return ahead of him.

She sat in her usual seat, one a bit apart from where he and Da usually sat. Why was that? He'd never asked her nor insisted she distance herself from them. He couldn't easily talk with her if they sat away from each other. He snatched up the plate meant for him and sat in the chair nearest hers. She looked confused but not upset. He took that as encouragement.

He chose easy topics to begin with: the ranch, the neighbors, improvements he meant to make around the house going forward. She seemed genuinely interested, offering thoughts and insights. She mentioned things inside the house she'd like to work on over the months and years to come. Some of the weariness in her expression eased as they spoke. He hoped that meant he was helping.

"I mean to start on my dress tonight for the calico ball. I picked a blue gingham. I've always wanted a blue dress."

"Blue will look nice with your eyes." He could easily picture it, in fact.

She smiled, the upward tilt of her lips so tiny he might have missed it if he hadn't been watching.

"My friend Caroline showed me a few dance steps. I've been practicing them in my room at night. I'm still really terrible, though." She laughed lightly.

Quinn let his smile blossom. "I've known the steps nearly all my life, and I'm still really terrible too."

Amusement twinkled in her eyes. "Perhaps you will distract everyone from my awkwardness."

"If that'd help you enjoy the evening, I'd be glad to." Friends did that sort of thing, after all.

She swallowed a bite of supper. "I plan to enjoy the calico ball either way. I've dreamed all my life of going to a dance. I finally get to."

She'd never attended a dance?

"And to be making a new dress for myself for a change... that is a fine thing as well."

It was good to see her in better spirits. Ma had always appreciated a new dress or a little bauble.

"I'm heading to Topeka in a few days," he said. "Is there anything I can bring you back from there?"

"You're leaving?"

"Sam and I need to fetch a few supplies before winter sets in for good." Da had often made trips to Topeka during Ma's final years, fetching her trinkets and adornments. "Are you wanting anything?"

She didn't look intrigued or excited or anything other than confused. "When are you leaving?"

He nodded. "In a little less than a week. We'll be gone about ten days."

Her mouth tugged downward. "The calico ball is in only two weeks."

"I'll be back by then."

"What if you're not?" The same look of heartbreak that had touched her face in the churchyard flitted over her features once more. An echoing pain filled his chest.

"I'll be back for the ball." He set his hand on hers where it rested on the tabletop.

"I've dreamed all my life of going to a dance. If I miss it..."

"I promise I'll be back," he said.

She smiled at him, a trusting and pleased sort of smile. Her hand remained in his. He liked the feel of her slender fingers beneath his, but the degree of pleasure he took in it caught him entirely by surprise. He'd been aiming for friendship; he'd do well not to overshoot the mark.

They sat like that as the evening wore on, hand in hand, speaking easily of whatever topic flew to mind. She seemed happier. He hoped she truly was.

He had sent for a wife as a matter of convenience, but he'd not appreciated the simple pleasure of a companion, someone to talk with, someone to listen. Someone to hold.

Someone he could feel himself beginning to truly care for.

· 11 ·

Quinn had not returned.

"The ball's started already," Tiernan said from his place by the fire. "But if you leave now, you'll not miss all of it."

Mirabelle smoothed the wrinkles in her blue dress. She'd been sitting, waiting, for a couple of hours now, and she had the rumples to prove it. "I was holding out hope that Quinn would be back in time. That doesn't seem likely now, does it?"

"He has his faults, but the lad keeps his word. If I had m' guess, I'd say he went straight to the gathering and is there wondering where you are."

"I know when the train comes in to town." She rose and moved to the front window. "If he were going to arrive today, he would have hours ago."

Tiernan rose and, to her surprise, crossed to her. He set his hands on her arms and looked at her tenderly, paternally. "He did promise you. I know my lad well enough to be certain he'll do everything in his power to be there, especially because we all know how much you were looking forward to it."

Her heart dropped. "I've been dreaming of this. He probably thinks me a little silly for it."

"He tries to be logical about things and pretend his head has all the say in his life," Tiernan said. "But I know that heart of his. It's more tender than he lets on."

"I think yours is as well," Mirabelle said.

His expression turned a little sad. "I loved his ma deeply, but we had a difficult go of it early on as we sorted things out between us, figuring out how to build a life together."

"I don't know how to do that with Quinn. Sometimes he seems to want something more than the arrangement we have between us, and sometimes I'm not certain he even remembers that I'm not the maid."

"Oh, he remembers," Tiernan muttered. He stepped away and to the door. "Come on, lass. I'll take you to the dance."

He was offering to take her? Tiernan never went anywhere. He seldom left the house, even.

"I am so touched that you would offer, but"—emotion solidified as a lump in her throat—"I don't think I could bear to go."

Tiernan looked concerned. "But you wanted to dance."

Misery clutched at her. "I wanted to dance with *him*." A hot tear pooled in the corner of her eye. "Clearly, I am *not* logical about things. I was ordered over the telegram like a piece of farm equipment. A man doesn't rush back to dance with a plow."

"He's a fool. I told him as much myself." Tiernan wandered back to the fireplace. "I've seen the way he looked at you when he left for Topeka."

"How did he look at me?" Even as she asked the question, she worried about the answer.

"*Not* the way he looks at his plow."

Oh, how she wanted to believe that. "Then why didn't he come home when he said he would?"

"I've every confidence there's a reason." Tiernan sat in his chair and took up his book.

Mirabelle made her way slowly to her bedroom. She pulled the blue ribbon from her hair, the same one she'd worn on her wedding day. She hadn't been certain Quinn would make the connection, but she'd hoped. And it had been such a perfect match for her gingham dress.

She sat on her bed, hands resting on her lap, and wrapped the ribbon around her fingers. Why did she let herself grow hopeful so often and so easily? She only ended up getting hurt.

Her next breath shook from her. She needed to pull herself together. There would be other opportunities to attend a dance. Quinn likely had a good reason for not returning when he said he would. Yet it still hurt. It hurt that he hadn't come back. It hurt that he'd gone despite her worries about the timing. It hurt that she was missing so many things she'd longed for: the dance, companionship, love.

She pulled her legs up on the bed and wrapped her arms around them, burying her face against her knees. What a fool she was, crying over a missed social.

Heavy footsteps sounded at the door. It was sweet of Tiernan to check on her, but she couldn't bear for him to see her sobbing like a child. The footsteps grew closer. The bed shifted beside her.

She wanted to tell him he needn't worry, but no words came.

Two strong arms wrapped gently around her. She knew then it wasn't Tiernan who'd come to comfort her, but Quinn. Every bit of control she had over her emotions evaporated. Her tears turned to sobs.

He pulled her closer. "I hate seeing you cry, dear, especially knowing it's because I broke my word to you."

"That's not why." She took another trembling breath. "It's not the *only* reason."

"Tell me what all's hurting you. I'll fix it if I can."

She turned enough to bury her face against his chest, her hand clutching his vest.

"I feel so foolish." Admitting that aloud helped calm her a little. "It is only a dance, and you've told me there will be others. It isn't as if I'll never have another chance. Yet I feel like my whole world came crumbling down while I waited for you."

He didn't say anything, just continued to hold her. The protective comfort of his embrace chipped away at her protective wall.

"Your father offered to take me to the calico ball so I wouldn't miss it."

"He did?" Quinn sounded as surprised as she had been.

"If it really was just the dance I was upset about, I would have gone. But I didn't. And yet here I am crying about it."

"Maybe you . . ." She had never heard such hesitation from him. "Maybe you wanted to go with *me*."

That set the tears flowing again, though without the shoulder-shaking sobs. "I know that's not our arrangement. I do. We each see to our work; that's what we agreed on. It's so silly of me to—" Her breath caught, and she couldn't continue.

"I missed you while I was gone," he said. "I thought of you. Not about your chores or the work you'd be doing. I wondered how your dress was coming along, if you'd had tea with your friends, if Da was being good to you. I wondered if you were upset with me for leaving when I did."

He'd thought about her. Worried. Wondered.

"I was late leaving Topeka, then snow down the line stopped the trains for nearly two days. I sat in a rail station, knowing I was going to be late returning home, and something became very, very clear to me."

She wiped at her eye with the back of her hand, not moving from her position tucked into his arms.

"It wasn't the delay or the inconvenience or the chores I wasn't seeing to that weighed on me most. I was disappointing you, and that tore right into me."

She turned a bit more, her bent legs resting against him, curled in a ball in his arms.

"I know perfectly well what our arrangement is," he said, "and it didn't matter one bit. Your heart and your happiness held greater importance to me than all of that."

She looked up at him, hope and uncertainty warring inside her. He brushed at the moisture on her cheek. How a man as large as he could offer so tender a touch, she couldn't say. But in that moment, she needed it. She treasured it.

"Maybe," he said, "it's time we rethought our arrangement."

She steeled herself. Hope had too often proved fickle. "You said in your telegram that you were not interested in an emotional or romantic attachment. You were very specific."

"Well, as my da often tells me, I'm something of a clodhead." He touched the pad of his thumb to her chin. "There's the smile I've been missing."

Though her eyes burned and moisture still clung to her lashes, she wasn't crying as she had been. She felt hopeful without feeling afraid. It was an entirely unfamiliar experience.

"I finished my dress." She held her breath.

"I noticed. You did a fine job of it. It's lovely."

A little heat touched her cheeks, though she wasn't embarrassed. Indeed, she was pleased. Touched. "I would have been quite the belle of the calico ball, you know."

He slipped his arms free and stood. She resisted the urge to ask him to come back, to keep holding her.

"You told me you hadn't ever danced, which is why I was late leaving Topeka."

That made little sense.

"I saw something in a shop there that I wanted to bring back for you, but I took too blasted long making my mind up about it. My own fault, really."

He pulled something from his pocket. She couldn't see what it was. It fit in his hand, mostly obscured. He returned to the bed and placed the item on her bedside table. A box-shaped something. Metal, with floral designs etched all over.

"What is it?" She scooted closer.

He looked at her. "A music box. It plays a waltz. I thought if you had music, I could teach you to dance, then you wouldn't be so nervous about attending the sociables. We should have had a couple of days for practicing, but the snow came and ruined everything."

"You bought this for me?" She shook her head. "It's too expensive. You have your debts to pay down."

He offered a soft smile. "I didn't go into debt for it. I simply sold a couple of things."

"For me?"

He held a hand out to her. She set hers in it, letting him gently pull her to a stand. With his free hand, he lifted the lid of the box. In notes soft and bell-like, a tune began.

"Will you dance with me, Mirabelle?"

"I don't know how," she reminded him.

He wrapped his arm around her waist and tucked her up to him. "We'll work on the steps later. For now, I just want to hold you."

"That's not part of our arrangement," she reminded him, her heart pounding in her chest.

"It ought to be part of our new one."

She set her arm at his shoulder, her other hand still in his. As the lilting music filled the tiny room, he swayed with her in his arms. No words were needed. They simply held each other with the promise of a new beginning.

· 12 ·

"It's an uncomfortable thing being here with the two of you." Da eyed Quinn and Mirabelle over his book.

They were sitting together on the sofa. Mirabelle was seeing to a bit of sewing. Quinn was enjoying a rare quiet moment. They weren't even talking.

"We're only sitting here, Da."

Da raised a brow. "Sure you are. And I'm the King of England."

"I think you mean the queen, yeah?"

Da rolled his eyes and returned his attention to his book.

Mirabelle moved a bit closer and rested her head against Quinn's upper arm. "Thank you."

"For what?"

She smiled broadly. "For making him uncomfortable."

Quinn laughed deeply. "I *am* just sitting by you."

She threaded her arm through his, embracing it. "You didn't used to sit by me."

He brushed his fingers along her silky hair. "I made a mull of it, didn't I?" With the pad of his thumb, he traced her jaw. "But we're finding our new arrangement. We're sorting it."

She closed her eyes, contentment in her expression. "Yes, we are."

He bent and placed a kiss on her forehead. He'd done that a few times since their dance the night before. The simple gesture brought such a look of relief to her face, as if a weight she'd been carrying for too long were momentarily lifted.

She needed tenderness, affection, gentleness. He would begin building their new relationship there, giving her reason to trust him and reminding himself how lucky he was to have her in his life. He had not a doubt in his mind that in time they'd grow to fully love each other. Not a doubt.

Someone knocked at the door.

Mirabelle sat up straight once more, setting her sewing aside. As she made to slip her arm from his, Quinn took hold of her hand. She smiled back at him as she stood.

"I do need to answer the door," she said.

"I know."

"As I said, you two are a bit uncomfortable to be around."

Mirabelle sent him an apologetic smile but didn't make any promises. Quinn leaned back on the sofa, amused and touched and hopeful.

She opened the door. Mrs. Howell, the preacher's wife, stood on the other side. "Please, come in," Mirabelle said.

Mrs. Howell did and offered greetings, which were returned. Da's contribution was a mutter and a dip of his head. No one was surprised. He'd kept to himself since Ma died. Everyone in town had learned to accept his grumpiness.

"Everyone was sorry not to see you at the calico ball last evening," Mrs. Howell said.

Quinn set his arm around Mirabelle's waist, keeping her at his side. "My train came in late."

"Sam Carpenter wasn't there to play the guitar. He must have been on the same train you were."

Quinn nodded. "He was."

"Let's hope you won't be gone for the Christmas ball."

"I don't intend to be."

Mirabelle leaned into his one-armed embrace. "There's a ball at Christmas?"

"A small one," he told her. "The snow is heavy by then, and the weather is unpredictable. Not everyone can make it to town."

Mrs. Howell smiled at them. "I've come for the dress," she said.

"What dress?" Mirabelle could not possibly have looked more confused.

"The dress you made for the ball."

"You want my dress?" Mirabelle choked on the question.

Oh, heavens. Hadn't he told her about that? Likely not. He'd forgotten himself until that moment.

"That is the most important part of the calico ball," Mrs. Howell explained. "The dresses we make are donated for the benefit of the poor. Many of ours will be sent to Cheyenne, where there are more in need."

"Oh." Mirabelle had turned both paler and splotchy with color. "I didn't know. It is the only dress I have other than this one." She picked at the skirt of her black dress. "I was going to save it for special days. It's blue."

She'd told him several times how happy she was to have a blue dress, and she'd been so pleased with how it had turned out.

"It is tradition," Mrs. Howell said. "Those who need the dresses are in far worse straits than we are."

"I—I hadn't intended to be selfish. I didn't know." The heaviness that had left her eyes returned. "I can get it. Just a moment."

Mirabelle slipped stiffly from his arm. She moved with

halting steps to the door of her bedroom. Quinn's heart broke watching her. She'd been so happy with her dress, and she'd worked so hard.

He looked to their visitor. "She really didn't know. I forgot to tell her that part."

Mirabelle would be heartbroken. She wasn't an ungiving person—far from it—but that dress meant a great deal to her. There had to be a way to make this right.

"Excuse me a moment." He moved swiftly to Mirabelle's room, unsure what he was going to say, but hoping he could think of something.

She stood near her bed, her beloved blue gingham dress in her arms. "I don't want to give it to her. Does that make me horribly selfish?"

"Of course not, Mira." He pulled her into his embrace. "You didn't know you were expected to part with it."

She leaned her head against his chest. "I can make another one, I suppose, the next time we can afford some more fabric."

"I'll talk with her," Quinn said. "Perhaps I could convince her to let you skip the donating this time or let me purchase something else she could send to Cheyenne."

From within his embrace, she shook her head. "I won't add to your debts. My heart will ache a bit, but I can part with the dress. I only needed a minute to convince myself."

"But it means so much to you." He knew it did.

"There are others who need it more." He heard the resolve in her voice, but he also heard the sorrow.

"I hate that you are hurting, my dear."

She reached up and touched his face, stretching on her toes and pressing a kiss to his jaw. "Dance with me after supper, and I'll feel better."

"Gladly."

Her lips trembled a bit even as she squared her shoulders. "I'd best not keep Mrs. Howell waiting any longer."

He took her free hand in his and walked with her back to the parlor, ready to support her as she parted with her treasured dress. He'd spent what little extra he had on her music box. He didn't regret the purchase, especially when it meant he could dance with her, but he hadn't money enough to replace her dress any time soon.

Da stood near Mrs. Howell, talking. He never did that. "The Quinns'll give a dress, sure thing, but there's no need to take it from our Mirabelle. She came to us with so little." He held out a green dress Quinn hadn't seen in years. "It was m' wife's. It's a bit out of fashion, but it's well-made and good fabric."

Da had packed away Ma's clothes when she died, and there they had stayed the past few years. The trinkets and decorations remained out, though he guarded them fiercely. Her more personal belongings he'd tucked away, just as he did nearly every bit of himself.

"Someone'll be right glad to receive it." Da set the dress in Mrs. Howell's hand. "Now, take it. I've a book to get back to."

He returned to his chair and his book and his isolation. Quinn couldn't look away. Da had parted with a dress of Ma's—willingly. He'd never imagined his father doing that.

Mirabelle managed some kind of farewell and saw their visitor out. The moment she closed the door, she turned back and rushed to where Da sat.

She wrapped her arms around him, her dress still clutched in one hand. She didn't say anything.

Da pulled her in for a brief hug. "You're a good lass, and we're fortunate to have you."

"Thank you." She pulled back, her smile tremulous. "Thank you."

"Quinn there'll offer you all the you're-welcomes you're wanting." He raised his book once more.

"Are you sure you won't be uncomfortable?" she asked with a twinkle in her eye.

"I will be, but I'll survive."

Mirabelle clutched her dress to her heart and turned to Quinn. "He saved my dress."

"I know it."

She moved to him. "But why?" she asked quietly.

He took her face in his hands. "He loves you, though I doubt he'll ever say it. And *I* love you." He surprised even himself with that declaration, but he didn't wish it unsaid.

"I've never been loved." She pushed out a deep breath with a smile. "I've always wanted to be."

"You are now." He bent and kissed her forehead. "You are now."

She set her hand on his arm. "Will your father slaughter us if I ask you to dance with me?"

"He could try, but he's not a young man anymore."

Mirabelle bit back a grin.

"Quit yapping and dance with the girl." Da flipped a page of his book. "Elsewise, I'll have Mrs. Howell come back so I can send *you* to Cheyenne."

Mirabelle looked back at Da. "I'll not let you send him away."

Quinn, standing behind her, wrapped his arms around her and bent over so his face rested beside hers. "I put the music box in the kitchen. There's room enough for dancing, and Da won't be bothered by us there."

She turned her head. "An excellent plan."

He walked with her hand in hand toward the kitchen

door. He looked back. Da was watching him. For the first time in ages, Da smiled.

"Thank you," Quinn silently mouthed.

Da nodded.

In the kitchen, Mirabelle carefully laid her gingham dress over the back of the rocking chair she sometimes sat in near the stove. She ran her fingertips over it. Emotion edged her eyes.

"He gave up something of your mother's to save my dress." She set her hand on her heart. "That was such a sacrifice."

"You've changed him for the better, dear. You've changed both of us."

She smiled at him. "Are you happy you sent for me, then?"

He opened the lid of the music box. The quiet waltz began on the instant. He reached for her. She didn't hesitate. Rather than assume dancing position, though, she reached up, her hands reaching nearly to his shoulders. He bent, and she slid her arms around his neck. He wrapped his arms around her and pulled her to him. Her feet lifted from the ground.

She was so tiny, yet so very perfect, even for a giant like him. Holding her that way, he looked into her eyes. His gaze traveled to her lips, so near his. Tentatively, hopefully, he kissed her. She didn't pull back but held more firmly to him as the warmth of her enveloped him.

"I love you too, Quinn," she said. "I really do."

"That sounds to me like the start of a perfect arrangement."

About Sarah M. Eden

Sarah M. Eden is the author of multiple historical romances, including the two-time Whitney Award Winner *Longing for Home* and Whitney Award finalists *Seeking Persephone* and *Courting Miss Lancaster*. Combining her obsession with history and affinity for tender love stories, Sarah loves crafting witty characters and heartfelt romances. She has thrice served as the Master of Ceremonies for the LDStorymakers Writers Conference and acted as the Writer in Residence at the Northwest Writers Retreat.

Sarah is represented by Pam Victorio at D4EO Literary Agency.

Visit Sarah online:
Twitter: @SarahMEden
Facebook: Author Sarah M. Eden
Website: SarahMEden.com

Isabella's Calico Groom

Kristin Holt

Dedication

For every woman who dared to be first so others might follow.

Historical Note

While researching the history of women in dentistry and specifics of late-nineteenth-century dentistry, many details surprised me. Not only had the "DDS" (like "MD") been in use since 1867, dentists in 1890 had *long been* using amalgam (metal) fillings, gold foil for filling cavities, treadle-powered drills, and full dentures made from vulcanized rubber and teeth (human or animal, or made from porcelain). Dental practices, including the use of laughing gas and injections to anesthetize, were surprisingly advanced . . . despite the lack of sterile, one-time-use needles.

· 1 ·

Evanston, Wyoming Territory
March 1890

Dr. Henry Merritt lived simply.

Despite requiring little for himself, his spending overwhelmed his earnings.

Dangerously so.

Until he paid all he owed, his creditors would not extend additional credit. He couldn't restock his dental cabinet nor feed his horses.

He rested his head in his hands and stared at the ledger's columns of numbers.

Late February sunlight, weak by nature, puddled on the hardwood floor. After his last patient an hour ago, he'd banked the fire in the stove and donned his winter coat.

No patients, no coal.

Something *must* change. Soon.

He fiddled with an envelope containing another request from the local newspaper fellow, Thomas Fisher. *It's not every day a talented graduate of Pennsylvania College of Dental*

Surgery settles in a humble railroad town and competes with a woman for business. Readers find such things fascinating.

The first three requests had flattered. The latest offered compensation enough to pay rent through March. Or pacify one or more creditors.

The bell over the door tinkled as wintry wind swirled inside. "Going out, are you?" Doc Joe, a medical doctor and Henry's closest friend, smiled without a care.

The coat told a tale, but not the correct one. "Thought I might."

Henry's stomach growled. He'd forgotten the box lunch Mrs. Linden had prepared for him.

"I'll walk with you. Glorious day. Marginally warm."

"Above freezing yet?"

"Positive thoughts, Doctor. Positive thoughts." Joe chuckled. "Or grow facial hair like a true Wyomingite."

That morning, icy wind had frozen tender membranes in Henry's nose during the four-block walk from the Linden home. "I'll survive another few months until spring."

He found his keys in the desk drawer, tucked order forms and bills inside the ledger, and shut the book to avoid prying eyes.

As he tugged on his gloves, he peered through the glass onto Main Street. A gentleman bundled in a heavy coat hurried past, revealing Dr. Isabella Pattison, DDS—the bane of Henry's existence.

A deep pink flowerpot hat, covered in silk flowers and ribbons, perched upon her head. Her costume, hidden beneath a figure-hugging black coat and matching muff, was likely the same shade of raspberry.

A flamboyant waste.

Mrs. Trolinger and daughters visited with Dr. Pattison and Joe's wife, Dr. Naomi Chandler, as if dear friends. The

Trolinger girls had been terrified of him. The children, apparently, weren't scared of *her*.

The women discussed fashion, evidently, as Miss Pattison raised the hem of her dark pink skirts to reveal high-heeled boots. She must've said something humorous, as Mrs. Trolinger and Doc Naomi laughed.

The girls took in the Parisian styles with awe.

He turned his back on the nonsense outside. "Why do ladies expend fortunes to dress fashionably?"

"Some, Naomi tells me, merely enjoy fashion."

"Evanston men outnumber ladies four to one. If she hadn't scared every bachelor away with enormous dressmaker bills, she'd have married long ago."

Married meant leaving dentistry, and that meant an end to Henry's mounting financial troubles.

Joe chuckled. "Whistling the same old tune?"

"You know how I feel. Women do not belong in a man's domain. Not in an office, and not in a coal mine."

"Jealous?"

Shame washed over him, hot and bitter. The woman's business grew by preying upon his own.

"Come outside." Joe opened the door. "I'll introduce you."

A stale topic of conversation if ever there was one. "No, thank you."

Hungry, grumpy, and broke. Now was not the time to pretend niceties.

Joe chuckled in his sunshine-filled way. "As you've said, my friend, for the last ten months. Make that eleven. Sooner or later, you must greet the woman."

"Why? I know who she is. And she, I."

"I'm surprised."

"No surprise here. I've not deviated in the year since Miss Pattison hung her shingle."

One glimpse, and he'd been snared by an attraction so strong, he'd followed, desperate to learn her name.

Only to be doused by a proverbial bucket of icy water.

The sign painter had sought to clarify the spelling of her name.

Dr. Isabella M. Pattison, DDS.

He'd abruptly returned to work.

"The surprise," Joe said, "is that you avoid a colleague for reasons you cannot explain."

"I can explain. I choose not to." To avoid further conversation, he led the way outside.

More men walked by, raising their hats. Over the friendly hellos and rush of Wyoming wind, Henry was drawn by Dr. Isabella Pattison's joyful laughter.

Why, after nearly a year had passed and numerous paying clients had quit him, preferring her, must he *still* find her captivating?

No, today was not the day for introductions. "Just remembered. I've an appointment with *The Chieftain*."

He hated to grant Thomas Fisher an interview, given all he'd read a year ago, when Fisher lambasted "the lady attorney", Sophia Hughes, née Miss Sophia Sorensen.

What choice did he have?

The offered sum might be his only salvation.

•••

Isabella slipped on the ice.

Linked at the elbows with Naomi and Sophia, she managed to remain upright.

"No one told me Wyoming winters last eight long months." How she missed the mild winters of Los Angeles.

Sophia chuckled. "Makes a New England nor'easter seem tame, doesn't it?"

"I survived the Great Blizzard." Naomi shuffled forward several more steps.

"Inside." Sophia, a stickler for details, seldom allowed exaggerations.

"I wasn't at home when the storm began." Good-natured jesting among the best of friends.

In mid-March the sun offered light until suppertime, but very little heat. "I've been frozen since October." Three flannel petticoats. A flannel combination. Two pair of wool stockings. Still, Isabella's circulation choked with ice floes.

"Your blood will thicken eventually. Or so Joe tells me."

Sophia, on the other end, muttered, "As will your skin."

"Thick skin? Extra pounds of padding?" Five pounds gained required Isabella to let out the seams of every costume. According to Mother's dressmaker, a lady's measurements *never* increased.

She noted a silent message between the others. "What?"

"Nothing." Naomi responded with finality.

"Obviously something. I do know the meaning of *thick-skinned.*" Her two closest friends were fierce protectors, and she loved them for it. "Tell me what you heard."

"I heard nothing." Naomi, ever the calming influence, smiled with reassurance.

"What did you read?"

Another look between attorney and medical doctor.

Four more icy, mincing steps along Main. Isabella caught the longing on Sophia's lovely features and her calculation of the time required to reach Evanston City's office.

"Planning a timely interruption won't protect you." Isabella aimed for light and careless but fell short. "I've heard and read plenty since announcing my determination to pursue dentistry. I'd rather hear the judgment from you than someone else."

A gust of wintry wind scampered by, piercing Isabella to the skin.

Sophia held her winter hat upon her head. "You know how I feel about Thomas Fisher and *The Uinta Chieftain*."

The weekly published today, Thursday. "What did he write?"

"Nothing new." More soothing from Naomi.

Isabella's pulse quickened. "Let me guess. Criticism of females who demand entrance into a man's world? Taxing ourselves with education?"

One of her tender spots, inflicted by cutting words. Many from those who should love her most.

The storm howled, but her friends remained silent.

"I'll find a copy of the paper. Perhaps at our meeting." One step farther. Then two.

"You win. I'll paraphrase." Sophia's sharp mind likely recalled every word. "It is only when she despises to be a helpmeet for man, a joy to the household—" Sophia's tone mocked a high-and-mighty man who knew everything— "only when she has lost all maternal instincts and determined to destroy all that tends to make her lovely and lovable to man—only when she has become a man-hater—"

"I've heard enough." Isabella swallowed a knot of fury. *That man!*

"You do realize this is rubbish?" Sophia always called a spade a spade. "Absurd. Absolutely farcical."

She'd heard this argument over and over. Some went so far as to label her choice in professions a moral depravity, a stark weakening of reciprocal love between a noble man and a pure woman.

Utter balderdash.

Naomi squeezed Isabella closer. "Joe swears by his good friend, Isabella. He's truly not as uncaring and cold as he seems."

Oh. *Him.* Henry Merritt. "He'll be at this meeting, won't he?" All professionals had been informed their presence was required.

"The comments in today's paper weren't Fisher's typical prattle." Resignation dampened Sophia's tone. "He interviewed Dr. Henry Merritt at length."

Henry Merritt. The dentist whose office stood one block from hers, across Main.

The man who refused to acknowledge her on the street. The man who had yet to allow introductions. The fellow who'd hated her on sight for no discernible reason.

She'd ask—again—what she'd done to offend Henry Merritt, but neither of her friends knew. They'd both asked their husbands—how did Joe and Chadwick consider Merritt a friend?—but obtained no answers.

"One direct quote," Sophia said. "'I'm a young man, doing fairly well in my profession, and hoping someday to have a home of my own with a wife to reign over it, but the Lord deliver me from one of these professional women! Our own beloved Evanston, Wyoming Territory, is near to overrun with professional women.'"

"All three of us." Naomi tried to lighten the conversation with a wry chuckle. "Three professional women, overrunning a city of two thousand souls!"

"Naomi, hush. This is the important line: 'My practice suffers to the point I may never afford to have that grandest desire—that home of my own and an angel wife to therein reside.'"

"He blames *me*?" Fury pounded with every quickened

heartbeat. "I've done *nothing*. How might I be responsible for his business or his lack of a wife?"

Dr. Merritt had proved discourteous, conceited, and cruel. Tonight, he'd earned *fiendish*. And wicked.

"Shall we take you home?" Naomi halted their caravan. "We'll return and tell the mayor and council you're unwell."

"Absolutely not." Indignation rattled Isabella's bones. "I will attend this meeting, even if that man will be present."

She'd show him she was made of sterner stuff. She'd show graciousness in the face of assault. She'd be herself, a contributing, helpful member of society.

"I fear," Naomi whispered, "both men will be present."

Fisher *and* Merritt.

"Thank you for telling me all you read. Let's hurry inside where it's warm."

•••

"Doctor." Fisher, the newspaperman, took a seat beside Henry in the city's council room. "Your piece ran today."

He'd not seen it yet, thanks to his first busy afternoon in weeks. Three patients made vague comments about his interview in the paper. Perhaps his luck had turned.

"I'll read it soon." The interview, less than a quarter hour in duration, probably filled a scant two inches. He'd locate it on page three, wedged between advertisements for patent medicines.

The compensation had been generous enough to keep his office open another month.

The upstairs room filled quickly. Two druggists, medical doctors from the new Wyoming Insane Asylum, three dentists, the city civil engineer, the county bridge builder, and four attorneys.

All three women had chosen prominent seats, front and center.

Between the people and the potbellied stove in the corner, the room slowly warmed. Waning light filtered through spotted windowpanes. Lamplight glowed from three wall sconces.

"Ladies and gentlemen." Mayor Raymond Gardner's heavy mustache curtained his teeth. Darkly stained hairs denoted chewing tobacco, a habit that spoiled a set of should-be pearly whites. "We approach the closure of a challenging decade. Wyoming Territory has faced the most difficult winters on record. This very season, our own county suffered yet another destructive season for our ranchers and their cattle."

What did the city's professionals have to do with ranchers and what newspapermen called the "Cow Killing Winter"?

The mayor stood a little taller. "Wyomingites are strong. Resilient. We've braved the worst, and we're still here. It's time we celebrate our tenacity and our spirit. Thus, on behalf our elected city officials, it is my pleasure to extend to you, our fine professionals, the honor of working in committee for the grand occasion of Statehood for Wyoming."

A rush of whispers and voices indicated excitement. Several men applauded.

The record books would remember 1890. Statehood had been a topic of discussion in every circle for years, especially since the constitutional convention convened in Cheyenne last September.

Mayor Gardner grinned widely, if the spread of facial hair could be trusted.

"Committee?" Leave it to Thomas Fisher to ask questions. "For what, precisely?"

"Evanston intends to celebrate in the grandest style. Statehood for Wyoming!"

A round of applause, muffled by the gloves many still wore.

The mayor acknowledged the applause as if he, and he alone, were to credit for territorial advances. "Numerous committees, involving every citizen of Evanston and Uinta County, will prepare a week-long celebration, from Independence Day through Friday, July 11. A parade with marching bands. Fireworks, suppers, a theatrical production. Bicycle and foot races. Musical programs. Military reenactment. And, as Wyoming will be the forty-fourth state, a forty-four gun salute. Speeches! And," he paused for emphasis, "a grand gala ball."

A dozen questions erupted.

"I know you're anxious to learn what your committee will do." Mayor Gardner rubbed his palms together.

Silence met the mayor's glee.

Eduard Sperry, youngest of the attorneys, pushed to his feet. "Seems to me the city might want to ask if her professionals would mind *volunteering* their time."

Mayor Gardner cleared his throat. "Why, yes, of course. That's—that's what I meant."

Sperry lowered himself to his seat.

Gardner cleared his throat again and rubbed his palms briskly once more. "We ask for your generous support in this valuable undertaking. The culminating event will be the honor of our city's fine professionals."

"The ball," Fisher stated.

Not one to attend dances, Henry hadn't the vaguest notion of the responsibility a "gala ball" entailed.

"What variety of ball?" Naomi Chandler's golden hair

shone in the lamplight. She'd removed her hat, a front-row courtesy. Henry had liked her from the moment they'd been introduced.

"That's for the committee to decide, Mrs. Chandler—excuse me." The mayor pressed a palm to his chest and bowed slightly. "My apologies, madam. *Dr.* Chandler."

Naomi nodded. "Are those present to constitute this committee?"

"Yes, ma'am."

"I suggest, Mayor Gardner, that we vote to answer the question posed by Mr. Sperry, and if all are in agreement, that we then presently determine the theme of the ball."

The mayor was notorious for interrupting, interfering, and unraveling diligent planning. Smart lady.

"Now that our city's finest know what the city's elected ask, all in favor—that is, uh . . . those who are willing to volunteer their time to the celebration of Statehood for Wyoming, say *aye*!"

A round of hearty *ayes* seemed to echo in the room.

"Very well." The mayor tucked his thumbs into his vest pockets and rocked back on his heels. "What do you propose?"

"Not so fast." Sperry again. He raised his hand, high. "I vote no." He turned his head about, seeking support from his pals. "Who else says no to this kindly offer to fill my week with more work?"

Sperry chuckled as several others, including the balance of the attorneys, raised their hands in unison.

"If we won't donate our time, I suppose you don't want us here." Sperry rose, buttoned his coat, and motioned for his fellow attorneys to join him. "Anybody else want to reconsider their vote?"

A few turned their heads about as if undecided.

Naomi didn't wait for numbers to diminish further.

"With our committee subdivided, responsibilities will be easily managed. I suggest a calico ball."

Fisher shifted in his chair. "A what?"

Questions buzzed throughout the assembled.

"Gentlemen?" The mayor scanned the men. "What say you?"

Dr. Edwin English, DDS, spoke up. "I say we follow Dr. Merritt's common sense, printed by Fisher." He winked at Henry. "Fine article, gentlemen."

Most of the men applauded, even as Sperry and his contingency exited.

On the front row, the spines of three female attendees stiffened. Dr. Pattison, the littlest one, didn't turn like her friends did. But her hat's ornamentation quivered as if she... laughed?

What had Fisher printed?

The city engineer stood. "Aren't balls a woman's domain?"

Last winter, Naomi had put on a splendid leap-year ball. But to say any woman could excel in this assignment would be false. Lenora wouldn't have attempted the feat, even to celebrate statehood. He shoved the unwelcome memories aside.

Male chuckling, inarguably good-natured, filled the lull.

"Precisely as Fisher and Dr. Merritt put in black and white."

Henry cut a glance at Thomas Fisher. They'd not discussed this subject, even in passing.

Another asked, "Don't balls plan themselves?"

The majority laughed, but not Henry.

Aggravation pinched Doc Naomi's and Sophia's expressions. Probably frustrated with Fisher's article and the demeaning banter.

Dr. Edwin English buttoned his coat. "I say we leave this to the ladies."

More raucous laughter, as two of the doctors from the territory asylum followed him toward the door.

A pang of ... anxiety? ... tingled down Henry's spine. He'd expected better from his colleagues. Naomi needed support. "I second the motion."

Three women turned as one and pinned him with fierce disappointment.

"The motion," Naomi repeated, her posture defensive, "to 'leave it to the ladies'?"

"You misunderstood. I seconded *your* motion. For a calico ball."

If Naomi was pleased, she didn't show it.

"Moving along." The mayor ignored Dr. English and the two docs from the big hospital up the hill. "Objections?"

Seconds elapsed without comment. The door shut soundly behind the three men.

"What's a calico ball?" This from the county bridge engineer.

"Mrs.—*Dr.* Chandler," the mayor caught himself, again. "Honor us with a reply?"

Always a lady, Naomi presented as the New York heiress she'd been. "A calico ball is the fashion from New York to San Francisco and in every locale between. Invitees wear new costumes of calico, rather than silk, taffeta, or velvet. Our purpose? To pass the once-worn garments to those grateful to receive."

Her bottomless heart matched Joe's. No wonder they made an ideal couple.

"Who?" the mayor asked. "We haven't tenements. Our churches have poor boxes to meet needs that arise."

"Mayor," Henry said, "if I may, I have a proposition. Our neighbors need the boon the calico theme provides."

Barefoot children, fatherless. Hollow-eyed widows in rags.

Henry recalled his parents' pride and refusal to accept charity ... and the deprivation. "We have an opportunity to make a difference," he insisted. "A legitimate difference." He swallowed, crushed anew by the pain he'd suffered upon hearing news of the disaster.

Beside him, Fisher shifted. "November twenty-sixth. Nearly four months ago."

Leave it to the newspaperman to recall the precise date of Almy's most devastating mining disaster.

Heads bowed. A few crossed themselves.

As Henry held Mayor Gardner's eye, memories of his own grief, buried in coal mines far away, crept in. "I can think of nothing finer than celebrating Wyoming Statehood with means to help our own. If any citizens of the soon-to-be State of Wyoming are deserving of our gift—" not charity, *never* charity—"the residents of Almy are."

"Aye," someone murmured.

"I'll second," a male voice stated with conviction.

Mayor Gardner nodded, as if his decision were the only that counted. "The motion carries."

"Wait." Thomas Fisher lumbered to his feet. "Will the widows and orphans we aim to help still be in Almy come summer? With their men no longer employed by the Union Pacific..."

How were these men so unaware? "They'll be there." Some had nowhere to go. Others ranched, and turned to mining for income.

"How do you know this?" The mayor tugged on his mustache. "We have months, yet."

"I know."

Chairs squeaked. Men shifted.

"I see." The mayor's mustache grinned.

Miss Pattison hugged Naomi tightly—her smile, brilliant and white, and filled with unmistakable happiness.

Must she be so lovely?

"A calico ball," the mayor continued, "will be held in the fine city of Evanston this coming July. By the grace of God, and with the diligent work of our congressional conference, may our city see the finest calico ball in the history of calico balls."

Over the last few minutes, Naomi assigned tasks to each subcommittee.

As the meeting disbanded, Naomi Chandler approached. Her lady friends flanked either side.

She took his hand in her firm grip. "Thank you, Dr. Merritt. I can't conceive of a more suitable recipient of the funds."

Funds? Wasn't this about dresses?

Uncertainty must've shown on his face, because Sophia, Chadwick Hughes's wife, stepped in. "Balls are an excellent revenue generator. Entrance tickets net significant funds."

All three women nodded.

Naomi released him, and Chadwick's wife, Sophia, shook his hand. Direct, firm, like an attorney.

Quite by accident, he'd turned to the third of their circle, the female dentist he'd successfully avoided for nearly one year.

The delicate fragrance of violets teased his senses.

Her smile punched him in the chest, hard and swift, and he found himself captivated all over again.

"Thank you, Dr. Merritt." She offered her hand.

Because he had no choice, he took her hand in his.

· 2 ·

WHEN THE COUNCIL of City Professionals next met, three weeks had passed. Winter had slowly released its death grip upon the high Wyoming plain.

Waterlogged earth could absorb not a drop more. Snowmelt ran in rivulets down the center of muddy streets, heading for pools in the lowest elevations. Enough snow remained on the river valley between Evanston and Almy, Henry doubted the wagon could make it, but the sleigh stood a chance.

The lone rider who'd carried a note last week had met him at the door of his office, pleading for him to come soon. If the weather held, he'd attempt the journey on Sunday.

"All in agreement?" Mrs. Sophia Hughes, the attorney, raised her hand to indicate all should vote.

Henry couldn't well cast his, given he hadn't a clue what she'd proposed.

"Dr. Merritt?" Sophia raised a brow.

"My apologies, madam. I had—"

The glare from Miss Pattison burned him from ten paces. She turned to face front once more.

He couldn't blame her. If he'd been in her tiny, high-heeled boots, he'd have been furious at the so-called "interview" Fisher had printed. What an utter falsehood.

After hours of deliberation, he'd determined Fisher had paid such an exorbitant price for the privilege of interviewing Henry for one reason, and one reason only—so he couldn't deny the interview occurred.

Between a bit of truth here and a scrap of reality there, Fisher had painted Henry as the worst of fiends, distrusting females in men's work. And that was precisely the problem. He did distrust professional females. But not for the reasons Fisher cited.

"I asked," Mrs. Hughes repeated, apparently, "if we agree to meet this coming Sunday evening at five o'clock to report upon the progress of our individual assignments."

Sunday. *This* Sunday. No. "Is it not possible to continue our meetings at the conclusion of a business day during the week?"

For the first time in three weeks, Dr. Pattison addressed him. "Where might you be, Dr. Merritt, that is more important than meeting your obligations to your community?"

Her dagger struck close to his heart. Precisely as she'd intended.

Drat professional women. Sharp-tongued, every last one of them. They'd forsaken every gentle nature, every bit of gentle persuasion their sex had ever owned.

"Personal obligations." In a room filled with nearly all of the town's well educated, he'd be loath to brag and hesitant to call attention to himself. A man had his pride, after all.

The woman stiffened, her posture screaming discontent and agitation.

He shouldn't care.

She had no say where he spent his Sundays, and he owed her nothing.

"Assignments, Mrs. Hughes?" Might as well admit he'd not heard a thing said. How could he, when the weight of everything else threatened to crush him?

"Your assignment, together with the other two dentists, is the invitation committee."

Other two dentists—

They'd assigned him to work with Dr. Pattison?

Sophia Hughes, like the professional she'd proven herself to be, regained control of the meeting. "We often meet without one or more members of our committee present, but this next meeting is essential, as we'll ensure committees are well on their way. We haven't time to lose. May I hear suggestions of an alternate date and time?"

Finally, with relative ease, the group decided upon a Friday evening one week hence.

"Will that Friday suit your busy schedule?" Dr. Pattison's tone exuded thinly veiled criticism. "We do hope you'll join us."

Though he wanted to respond in kind, his mother had taught him better. He drew a breath to center himself. "Friday next will suit quite well, thank you."

•••

Once spoken, words could not be called back. How Isabella regretted failing to hold her tongue.

Unfortunately, *that man* had needled her. First, the newspaper interview with hot-tempered Thomas Fisher, and second, his insistence that the committee change plans to accommodate his inconsequential social commitments.

Rudeness in the newspaper had kindled rudeness in her. Granted, Fisher and Merritt had made a target of her, but that didn't excuse unladylike behavior. No one provoked her like this. Not Mother. Not Dudley.

Shame heated her cheeks.

"Isabella?" Sophia offered a steaming bowl of glazed carrots.

"So sorry." Isabella accepted the china dish and served herself. The roast beef supper filled the dining room with luscious aromas.

They'd gathered at the Hughes home after the meeting, including Doc Joe, Naomi's husband, and their host, Chadwick Hughes, a talented cook. Chad had wed Sophia last Valentine's Day.

The closest of friendships existed between the women and the two men who'd won the ladies' hearts. Isabella imagined they'd remain friends through the years, their private supper parties providing an opportunity to discuss personal matters. Inviting a bachelor would be of no benefit, except to assist in passing dishes.

Tonight, the men discussed supplies for the clinic, delayed in transport by the Union Pacific.

Her mouth watered as she spread butter on a hot roll.

Naomi caught Isabella's eye. "Are you comfortable on the invitations committee?"

She would not let *that man* interrupt her digestion.

"Dr. English, Dr. Merritt, and I will work together without . . ." Truth be told, she couldn't promise the absence of friction. "Without disappointing the committee."

Sophia set down her water goblet. "I saw your reaction tonight."

In her estimation, all she could control was her response. Shame dampened her appetite.

"I'll persuade someone to trade assignments with you. You needn't pair with Dr. Merritt."

She adored Sophia, particularly her protectiveness. She

bit into the tender roll, savoring the delectable, homemade freshness.

"You're most kind." Assignments had been made by profession. To ask for adjustments now would draw attention. "You needn't go so far. The worst that might happen is I'll be forced to do all the work myself."

"Are you certain?" Naomi set down her knife.

"Yes." How she adored these women, who understood her challenges with perfect comprehension. "I'll see this through."

"A trait we love about you." Naomi raised her wine glass in salute.

"To the calico ball," Joe toasted, "and its success."

Chadwick followed suit. "To the calico ball. With the lovely women at my table hard at work, the occasion *will* succeed."

"Thank you." Sophia meant her words for her husband alone. The connection between them, at the head and foot of the table, seemed a living thing.

Longing knocked on her lonely heart. Wishing for that kind of a match seemed nearer the surface of late. She'd long ago given up on finding a man who would honor, respect, and love her for who she was.

Last to raise her glass, she took in Chadwick and Joe, Naomi and Sophia. Her replacement family. "To us."

· 3 ·

On Sunday morning, Henry determined that winter's snows had receded enough. The team could make the journey, pulling the loaded wagon, if the vehicle were on sleigh runners. So he'd taken precious time to affix the runners, then loaded up with needed supplies, tool kits, dental engine, and chair.

Not fast enough, though. Two competing church bells clattered, announcing Easter morning services had concluded.

Aggravation locked its claws tightly about his gut. For years, he'd kept his weekend trips unknown to the gossips. He'd quietly roll out while men slept off Saturday night drinking. If only last night's storm hadn't demanded he scout the conditions before attempting the journey with a loaded wagon.

Come quick as you can, Doc. Winter's been long.

Fisher's payment had made it possible to accept the call. He couldn't wait another week.

A stream of colorful bonnets, well-dressed ladies, and men in tailored suits paraded past. No one drove buggies with the streets sure to swallow wheels to the hub.

One last trip inside to douse the lamps, close the shades, and lock the door.

"Dr. Merritt, good morning." Mayor Raymond Gardner, not three feet away, spoke loud enough to be heard across the street. "How are you this fine Easter morn'?"

"Well, thank you."

The mayor noted Henry's cap to his boots, no doubt realizing he'd dressed for the mines, not church.

Religion, Henry had long believed, was where one found it.

The mayor turned to the wagon bed, covered with canvas and tied securely, upon its runners. "Problem, Merritt?"

"No, sir."

A knot of ladies passed by, some holding children's hands, calling good mornings. Henry lifted his hat, responding to several by name.

One of the men in their company engaged the mayor in conversation, so Henry grabbed the opportunity to nod his farewell, circle the congestion on the boardwalk, and gather the reins from the hitching post.

"Henry Merritt!" Doc Joe, with his perpetual warmth—and his wife on his arm—offered a handshake.

Sure enough, immediately behind came Chadwick Hughes, his wife also on one arm, and Dr. Isabella Pattison on the other.

Would nothing go smoothly? This was precisely why he left town under cover of darkness and while Main Street yet remained quiet.

Henry shook Joe's hand, then climbed to the wagon seat. He raised his hat to the women. "Morning, ladies."

At this, Chadwick laughed, good-natured and friendly. "Am I one of the ladies, now?"

"Sorry, Hughes." Henry gripped the reins.

"Couldn't see me for all the Easter bonnets?"

Actually, yes. The ridiculously festooned bonnet perched on Isabella Pattison's dark head distracted him.

With royal-blue ribbons tied in bows, feathers, and flounces cradling robin's eggs so real in appearance, they might've been natural. A stuffed red-breasted male robin, accompanied by a nut-brown female, perched on the edge of their nest and their eggs.

How... *domestic.*

Why a bonnet like that would appeal to a professional woman, who had no interest in a home of her own, he hadn't the vaguest notion.

Perhaps the royal blue of the hat itself, tall and—from the looks of other hats upon the street—highly fashionable, matched the royal blue of her costume. She'd clutched her skirt and multiple petticoats in her free hand to save the hems from the muck of the streets.

Every time he had the distinctly unfavorable experience of glimpsing this woman, she wore another vivid color. Why, if he had access to the fortune she spent at the dressmaker, millinery, and shoemaker, he'd never want for gold foil or nitrous oxide again.

"No offense taken," Hughes insisted. "Say, won't you join us for Easter dinner? We're headed home now."

Noon, already?

With impeded travel, he'd be lucky to see only the most desperate. "I thank you for the invitation. I'm not able to, not today."

"Where are you headed?" Doc Naomi asked.

Apparently Joe didn't feel the need to ask where—or for permission. He lifted the canvas and peered inside. "Removing your offices? Where to?"

Jesting, yes. But the guess speared Henry's gut. Twenty-four days remained until the rent must be paid. "Not today."

The bright blue bonnet bobbed in his peripheral vision, as if Dr. Pattison did her best to see over the taller persons in her company. The little miss barely reached Chadwick's shoulder. Unless one took into account her stylish high-heeled boots and absurd bonnet.

"If I didn't know better," Joe said, laughter lingering in his words, "I'd say you're setting up shop in a tent."

"No tents. Now, if you'll excuse me, I'll bid you a fine day."

While he'd been careful not to glance in her direction, Dr. Pattison and her fancy blue costume made her way to the front. At Joe's side, she peeked into the wagon.

Henry's gut pinched. Hard.

Joe had earned the right to pry and to ask questions. He'd paid for that right with years of genuine friendship.

Dr. Pattison had not.

He clamped his mouth shut rather than break every rule of decorum his late mother had drilled into him. Let the lady show her lack of manners—no one expected a professional woman to behave.

"Are you sure you won't join us?" This from Sophia Hughes.

Already, his stomach grumbled. "I do wish I could."

"My husband is a fine cook. We have more than enough."

"Yes, ma'am." He'd heard tell of Chadwick Hughes's skills in the kitchen. What an odd couple they were. She, a professional, wage-earning woman—though not as successful as Doc Naomi. And he, a successful Station Master for the UP.

"Why, you've loaded your dental office, Dr. Merritt." Dr. Pattison kept peering beneath the canvas. He itched to drive away and pull the cover from her nosy fingers.

But her tone held only curiosity, as if he were a puzzle to be solved.

Today was not the day to reveal his secrets—especially not to her.

She looked up from the wagon bed and held his gaze with a mixture of surprise and ... triumph? Her hazel eyes sparkled.

Oh, no.

"You're taking dental care to those who cannot come to you." Gears turned in her mind under a full head of steam. "It's Sunday, and you're prepared with runners for a distance beyond Evanston."

The others had fallen silent, taking in her assessment.

"At this hour," she continued, "you can't plan to go much more than five or ten miles. Nor are you headed along the road, or you'd have purchased a ticket and loaded crates into the baggage car."

The road, meaning the UP line east to Rock Springs or west to Park City, or the spur northwest to Almy.

She spoke casually of the train and baggage car as if money were no object.

For her, obviously, no object at all.

What could she possibly understand of his mission?

Every bit of snootiness embodied by matching, fashionable costumes, slipped away. She blinked remarkable hazel eyes. "You're headed to Almy."

His jaw loosened. "Now how'd you figure—?"

Joe shifted. "You're not setting up shop in Almy, are you?"

"No." A little shake of her head sent her bold hat bobbing.

Were those stuffed robins on springs?

Dr. Pattison spoke to her friends. "I'm certain of it. He's taking dental care to the residents of Almy, none of whom can travel to Evanston."

How had she drawn that accurate conclusion?

If anyone put two and two together, it should've been Joe, who understood the miners' troubles. Twelve-hour shifts, Monday through Saturday. He and Naomi often rode to various mines when disaster struck, to treat the injured.

"But," Chadwick Hughes began, "on Easter Sunday?"

"I want to go along." Dr. Pattison bounced on her little feet, her eyes bright.

"Impossible." She could not go with him. Absolutely not.

"Of course it's possible." She refused to acknowledge his answer. "With two of us seeing to the needs of the residents, the work will go much faster."

She intended to steal his nonpaying patients, also? Or did she assume the miners paid him?

"Your noble endeavor is most deserving. Pull your wagon around to my office, and we'll load my implements and supplies."

She ordered him about, as if he worked for her? He'd put her in her place, but she wouldn't have heard.

In the fracas, he met Joe's eye. His unspoken question conveyed with ease, for Joe laughed. His eyes crinkled in that way of his. Laughing at life's inconveniences.

"*Miss* Pattison," Henry spoke over the top of her as she huddled with her kind. The three professional women were no doubt hatching a plan to take over the county.

She stilled. She squared her shoulders in her smart costume, and almost as if someone tightened her corset another full inch. She turned to him. "*Dr.* Merritt?"

He wanted to groan. And throw his hat to the muddied street. And stomp on it.

She'd railroaded over him, ordered him to see to her wishes, invited herself along.

Unpredictable.

Bossy.

Troublesome.

Precisely why he didn't care for women like her.

Well, one of the topmost reasons. He had plenty.

His mother's insistence on proper decorum around ladies nagged at his conscience. "I apologize, Dr. Pattison. I misspoke."

She radiated triumph.

Because he'd acknowledged her education? Fool woman.

"If you'll be so kind as to allow me, I'll contribute my ready supplies. My own chair, implements, machine. I am well supplied."

Unease curled in his gut. He'd loaded his case that morning, agonizing over the number of doses, and fearing his lack would render the trip useless. Yet, to accept help from a woman, especially like this, trampled his pride.

He grasped at the one remaining argument. "I work late, by lantern, and won't return until tomorrow." Before she could argue, he insisted, "I won't risk the horses."

She nodded. "Seems wise."

"Don't you care for your reputation?" Proper ladies did not travel overnight with a man.

Without so much as a glance at her friends, she took one dainty step closer. "Allow me to ask, Dr. Merritt. What is your age?"

Where had *that* come from? "I'm twenty-seven. Twenty-eight in June."

"Why do men consistently include the not-yet-achieved year?" A rhetorical question. "I am age thirty, Dr. Merritt. I go where I wish, I sleep where I wish, and I make my own decisions. I need not a father or brother to look after me."

Henry looked at the others—Mr. and Mrs. Hughes and Dr. and Dr. Chandler. None seemed surprised. Or uncomfortable.

"My offer of help, Dr. Merritt, is for the children and women of that mining town. Not for you."

His resolve softened, sure as snow on a late spring afternoon. "What of the men?"

"I don't see why not."

"They'll prefer my care." His insistence rang false. How many male patients had he already lost to her?

"I understand."

Did she? He doubted *he* understood.

"I'm leaving now. In conditions like these, I face hours of travel, many on foot." He paused for emphasis. "No chaperone. No ability to return until tomorrow."

He expected her to hesitate or to change her mind.

He'd banked on it.

"I'm a professional, Dr. Merritt."

Precisely why he disliked her.

The diminishing stream of passersby trickled to almost nothing. Clouds, swept on brisk Wyoming wind, scuttled across the sun. The day was wasting.

From the looks of her entourage, particularly Doc Joe, Henry hadn't an icicle's chance in August against this woman.

He'd show her the truth of dentistry away from the comforts of an office. She'd not ask again. "Very well."

Her grin erupted with the force of a mine explosion.

She took two long strides back in the direction she'd come. "Pull up in front of my office. I'll bring out my gear."

· 4 ·

MELTING SNOW CHOKED the engorged river, swelling over its banks and puddling deep in the low spots. Isabella tugged her warm gloves on more snugly, grateful for sturdy boots and a winter bonnet designed to keep her head and ears warm. Compared to southern California, Wyoming Territory was a frozen wonderland.

Beside her, Henry Merritt dressed like a common man. A rancher, or maybe a miner. In Evanston, he wore one of two modest suits of clothes. Always clean, well-brushed, and orderly. Plain, simple, utilitarian.

Since her outburst at the committee meeting, she'd sought an opportunity to apologize. No time like the present. "Dr. Merritt, I owe you an apology."

Beside her on the wagon seat, he held the reins in a loose grip, his elbows resting on his knees. From his inclined position, he couldn't see her. That suited her fine.

The man didn't like her. He'd made that woefully clear.

"Apology accepted."

Didn't he want her to acknowledge her weaknesses? Detail all she'd done wrong? "Do you know what trespass I apologize for?"

He tossed a thumb over his shoulder, indicating the wagon bed. Her forceful request to come along.

How could she explain the overwhelming urge to contribute to his dental dispensary?

He hadn't confessed to providing dental services free of charge, but she knew.

"If you believe I owe you an apology for requesting you bring me along to Almy, then yes, sir, I do apologize for my forceful request."

"Forceful." He muttered.

"I was direct, wasn't I?"

His arm brushed hers, though she sat as far to the opposite edge as possible. The man's presence surrounded her, pressed ever closer.

No answer. She drew a breath for courage. "I recall the vehemence with which you suggested the calico ball's proceeds benefit the residents of Almy, the many widows and fatherless children. Your plea touched me that day." She'd thought of little else since. "I want to help."

He seemed to ponder. The horses plodded on, their hooves squishing in the waterlogged earth and sloshing through puddles.

"If not for inviting yourself, why apologize?"

The roughness of the trail rocked her from side to side and into Dr. Merritt's solid form. "I apologize for my rude behavior last Wednesday night. I spoke without tempering my words, and for that, I'm genuinely sorry."

He glanced at her from the corner of his eye. "Insisting I attend the follow-up meeting. Tonight."

He'd planned this journey to provide help to those in need.

"Yes. I assumed the worst of you. I've never behaved so poorly." Not even when a child.

True, he'd provoked her with that horrid newspaper article. But she'd determined long ago, before dental school, that she'd not allow naysayers to steal her dignity or her happiness.

Why did this man elicit her worst?

No, that wasn't quite right.

Why did she *allow* this man to elicit her worst?

"Perhaps it is I who owe you an apology, Miss—" He flinched. "*Dr.* Pattison. I granted an interview to Thomas Fisher." He turned to her again, briefly. "Our conference that night lasted a mere fifteen minutes and barely touched upon you or your practice in Evanston."

"Mr. Fisher took liberties?"

"Precisely. I never said most of what he published."

"It's easy to believe Mr. Fisher elaborated, thus printing his own beliefs and agendas."

"You heard about Mrs. Hughes's experience."

"Yes." Sophia had shared details of the persecution she'd suffered as well as Fisher's unexpected apology. Both before and after Fisher's interview of Dr. Merritt ran in the paper.

Why would a man apologize, then return to the same behaviors?

Dr. Merritt steered the team around a pool of standing water. "I called on Thomas Fisher after I read his pompous article."

She'd have liked to witness that.

"He twisted my words and presented me as a man I'm not."

A moment passed in silence. "That must've hurt."

"He agreed to print a retraction."

A retraction! "You're most persuasive."

"Perhaps not so persuasive as you."

Was that a smile on his smoothly shaved face? A *smile?* For her?

Dr. Henry Merritt had surprised her once more. First, the heretofore hidden trips to Almy. Then, persuading the newspaperman to acknowledge wrongdoing.

The sequence of events made more sense. "Forgive me. I see now that I mistook your seat beside Mr. Fisher, and your apparent comfort, as signs that the article reflected your opinions."

"You should know one more thing." He kept his focus on the terrain ahead. "Fisher offered me a tidy sum for the interview. I'm not proud of it, but I accepted his money." His tone soured, as if the confession tasted foul. "I regret that."

Her softening heart melted further. Dr. Henry Merritt had proved himself far more than handsome, cocky, and arrogant. Beneath the critical and brash exterior, it seemed a fine man resided.

A comfortable silence accompanied them for a quarter mile.

He turned to her, a hint of a grin on his too-handsome face. "Will you accept my apology?"

She hadn't answered, had she? "Yes, though I recognize you're not at fault. Thank you for impressing the matter upon our friend at *The Chieftain*. And you accept my apology?"

"Yes, ma'am."

Beneath the misunderstandings and bluster, the man was reasonably nice. And generous-hearted. Who else would volunteer one day in seven and give away his services?

He'd comprehended her reaction to the awful newspaper article. He'd shaken off her rudeness, then corrected matters with the source.

If only she weren't tempted to *like* him.

•••

"You're doing well, Mrs. Johnson." Dr. Pattison's soothing voice, coupled with her competent dentistry, put Henry in his place.

Well, perhaps not in his place, but definitely at ease.

She'd already won over the grieving widows and half the children—who hated having teeth pulled or drilled more than they hated almost anything. The kids had been through the jaws of hell. They didn't need more from dental caries nor from incompetent dentistry.

Henry returned his attention to his own patient and worked the treadle-powered drill at the correct pace.

Lamplight brightened the kitchen of the Crompton home, the customary space used for the long line of those awaiting their turn. Squeezing in a second chair and set of equipment brought Dr. Pattison into close quarters.

Her patient reclined immediately beside his. If only he could ignore the myriad distractions Dr. Pattison presented.

He heard the tell-tale crack as a diseased tooth separated from the mandible.

Mrs. Johnson gave a wordless sound of relief as Isabella set her forceps upon a towel-covered tray in exchange for a folded square of flannel.

"Bite down. There you are." Her little hands moved with grace and practiced skill, her talent showing in an economy of movement.

In the forty-five minutes she'd worked on Mrs. Johnson's badly decayed teeth, she'd succeeded in pulling four molars. Outstanding, in that the woman hadn't expressed pain. Doubly so, given the woman had been unwilling, previously, to allow Henry to examine her. She'd suffered in agony through all of last year.

He didn't know whether to bask in relief that Mrs.

Johnson had, at last, taken a healing step toward dentures, or to resent Isabella's success.

He'd learned his lesson about female dentists.

But Isabella Pattison didn't fit the mold he'd fashioned.

She possessed an uncanny knack for nurturing. She'd explained, reassured, asked and answered questions, held women's hands, and hugged nearly every woman as she'd left her chair.

The gentle care she showed the children, despite their dirt-streaked, coal-stained faces and poverty apparent in unwashed bodies and old clothes that fit poorly.

She soothed scared children, defiant adolescents, and newly widowed women with the deference she'd show royalty. Almost as if she—wealthy, well-dressed, and stylish—were no different than they.

What could she know of poverty?

He had no answers as the night drew to a close.

Word had spread through the community. A lady dentist had accompanied Henry, and folks came for treatment they'd never accepted from him.

That hurt.

But overall, the night had been a success. Between the two of them, they'd treated twenty-one people.

"Will you both return next week?" The hope in William Crompton's voice pleased Henry.

Isabella's sleeves were rolled to her elbows, and her apron far less pristine than when they'd begun. Her dark hair no longer curled, but frizzed about her face. The woman had worked herself into a state of exhaustion.

The female constitution, according to some, simply wasn't up to the rigors of dentistry. Beyond the gore, odor, and anatomy coursework, what of the physical exertion required to pull teeth?

Isabella smiled as she untied and removed her apron. A warm, world-encompassing smile that spoke of satisfaction and happiness.

Precisely the emotion buzzing in him. The nonmonetary reward kept him returning week after week as long as the weather allowed.

Because here, he made a difference.

Several women remained in the Cromptons' kitchen: Mrs. Crompton and a couple of neighbors with two nearly grown daughters.

Two ladies spoke at once. "Oh, won't you?" and "Please?" The very women who'd been lost in grief, barely able to greet him or Dr. Pattison upon arrival.

Isabella embraced her new friends. Friendships forged in the dental chair, based on trust.

Did she know she possessed a rare gift? The people of Almy had met her mere hours ago, and already, they welcomed her return. Watching her work answered every question as to why his patients preferred her.

She turned her tired yet dancing hazel eyes to him. "May I accompany you, Dr. Merritt?"

He couldn't speak. The tightness in his throat couldn't be emotion. Must be weariness and exhaustion after a long week.

One small reservation raised its head, like a weed in a flower garden. "I leave before sunrise. I can't wait for you to attend church services first."

"Not a problem. I'll be ready."

He granted permission with a nod.

Dr. Pattison's happiness blossomed. "It seems my answer is yes, ladies."

Female chatter and words of appreciation enveloped her.

Henry disassembled and packed the equipment. As

usual, he'd load the wagon of everything they brought to give Mrs. Crompton back her kitchen.

"Won't you stay in my humble home tonight?" one woman addressed Pattison. Her name eluded Henry, but he recalled she resided two doors down from Mrs. Johnson. Everyone in that row of dugouts had been widowed by the terrible explosion last November.

"That is . . ." The woman lowered her eyes to her hands, or perhaps to her tattered boots. Her skirt hung several inches too short, heavily stained to a dirty brown. "If you haven't elsewhere to go. I have only me and me girls. You'd be safe with us."

The moment of truth had arrived.

Henry itched with unease. She might not intend to, but she'd show a glimmer of distaste, behave a little more like Lenora . . .

The goodwill would explode to bits.

Pattison took the woman's hands in her own, squeezing them as ladies do in the most intimate of circles. "Thank you, Mrs. Nye. I'm most honored."

Take care, Pattison.

"Yes. Thank you for your generous offer."

Mrs. Nye chuckled with delight and relief. Never mind the terrible state of her teeth—broken, darkened, and worn.

He couldn't help but take heed. He made his living from dentistry.

If Isabella noticed, she didn't so much as glance at Mrs. Nye's mouth. Nor wince at the foul odor.

"Me name's Gladys, Dr. Pattison. Just Gladys."

"Thank you, Gladys."

Henry nearly choked on his tongue as Isabella Pattison, a woman he'd sorely misjudged, threw her arms around Gladys Nye.

"You must call me Isabella."

He looked to Crompton and the others, finding them as enchanted as he.

Entranced.

Grateful.

Wanting more. *More* time with her, *more* friendship.

Just . . . *more.*

No. *No.*

She'd earned his professional respect. But there could be nothing personal between them.

Lenora had taught him that painful lesson.

· 5 ·

"Precisely my point." Isabella turned on the wagon seat, apparently to face Henry better. Excitement animated her features, and most of the twinkle in her eyes had little to do with sunlight sparkling upon the snowbanks.

"W. D. Miller wrote of this challenge last year—have you read his findings?" She nearly bounced on the seat, and her words spilled like the rushing Bear River.

He hadn't yet read the publication, but he'd make the time. How could he not prepare for an invigorating conversation with her?

Today, he'd rather listen to Dr. Isabella Pattison's viewpoint on dental caries and their causes than contribute to the conversation.

Observing her work in the Cromptons' kitchen over the past three weekends and her uncommon and immediate connection with the women and children, he found himself more than enamored with her skills.

And brain.

And fascination with science.

The hours spent driving there and back had become filled

with stimulating conversation on virtually every dental subject. He'd found renewed interest and energy for formerly dull concepts.

"Dr. Willoughby D. Miller, DDS, is an American. You know of whom I refer?"

He nodded.

Her focus, which had flitted from the scattered and wind-curved trees to the river, to the motion of the horses before them, landed on him for a moment.

"This American published an article in German, last year, challenging dentistry in myriad ways, enlightening the cause for which we labor."

"You read German?" Had this woman's education no limit?

"No, but I had the good fortune of attending dental college with two brothers, German by birth. We remained in contact, and upon discussing the matter, the two translated Dr. Miller's research."

One woman among a class of men...

Once more, this lady dentist reminded him of another. The joy in stimulating conversation dissolved with the rapidity of sugar whisked into hot tea.

"I could not wait." Every ounce of desperation carried into her words. "Various dental periodicals have mentioned the English format would be published this year. I needed to know everything immediately. How could I wait?"

She paused for a long moment, as if she wanted an answer.

He chuckled, caught up in her enthusiasm.

"His discoveries are fascinating. Contrary to the common belief that sucrose, so prevalent in the modern diet, is the primary villain, Dr. Miller's findings prove that carbohydrates are." Her knee bumped his, then rode against him.

She hadn't noticed. "The sugars are readily diluted by saliva, while carbohydrates—frankly, the staples in the diet of our patients—adhere to teeth and spaces between, causing subsequent caries."

"The people of Almy haven't the resources for more protein." Who would hunt? With their earnings decimated, how could they buy?

She turned solemn and introspective. Fascinating, how her animation dimmed and surged, so like gusts of wind on the high Wyoming plains. "I do believe, Dr. Merritt, the challenge lies not in adjusting the diet of the Almy residents, but in helping them to understand the necessity of oral hygiene."

"How do you propose to convince them that improved oral hygiene will result in fewer lost teeth?" He couldn't pass on this point of contention. How did she address it with her patients? He'd tried, failed, and tried again.

He attempted to keep his eyes on the road, stunned to realize the team had brought them nearly to Bear River Bridge.

"It's a matter of education," she insisted. Vivaciousness in her tone struck a new high note. "Without instruction, how might they know the importance of brushing and flossing regularly?"

He couldn't help but smile. "They argue such things aren't natural."

Her laughter surrounded him, banishing doubt. "Dentures? Dentures are natural?"

He chuckled, despite his wish to remain beyond her influence. "Of course they are. Every component is indeed natural, from vulcanized rubber to porcelain."

At his reply, she lit up, from the crown of her head to the soles of her boots. She'd worn "country" clothes, simple, plain, warm, and durable. Almy's mud clung to her hems and boots.

She didn't need vivid raspberry or royal-blue wool. She didn't need dyed feathers or ridiculous stuffed birds. The woman's natural state was filled with life, energy, and color.

From that first moment he'd noticed her on Evanston's Main Street, he'd been wildly attracted. He'd wanted to discover her name and her place among the citizens. Whose visiting sister? Was she wed?

He'd reacted with haste and pain upon discovering her identity.

Now he needed to know everything about her. Beliefs and perspectives on matters from amalgam to dentures, food preferences, and why she wore a new costume every time he noticed her.

"So you agree with Dr. Miller's microorganism theory?" She seemed braced for criticism.

"I do." Possibilities unspooled before him. Someone to discuss ideas with, discover solutions, develop improved practices . . .

And so much more . . .

"You agree?"

"Naturally. I've read Lister's work at length. With bacteria causing suppuration of wounds and surgical incisions, the success of his antiseptic technique—this school of thought makes sense."

"Dr. Merritt . . ." She tugged her gloves on more snuggly, shifting in her seat with restless energy. "I'm thrilled to discover your beliefs are much like my own."

"Likewise."

She slid him a knowing look.

He grinned.

How unfortunate that he'd lost the previous eleven or twelve months, when he might have had the association of Dr. Isabella Pattison's sharp mind.

She returned his smile. Warm and open and genuine. "I shouldn't be surprised."

This woman's smile transformed her from lovely to dazzling.

He turned back to the path ahead, his senses attuned to the music of nature: the rushing melody of water over rocks in the riverbed and the wind singing over the plain.

The wagon seat, barely large enough for two, put her person in close quarters. The wagon rocked frequently, the back-and-forth motion brushing her shoulder and thigh against him. Often.

"You're doing a good thing in Almy." Her tone underscored her sincerity. "Mrs. Nye told me what you've done for the coal miners and their families these past five years. And how you persisted until they accepted your services."

How had he once thought Isabella and Lenora too much alike?

Beyond gender and choice of careers, what had they in common?

Not once had Lenora understood his reasons. She would not have approved of his determination to help ... nor his choice to give away services that should've netted a tidy income.

Perhaps that's why he'd kept his Almy visits a secret. If no one knew, he'd not take the brunt of their criticism.

He fiddled with the reins, uncomfortable with Dr. Pattison's praise.

Her little hand, gloved in brown calfskin, settled upon his. He shouldn't be able to sense her heat between their mismatched gloves, but he did.

She squeezed, rested there for a long moment, perhaps the space of ten seconds. She released him far too soon.

The oddest warmth expanded in his chest.

Soil slipped beneath his proverbial feet, giving way in an alarming rush.

Now here he stood, again, on the cusp of repeating that greatest mistake of his life.

He must *not* fall for the wrong kind of woman, not ever again.

•••

Isabella bit into a crisp apple, savoring the sweet-tart flavor. Late April sunshine heated her back through her many layers of clothing as she strolled, slowly, in the direction of the office.

Restlessness nipped at her heels.

If someone had warned her, on the eve prior to Easter Sunday, that her life would change so significantly, she'd have scoffed.

Until Dr. Merritt, she could have held her life's significant detours in a thimble.

Two and one-half weeks.

Three Sundays in Almy and three Monday-morning return drives.

Hours of invigorating conversation.

Given where they'd begun—with him unwilling to acknowledge her on the street nor make her acquaintance—they'd somehow become esteemed friends. At ease, laughing and talking about science and shared challenges.

Never had she made the acquaintance of a man who claimed her awareness so completely. Never before had she wanted more than friendship.

She nipped off the last good bit of apple and fed the core to a patient mare tied at the hitching post before Davidson's Drugs.

The drugstore's doors stood open wide, welcoming fresh

air and warming temperatures. A paperboard sign hung on the window's frame, swinging gently in the breeze.

Premium Office for Rent.

A calligraphic arrow pointed up.

Up?

She tipped her head back and discovered a matching sign in the second-story window.

Between the pharmacy and a merchant tailor shop, a door opened to an interior staircase, smelling of fresh paint. Natural light entered the stairwell from windows at both top and bottom.

Satisfactory accommodations couldn't preclude wishing, right?

Midday sunlight spilled through four tall southwest facing windows and illuminated the grand room with its high ceilings and new hardwood floors. The space smelled of fresh plaster, sawdust, varnish, and paint. The workmen must've left a window or two open to clear the air, because a fresh breeze teased fine hairs at her temple.

A washroom in back provided running water and indoor facilities.

With ease, she imagined her chair and footrest, dental cabinet, and drill in this palatial space . . . filling less than half.

If Dr. Henry Merritt joined her . . .

Their Sunday forays north were filled with stimulating conversation, insightful questions, and a budding friendship.

The best parts of her Sundays and Monday mornings could easily become the best parts of her weekdays.

She really should lock away her affectionate feelings for the man—a remarkable fellow who'd make some lady a wonderful, faithful husband.

Not her, naturally. Never her.

Their friendship and working relationship was based on mutual appreciation of intellect.

Their Almy runs were the furthest thing from a courting ride as could possibly be.

She had no business wanting more.

But . . . *what if?*

What if they could have more, *be* more?

She turned from the sunlit space. At the bottom of the stairs, she shut the exterior door with a smart snap.

If she were prudent, she'd halt this nonsense, immediately. Before she ended up on the fast train to heartbreak.

The same mare who'd shared the apple tossed her head and whinnied.

"No more apple, girl." The horse's muzzle was warm velvet beneath her hand. "Though I understand you'd like more."

Longing tugged her view upward. From here, the screen on the open window was visible. Funny, she hadn't noticed that convenience from inside the room.

Perhaps a different perspective was all she'd needed.

The many hours in Dr. Merritt's company had given her that new perspective. He'd awakened much more than a desire for intellectually challenging conversation.

She *wanted* more. Easy to admit, at least to herself.

Somehow, in the space of five minutes, she'd made a decision. Perhaps several.

She wanted to work alongside Dr. Merritt and spend more time with him. That meant she wanted the rental.

With one last pat on the mare's muzzle, she whispered, "Thank you, lady, for your fine advice."

Inside the pharmacy, she made her wishes known, and paid for the first three months.

Now to inform her patients of her new address, and to invite Dr. Merritt to join her there.

· 6 ·

IN SIX SHORT days, April would come to a close. He closed his eyes against the inevitable.

Bells tinkled above his office door. He turned, surprised to see Isabella. Black piping adorned her fawn-colored wool suit. Black buttons marched along the edge of her asymmetrical jacket. Stark lines emphasized her feminine figure.

"Dr. Pattison." He rose, delighted by the surprise visit. "To what do I owe this pleasure?"

"I believe I left my kit in your wagon last Monday morning."

"My apologies. Yes." He'd forgotten it—but not her. "Your dental kit."

She held the instruments in gloved hands. Tassels on her reticule swayed. "Am I interrupting?"

"No, ma'am. I've been reading." *The Chieftain* lay open on his desk, the promising advertisements circled with red pencil.

Her scrutiny touched the paper.

Maybe she wouldn't see the neat stack of unpaid bills, nor the tell-tale newsprint.

Especially if he misdirected. "Did you see the article about the progress of our pavilion, built under the direction of the Council of City Professionals? Our city engineer and county bridge builder have done fine work, according to *The Chieftain*."

"I did see that notice."

"Very good. I understand they're on schedule to complete with plenty of time to spare before the celebration events scheduled there."

She nodded, evidently willing to allow the topic to conclude. Confidence squared her shoulders and lifted her chin. "I've a matter I'd like to discuss."

Sweet, dainty violets teased his senses. The fragrance suited her.

"Will you sit?" He gestured to chairs once used for waiting customers.

"I thought we might walk, enjoy the fresh air, and discuss my proposal over a meal."

On cue, his belly grumbled.

She chuckled. "I see your stomach approves."

"I have a box lunch Mrs. Linden sent."

"Your landlady."

"Yes. You know the Lindens?" Had they defected to the sunny lady dentist?

"Can't say I do." She watched him for a second or two. "Dr. Merritt, you are an enigma."

"You unearthed my greatest secret. What more could there be?"

"I suspect you hide many more layers." Delight winked in her eyes. "You board with the Lindens, four blocks from here. Mr. Linden is employed by Union Pacific, and they rent a small home."

She'd graciously avoided mentioning the poor rent district and the undesirable neighborhood. "True."

"I'm curious to comprehend why you spend a large portion of your income for Almy residents. I've thought of little else."

She'd thought of him, all week? Should this please him or cause him anxiety?

"Perhaps it's time I state my business."

"Yes." He could handle business.

"Our shared experiences these past Sundays have brought another joint venture to mind. Are you aware of the newly finished rooms above Davidson's Drugs?"

He'd seen the ad, but immediately passed by. He managed a nod.

"I visited that sunlit, airy space—too large for me, alone. I considered... Will you join me?"

"Join—" his heart bolted—"you?" Lightheaded, he grasped the back of a chair. "Please, sit."

She perched on the front edge of a chair.

He spun his chair to face her, ensuring several inches between them.

"We'll maintain our own businesses," she said, "within the same room. We'll enjoy working side by side."

Her words sketched an appealing scene.

"You truly would be a great help."

That made no sense, and he nearly told her so. *Manners, Henry.* "To be blunt, Dr. Pattison, I can no longer afford these accommodations." The admission stung his pride. "If I cannot afford this, how will I afford fifty percent of the most attractive retail space in Evanston?"

She scooted closer to the edge of the chair. "I have more patients than I can comfortably see. I'm hoping that by bringing a second dentist into my—no, I've misspoken. Separate businesses—" she waved a gloved hand, as if to erase her words—"same office."

"Many of my former patients, I believe, now see you. They've made their choice."

"Allow me to speak freely." Her cheeks pinked, and for the first time, uncertainty flitted through her expressive eyes. "Women and their children have flocked to me, and that can be explained. My problem lies in the single men, of which this town has an excess—"

The picture came into sharp focus.

"—who assume familiarities. Their behavior has become wholly inappropriate, as they recline in the dental chair and I lean near." She trembled. "As required of a dentist."

His desire to protect her warred with his determination to protect himself.

She straightened her spine. "If we worked alongside one another, you might take some of those men as your patients. If they remain mine, I doubt they'll make inappropriate remarks in your presence."

Simpler solutions existed. "Why not hire a secretary with a firm hand to safeguard you? He'd prevent inappropriate behavior."

"Why, indeed?" She held his eye for several long moments, and seemed to debate revealing more.

Had she endured something so significant that she'd invite more gossip?

She twisted her reticule cords. "I couldn't find a single dentist in Los Angeles who would accept me as a partner in their practice. Or in San Francisco. Or Salt Lake City."

Her pain pierced his conflicted heart.

"Nor would any, not even newcomers to our profession,

consider working in the same building—keeping our accounts and businesses wholly apart."

Precisely the arrangement she'd offered him.

Like so many others, he'd declined.

The awareness brought shame in wagon loads. "A man has his pride."

"Perhaps. But you're not like the others."

Her compliment added to his guilt. Wouldn't a gentleman have been quick to help, rather than hold fast to selfish reasons to keep his distance? "I believe I'm quite common."

"You're most uncommon, Dr. Merritt. I suspect I've discovered your motivation for providing a dental dispensary."

"Oh? Let's see how close you come to the truth."

"You grew up in a mining town. You witnessed depravity and how few hours miners have outside their shifts, and determined to bring dentistry to them."

True, he never charged for his services. Or materials. Or medicines.

"You're partly correct." He'd grown accustomed to hiding his past. Why did he want to confide in Dr. Pattison?

Cocooned as they were in his little storefront, the outside noises of passing wagons and a train whistle in the distance seemed muted.

She waited, curiosity lustrous in her eyes. She leaned nearer. "Oh?"

"I'm descended from a long line of coal miners, first in England, then in the United States."

He'd disclosed less to Lenora, and she'd immediately silenced him.

Instead of disgust, Dr. Pattison nodded with certainty. "You help because you *know*."

Partly. His reasons ran deep. "Dad enlisted, alongside

every patriotic man in Penn. I was born while he fought for the Union." Still, no balking. "He lost his dominant arm, but he returned to the mines after the war."

"Your father is a fine man."

"Was."

She nodded. Gentleness filled her expression. "Please continue."

How much did he trust Isabella Pattison?

"My mother worked herself into an early grave. She cleaned houses for the rich, gardened every inch of soil possible, took in laundry..."

Sweet understanding shone in her eyes.

No pity, or he'd have halted.

He leaned his elbows upon his knees and his face in his hands. "My brother was killed in a cave-in at age fourteen." He managed to avoid emotion.

To acknowledge his heritage, and his brother, felt... freeing. Lenora hadn't allowed him to remember with her.

In sharp contrast, Dr. Pattison waited, showing no glimmer of discomfort.

"Dad determined I'd make something of myself. He sent me to Philly to dental college, where I worked the docks every minute I wasn't in lectures. I found a willing supporter or two. I repaid every dime."

"Your dad?"

"Crushed by falling rock six months before commencement."

One, two, three counts to the inhale. Slow exhale.

Years had passed. Would more time heal the pain?

Fabric rustled as she leaned nearer, bringing the scent of springtime and violets. Her hand settled on his shoulder and soothed. He hesitated to move, for fear she'd come to herself and pull away.

"Your father's greatest wish was to free you from the mines. *He succeeded.*"

"Yes." His voice cracked.

"I assumed wrong," she said, after moments passed. "Your motivation for donating so much in Almy is far more honorable."

He shrugged.

"Your work honors your parents' and brother's memory. They would be proud of you, Henry Merritt." She whispered, her words intimate. "I am proud of you."

Those five little words tiptoed past his defenses and settled dangerously close to his heart.

He'd needed the reminder. The story of who he'd been, where he'd come from, and all he'd overcome made him a man engulfed by acute loneliness. And a plan to ensure he'd fill that greatest desire in the right way, and at the right time.

Years ago, he'd made a grab for a real home and a place to belong. The try had ended badly. He'd come to understand that the best way to honor his parents' sacrifice would be to ensure his own children were raised in a real home, with a mother who wasn't forced to sacrifice everything . . .

Who but Isabella Pattison could have shown him the honor in his past?

Slowly, he scrubbed his eyes, relieved to find them dry, and sat back.

"Forgive my selfishness." Her voice returned to normal volume. "I simply must insist. I need to work with you on Sundays in Almy, and I need you to work with me in Evanston."

How could he refuse her, after all she'd confessed?

"As you provide transportation to Almy, I will pay our rent."

"Absolutely not."

"Consider it payment for your protection."

"That's absurd."

Her expression hardened.

He far preferred her smiles, vivacious conversations, and secrets she told no one else.

"Forgive me, Dr. Pattison. I misspoke."

Did he dare risk working beside this woman nearly every day of the week?

"No offense taken." Her countenance filled his heart with light. "Come with me. I'm anxious to show you our new office."

●●●

"I'm of the solid opinion," Isabella stated, her tone ripe with aggravation, "that *The Chieftain* is not worth the paper it's printed on."

Henry looked up from sweeping the floor. Late afternoon sunlight streamed through the open, southwest facing windows, kissing her curls.

Sunshine burnished the gray-green of her costume into the hue of Pennsylvania, like home. The breeze teased her hair, bobbing it this way, then that.

Focus. On *anything* but Isabella's person. Or *Isabella* and *home* in the same sentence.

Heat.

Windows.

Yes. See how quickly he'd interrupted the inappropriate train of thought.

Windows. Summertime.

They'd need blinds before the full heat of summer, or this upstairs location would be an oven. But the past two weeks since moving in, they'd enjoyed the pleasant breeze and springtime temperatures.

He opened a hand, silently asking for the paper.

She passed it over. For such a little thing, she was a bundle of energy. "That Thomas Fisher is a troublemaker. I swan, he stirs up sediment, with the express purpose of causing a sensation."

"Well said." He found the notice she referenced on page two. *Dr. Pattison, Dr. Merritt Join Forces.*

He skimmed the "news"—the fact they'd both removed their respective dental practices to this singular address.

Anyone with sufficient eyesight and the ability to read could've discovered this for themselves. Precise gold and black paint adorned second-story windows and a street-level door. *Dr. H. M. Merritt, DDS, and Dr. I. M. Pattison, DDS. Modern & Painless Dentistry.*

He skimmed Fisher's article. *Dr. Pattison and Dr. Merritt combined two dental practices into one.*

Inaccurate and false. But not enough to upset her.

The next two paragraphs hinted at a long list of improprieties, unchaperoned as they were at moments such as this.

The accusations didn't stop there. According to Fisher, they'd abandoned all decorum, discarded every rule, and caused a Wyoming-sized scandal.

The "news" of their indecent behavior stank of retaliation.

"You know the old adage, 'Never pick a fight with someone who buys ink by the barrel.' I fear I used flawed judgment. Again, I ask forgiveness." Would he forever say and do the wrong thing around this woman? "If I'd not agreed to the interview, if I'd not pressured the man to retract—"

"Stop." She seemed far more weary than angry. "No apology necessary."

How could he not admire a woman who accepted apologies easily and seemed incapable of holding a grudge? The novelty endeared her to him.

Yet the angelic quality of ready forgiveness wasn't the same thing as tolerating a fool.

"For the record," he dropped the paper on her dental chair, "I never liked Fisher."

He grabbed the broom and resumed sweeping, expecting Isabella to wear the topic to shreds. She had every right to be agitated. Some people believed everything *The Chieftain* printed.

"Neither have I."

He braced for the storm.

She picked up the paper, folded it in half, and in half once again. Determination radiated from her posture and the set of her jaw.

Here it came.

"I'm pleased mornings remain chilly." She pushed today's *Chieftain* into the corner of the well-stocked kindling box. "Tomorrow morning, when I start the fire, Fisher's gibberish will be reduced to ash." She dusted her palms against each other. "Most rewarding."

Surprise tickled through him. What? No long-winded rant? No hysterical bout of tears?

No, of course not. Why did he assume all lady dentists behaved like Lenora Baily?

He laughed in delight.

She winked.

From the moment she'd peeked beneath the canvas covering his wagon bed, she'd been one pleasant surprise after another. She'd exceeded his expectations in the best of ways.

What a remarkable woman. If Lenora had been like her . . .

"I'll strike a bargain with you, Dr. Pattison."

"Such as?"

"Let's discredit Thomas Fisher by showing ourselves a

capable team of professionals in our visits to Almy and by the way all townsfolk see us interact here."

"Fine idea."

"Whether we're seen at meetings of the Council of City Professionals or taking fresh air as we circle the block, residents of Evanston will see nothing but utmost cooperation and decorum."

She offered her hand to shake on it. "It's a deal."

· 7 ·

"Oh, darling—are you all right?" Sophia embraced Isabella in a sisterly hug.

Who needed blood relatives when one had remarkable friends?

"Come in, out of the hallway." She urged Sophia and Naomi into the private boardinghouse bedroom.

The walls were thin, but Isabella didn't need to remind her friends. Sophia had lived in this same boardinghouse prior to her marriage. Their voices immediately dropped to whispers.

"We read Fisher's article." Naomi took a turn hugging Isabella.

And by sundown, they circled the wagons around her. How could she not adore these women?

Sophia's fury sparked. "How dare that man apologize to me, then treat you badly?"

"It's all right. Please, sit."

The ladies claimed the two upholstered chairs. Isabella took the settee, beside the dental periodical she'd been reading.

"It's *not* all right." Sophia rarely lost her temper, but where Thomas Fisher was concerned, emotion clouded her vision.

"You two would go to war for me, and I love you for it."

The three clasped hands in a circle.

"How much of Fisher's article is true?" Sophia asked. "We'll love you, no matter what."

"You didn't believe any of it, did you?" Isabella chuckled. An old woman with the adjoining bedroom had excessively good hearing, enjoyed nosing about, and thrived upon complaining to the landlady about noisy residents.

"Dr. Merritt and I," Isabella whispered, "have determined to ignore Fisher, burn today's edition to ashes, and allow all to witness that our behavior is above reproach." Though some would never approve of their visits to Almy.

"We want you to be happy." Lamplight reflected in Naomi's eyes. "We believe Henry Merritt may be what your heart needs."

They knew she hoped one day to find the right man, one who understood and loved her anyway.

Joe and Chadwick were proof such men existed.

"I want to be happy."

"From everything I've seen," Naomi whispered, "Henry is a good man. Joe confirmed my diagnosis."

The joy of dentistry, alongside Henry, had been magical. "Sharing an office has shown me more of who he is, beneath the bluster and fear." She searched both friends' faces, noting encouragement and hope.

"Our time traveling to Almy and back, and now in the office each day, are the best hours of my week. We laugh, we debate, we discuss science in a manner that fills me to overflowing."

Both ladies nodded. They knew, perfectly.

"I'm anxious to go to the office each morning. I'm loath to return here at night." She paused, weighing the secrets she guarded closely when near Henry. "I want to risk letting him in."

"Oh, Bella."

Naomi's sisterly affection provoked Isabella's tears. She chuckled through a sob. "No nicknames."

Both ladies squeezed her hands. Here, she'd found home, family, and belonging. Was romantic love too much to ask?

"Am I foolish to hope?"

Sophia smiled. "If you don't take a chance, you'll never know."

•••

The following morning, Isabella waited for Henry at the gate of the Linden home.

"Dr. Pattison?" Worry lined his features. "What's wrong?"

"Accompany me to the Job Office, will you?"

"Certainly. May I ask why?" He shut the gate behind them.

"After Mr. Fisher's ill-mannered behavior in yesterday's weekly, I don't trust him to give the calico ball proper attention. You and I, the dentist subcommittee, were charged with invitations. I intend to do the job well, despite Fisher." She leaned in and lowered her voice. "He might *forget* to publish the calico ball, midst all statehood events."

"Smart thinking." He offered his arm, took his habitual place closest to traffic, and let her set the pace. "The Job Office. The one alternative press in town."

"I knew you were a bright man."

His grin caught her in the middle. Must he be so handsome?

Concern lined his features. "I thought Fisher planned to print the invitations."

"I'm certain he does. But as he's not begun, and my concept for a specialty invitation involves materials he's not accustomed to."

He chuckled—rich, deep, and warm. "Thus the Job Office."

"Indeed."

"How many invitations?"

"We'll need enough to be delivered to every residence, UP line shack, and soul in China Town . . . everyone in Almy, everyone in the greater county at large."

"That many?" he asked.

"Yes." His broad grin kept butterflies swirling in her stomach.

"What plans have you for delivery?"

"Ideally, we'd hire a reliable team to deliver the invitations to everyone in the county."

"But?"

"This isn't one of my mother's annual parties, with a guest list of two hundred. So help me decide. The post office? A delivery service?"

"I trust your judgment."

So different from *don't women handle these things?* "Thank you."

At the Job Office, a young clerk obtained particulars and filled out a form.

"I want the invitations printed upon calico."

"Calico?" The fellow blinked, his eyes magnified behind spectacles. "Fabric?"

"Precisely."

"We've printed grain sacks . . ."

"Yes. Fine printers, such as this establishment, do print

upon fabric. In Los Angeles, my family received a calico ball invitation made of calico."

The young clerk blinked. "The fee will nearly double."

"Fabric costs more than fancy paper?" Henry's surprise bordered on accusation.

"Not merely the cost of the cloth, Dr. Merritt. See, calico is harder to print on. Takes a different method. And more time."

At nearly twice the cost, the allotted budget was insufficient.

True, she could ask for an increase, but every dime spent on the event meant a dime lost to widows and orphans.

Disappointment had been Isabella's frequent companion. She knew how to cope. "Plain stock will suffice."

"Dr. Pattison?" Henry interrupted, ablaze with discovery. What solution had he devised?

He settled a warm, strong hand at the small of her back. "Young man, do set our order aside, will you? By the end of the day, I'll bring in our deposit and finalize everything."

Henry's unwavering confidence proved mighty appealing.

Outside, she blinked in the sunlight. "Tell me your idea."

Throughout her life, friends, classmates, and acquaintances had falsely assumed she could buy anything she wanted.

Father's money had purchased her education, but hadn't brought her love.

If Henry proved as narrow-minded, she'd be disappointed.

Excitement animated Henry's brown eyes. "Everyone in town will benefit from the calico ball—not only widows and orphans of the Almy mines. I suggest we approach a merchant or two and invite them to donate calico in trade for their company's name on the invitations."

Why hadn't she considered this? "I like your idea. Because of our ball's theme, they'll sell a good quantity to women preparing their costumes."

Henry wanted to help find solutions. How could she not fall, a little bit more, for this remarkable man?

"Let's do the same with the Job Office." He put his hand at her back, urging her toward their dental office and their waiting work. "I'll speak to the owner and persuade him to reduce the fee by half. We'll credit him generously on the invitations—superbly printed upon calico."

"Thank you." She wanted to halt their progress along Main Street and embrace him.

"You're welcome." The genuine warmth in his eyes promised he'd lasso the moon if doing so would bring the plan into reach. How endearing.

He doffed his hat to a matron who stepped out of Blyth and Fargo.

"Which is more expensive?" she asked him. "Post office or delivery?"

"We might deliver them ourselves." His manner bordered on teasing. Or perhaps he meant it. "Don't look at me like that. I'm accustomed to hard work."

"Yes, I know." She couldn't help chuckling.

"We'll distribute Almy's through mine foremen."

"An excellent idea."

"And mail to the outlying ranchers, smaller mines, and communities in the north."

"Good." Already, the plan seemed more workable. "And in the city?"

"Deliver them door-to-door with me?"

"You'd better be teasing, Henry Merritt."

"Yes. I received a note this morning at the breakfast table. Dr. Edwin English is unable to see patients for the foreseeable future."

She didn't need confirmation to know Henry had agreed to help. "What happened?"

"His wife is unwell." Henry rested his gaze on hers. "We'll have more patients. Later nights in the office. No personal deliveries."

"I'm sorry for Mrs. English." She tipped her head, enjoying looking up, up, up. "Work before play."

"With you," he winked, "work seems like play."

Waiting at the corner to cross the street, she couldn't help glancing at his strong profile a time or two.

A heavily loaded wagon lumbered past, then a man on his mount.

"I've heard," she told him, "women are already placing orders with dressmakers."

A twinkle shone in his eye. "You?"

"Not yet." With so much to do, she'd not pursued it.

"I thought you enjoyed purchasing costumes." He skimmed the slim lines of her new springtime-green ensemble, sans bustle. She knew how sunlight shimmered on the soft draping. "You're lovely in this new dress, Isabella."

Compliments? On her personal appearance? She looked down, made anxious by his absorption in her.

"My mother sent it. She orders one thing after another and ships crate after crate." Embarrassing, how Mother still chose everything Isabella wore. Worse, the long-armed reach reminded Isabella every day how little Mother trusted her to dress herself.

Something flitted through his warm eyes. "Your mother runs a constant account at the dressmaker, in California, for your costumes and matching hats?"

"I'm embarrassed to admit my mother treats me like a child." She checked the street, finding no one near enough to overhear. "Or a debutante, twelve years past her debut."

He blinked. "You misunderstand. I only meant to convey my compliments. And express curiosity. I find myself desirous to know everything about you, Isabella Pattison."

A break in traffic came. She accepted his arm as they crossed the street. She'd heard empty flattery before. Henry's statement was the furthest thing from it.

He matched his pace to hers, guiding her carefully around the worst of the mess.

At the opposite sidewalk, she dropped her handful of skirt and petticoats.

I want to know everything about you, Isabella Pattison.

A few steps farther and he slipped a key into the lock of their street-level door.

Isabella decided she could grow quite accustomed to Henry Merritt's kindness.

· 8 ·

Two weeks later, Henry found himself occupied with a complaining twenty-year-old man suffering his first broken tooth.

Isabella met the delivery boy, signed for crates filled with invitations, and went to work prying them open.

Henry's forceps slipped on the damaged tooth.

"Doc!" In his outburst, the fellow chewed on Henry's fingers. "That hurts."

"Be still. We'll have this over within a minute."

Sure enough, by the time Isabella read an invitation in the sunlight, Henry had pulled the hopeless tooth, stopped the bleeding, stitched the man's gum closed, urged him to keep the area clean, and collected payment.

Henry washed and dried his hands. "Let's see."

He wouldn't have cared if the invitations had been printed on card. But Isabella cared. And he enjoyed her pleasure in something so easily accomplished.

The calico's blue dots and trailing vines of light green decorated the cream background. As desired, the necessary information stood out in stark relief.

"Well done, don't you think?" She hadn't stopped smiling.

"Very nice." Friday, July 11, would feature the calico ball at the conclusion of a jubilant week. "Congratulations, Dr. Pattison."

"Thank you."

He reached for the fabric rectangle, trimmed with a pinking iron, and rubbed it between forefinger and thumb. Nice quality. A decorative frame around the important details gave credit to the Job Office, and recognized both the Blyth and Fargo and A. C. Beckwith stores for their donation of calico for printing.

"Ready for addresses." From an open crate, she lifted a cardboard box filled with creamy envelopes.

"I have horrid penmanship."

She laughed with disbelief. "Oh no you don't. You and I, thanks to Dr. Edwin English, are the invitation committee. Besides, you promised to help."

"And I will. Beginning day after tomorrow when I'll hand a stack to the foreman of each mine."

"That's helpful, but the northernmost county residents will travel more than two hundred miles. Journeys like that require time, and arrangements must be made. I want their invitations to go out in Monday's mail."

Good thing Dr. Pattison made up half of the invitation committee—or he would've messed this up. "You're right. You have the information?"

"You know I do."

No, he hadn't, but he shouldn't be surprised. This woman took responsibilities seriously. He admired that trait.

Within a quarter hour, they'd set a table where light was best. With fountain pens, envelopes, and the list between them, Henry addressed his first invitation.

"What do you think? Acceptable, Doctor?"

She'd completed two to his one, her script perfect and spacing ideal. Lovely penmanship for a lovely woman.

"Yes. Do continue."

Quiet minutes slipped past, the scratch of their pens the only noise.

"I've a question," she said, "and I'd like an answer, if you're willing."

He finished the address and placed a check mark beside the corresponding listing on her sheet. "If I can, I will."

"Joe and Naomi tell me that you've liked Naomi well from the moment you were introduced. Naomi is a medical doctor."

Guilt pinched, hard. So far, no question, but he knew, when the question came, he wouldn't find it easy to answer.

"You avoided me quite successfully for nearly a year after I arrived in Evanston. I'm relieved to discover," playfulness graced her tone, "you're reasonably nice."

He chuckled. "Glad to hear it. And I'm glad to discover you're reasonably nice."

"Why avoid me?"

He'd been horrid. "I'm sorry for my rudeness."

"Had I offended you? I ask, because you evidently didn't like me. You liked Naomi, despite her education and choice to practice medicine, but . . ."

"First, let me assure you that you'd done nothing to offend me." How could he explain something he didn't understand? "Mrs. Joe Chandler had been introduced to me exactly as such. A married woman—and a physician."

"So, it's unwed women you have no liking for." Sadness showed in every plane of her face.

"I see now why you called me an enigma. I am quite difficult to understand."

"Quite."

Flashes of that first sighting, coupled with sudden and overwhelming attraction, struck him once again. He chose to tell the whole truth.

"I'd noticed you, found you lovely and appealing. Then I overheard you talking to the sign painter, clarifying the spelling of your name."

"You discovered my profession."

"Yes. Please understand. It wasn't you. I saw the world, and everyone in it, through the lenses I'd learned to wear." How narrow-minded he'd been. "Among my dental college enrollees was one woman."

Isabella completed another name and address. "You didn't care for her?"

"Quite the opposite. She was bright, competent, and charming." He didn't want to remember the best of Lenora nor the worst. But memories protected him from repeating lessons learned.

"You felt threatened?"

"Oddly, no. I found her intellect stimulating. Much as I do our conversations and debates." He joyfully anticipated time with Isabella. Infinitely more than with Lenora.

Interesting, the discovery he could remember Lenora without pain. Though he'd believed he'd love her forever, his love for her had faded into the past.

Isabella listened with her eyes, ears, and soul. "She returned your regard?"

"Yes, I thought so." He beheld this woman who'd become dangerously dear. "Love wasn't enough. She wanted to be a dentist more than she wanted me."

He searched her face, desperate to glimpse understanding. He must try harder. This painful past had driven him to state that *women do not belong in dentistry*, and that misstep had provoked Fisher to publish embellishments.

If anyone deserved an honest explanation, Isabella did.

"When news of my father's death came, I was inconsolable. I'd been born to parents who loved me and did their best. I was alone." He glimpsed understanding in her eyes. "Every day spent in school, rather than the mines, distanced me from former friends."

She nodded, waiting.

"In my destitution, I craved someone to call my own. I wanted marriage and family. At the cusp of graduation, I acted in haste and asked Lenora to marry me."

Her rejection had stolen his last spark of hope. As if the loss had been yesterday, the pain resurfaced, a tight fist about his throat.

He'd already voiced the hardest part. *Lenora hadn't loved him enough.*

"I'm sorry." Isabella whispered without censure. "Perhaps she believed marriage and career are mutually exclusive."

Weren't they? What dentist-wife could embrace both loves? No woman could keep a comfortable home *and* treat patients.

Home.

The immense craving resurfaced. Husband and wife, father and mother. Precious bonds between people committed to one another. He had to believe he'd find that miracle. Somewhere, sometime.

As he tended to do when he ached for that elusive dream, he fingered the watch chain given to him by Dr. Ullman. While a student, he'd been invited a handful of times to dine in the professor's home. Not only was the household well-run and comfortable, but both Dr. and Mrs. Ullman showered their children with unabashed affection. Dr. Ullman attributed the success of his marriage, home, and children to his wife: *the mother is the heart of the home.*

With each visit, Henry had become more and more certain that he'd glimpsed heaven.

As Lenora Baily didn't want what he did, he'd determined to find the right kind of girl, one who cherished the same priorities as he. But not until the right time, when his business was established and he had the financial security to support a wife and children.

"Do you?" Isabella tipped her head to the side. Sunlight turned her tight brown curls to bronze.

Did he what? Where had the conversation been? Oh, yes, that elusive sense of home. Of course he wanted that. With all of his heart. "Yes."

She might want those things also.

She capped her pen, and set it beside the stacked envelopes. "I believe you've opened my eyes."

He waited, his heart pounding.

Isabella turned in her chair, to face him. "Are you aware that Joe sent for Naomi, as a mail-order bride?"

"Yes." Joe had spoken of his happiness with Naomi and the circumstances that brought them together.

"In contrast, consider Sophia and Chadwick. He's an unusual man, one who sees no lines between women's work and men's." She studied him. "I'm startled, and a bit ashamed, to realize I'd not recognized yet one more school of thought."

His heart pounded, harder. What school of thought?

She examined him with care. "I believe I see your view."

"You do?"

She seemed ready to reply, as if something wonderful were nearly said . . . but not.

After all they'd shared, the secrets he'd told no one else, every hour in the wagon, discussing similarities and differences of medical opinion, setting up adjoining businesses... he'd taken her into his confidence. He'd trusted her with everything.

For so long, he'd believed he wanted a traditional wife, but the past months had reopened his eyes to the joy found in a woman with a quick mind. After meeting and coming to care for Isabella Pattison, could he be happy with anyone else?

Dare he open his heart to the possibilities?

"Please. Call me Henry."

"Oh no. If you are now Henry, you must call me Isabella."

"Not Izzy? Not Belle?" He squinted at her. "Isa?"

She laughed—sudden and intense joy. "My name, Henry, is Isabella."

"Might I call you Bella? Is that better than Belle?"

"If you stoop so low," teasing restored to her light tone, "I will address you as Hen. You'd like that."

He chuckled. "Understood. You were saying?"

"Henry." Her smile was bittersweet. "I believe, at last, I see."

· 9 ·

THEY'D JUST LEFT Almy behind, and had the entirety of the return drive before them. The early June sun felt weak and the air decidedly chilly.

"You do realize, Isabella, you owe me a story or two."

She enjoyed, far too much, the musical quality of her name on Henry's lips.

In the week and a half since he'd asked her to use his given name, he'd shown respect and deference, consistently addressing her as *Dr. Pattison* or *Doctor* when in the company of patients.

But when they were alone, he used her given name with relish.

Most definitely not something a good man like Henry would do if he believed them to be business acquaintances and nothing more.

"A story? What would you like to hear? A fairy tale?"

"I told you everything about me. You know all my secrets." His eyes sparkled with keen interest. "It's time you do the same."

He'd maintained composure when speaking of heartbreak. Could she, as well?

"I'll begin." He cleared his throat. "I decided to pursue dentistry..."

She laughed at his silliness. "Do you want my story, or not?"

"I do. I want to know everything about you."

Her heart thumped at his flirtation. Was he in earnest? "Then you mustn't tease."

He traced a solemn X over his heart with one fingertip. A promise made.

The wagon rolled onward, the team's pace easy on the dry road.

"My father is a physician in Los Angeles. I grew up watching him receive patients in his medical rooms in our home. Like him, I was drawn to healing. We talked of medicine, his greatest joys and greatest heartaches. He believed I'd make a superb doctor's wife."

He listened, interest showing in a nod here and there.

"I decided I wanted to be a dentist while still in school. I'd suffered from a toothache, and through the experience with a dentist near our home, discovered my passion."

"How did your parents react?"

"With surprise. And objection. They'd seen my curiosity in Father's work as acceptable, for every mother benefits from basic medical knowledge." The expressions her parents had worn—disbelief mixed with a good portion of doubt—had haunted her since. "Father was always more indulgent than a father should be."

"Said who?"

"Mother."

"Ah."

"Indulgent, he granted permission for me to attend dental college and paid every penny. He purchased my equipment, paid my room and board."

"Generous."

She nodded, reflecting on that difficult time. "He insisted I consider my decision with care. He warned that by choosing to study dentistry, I chose to relinquish marriage."

Henry's expression conveyed understanding and compassion.

"Father warned the best men wouldn't be looking for wives among their classmates." He'd been right. "He believed dentistry could never provide the same fulfillment as marriage and motherhood."

That conversation had been etched upon her memory in vibrant color. She'd sat on the patient's side of his desk. Father had pushed his spectacles high on his forehead. She'd pleated her burgundy wool skirt with her fingers. Pleated and smoothed, pleated and smoothed.

Because of the memories branded into that skirt, she'd never worn the favorite burgundy wool again. Longing and determination had fortified her then, preparing her to fight for what she wanted.

"Was he right? Or have you found fulfillment in your career?" Henry's questions resonated with kind support. And encouragement. Henry truly understood the joy she'd found in dentistry.

"Indeed. I have."

"Your parents preferred you wed?"

"Naturally. My whole childhood, every privilege prepared me for my life as someone's wife and someone's mother. Quality education. Cooking lessons. Musical training."

"Yet they deferred to your wishes."

"Yes." If only she'd retained their affection.

"Brothers? Sisters?"

"One sister." Perfect in every way. "Florence is two and

one-half years younger. She and her banker husband, Mr. Dudley Ketton, have three sons and one daughter."

He needn't know she hadn't seen the children for several years. She'd returned home one Christmas to nurture family relationships. But she'd been unable to withstand their constant pity.

Or mother's tearful entreaties. *Please, darling. Come home. It's not too late for marriage. You'll find a good man, an upstanding member of the community, once you leave dentistry behind.*

As if any other life path were a travesty.

"How old are they?"

"The children? Nine, seven, six, and three." Rough estimates.

"They must adore you."

"Truthfully? No."

Her confession hung between them.

She'd come this far. Why not purge her heart? If anyone might understand, Henry would. He knew how much she needed to work in her chosen field.

"Through school, and every year afterward, I spent the holidays with family. Mother wept and pleaded with me to withdraw from school, allow her to introduce suitable marriage candidates." Pain still burned, hot and deep. "She believes my foolishness prevented me from marriage."

"I'm sorry." He settled his hand on her back, like he might with a child in need of comfort. But his soothing didn't feel patronizing. His touch felt ... *right*. So very right, and beyond wonderful.

"Florence and I grew apart. She loves her life and cannot understand why I discarded the privileges and blessings of our sex to invade a man's world."

"Common belief. But commonality doesn't make it

right." He rubbed one more circle upon her back, then eased away. "Your brother-in-law agrees?"

"He dislikes my independence and believes my desire to earn wages is unnatural. He forbade me to influence his children."

"Narrow-minded fool."

Henry's quick reply, condemning Dudley, evoked laughter. "That he is."

The wagon wheels turned, the river rushed, and Isabella tipped her face to the sunlight. She might not have family, but she had this beautiful, wild corner of Wyoming Territory, free of coal soot and crowded streets, where she wasn't expected to dine every Sunday with displeased family members.

"When you turn quiet, I think you're keeping parts of the story to yourself." He gave a gentle nudge. "Tell me what you're thinking."

"I'm thinking that I love Wyoming and Evanston, the wide, clear skies. And before that, remembering one last uncomfortable visit at home, after graduation. Around that dining room table, with every member of my family, I was the only one celebrating.

"To everyone else, my graduation signaled an end to my self-indulgence. I'd lost too much time. I needed to set aside distractions and focus on regaining all I'd lost." An ache throbbed behind her breastbone.

"What did you do?"

"Nothing would change if I remained in Los Angeles, so I packed my trunks and left. I lived for a time in San Francisco, then Salt Lake City."

"Sounds lonely." If anyone understood, Henry did.

"I found patients wherever I went, but never a place to belong."

She'd already told him about the difficulty in finding

someone—anyone—who'd welcome her into their practice or share a building. Those had been discouraging days.

"That all changed when I read a newspaper article in *The Salt Lake Tribune* about Wyoming Territory's stance on women's rights. I read of Evanston's female medical doctor and female attorney and their well-attended leap-year ball in '88. I wrote to Naomi and Sophia, and before long, the three of us were far more than acquaintances.

"Time passed, then Naomi and Sophia invited me to visit Evanston. Before I left Salt Lake City, they'd suggested I plan a long visit to discover if Evanston and Wyoming Territory could be the place for me."

"You're smiling."

"Indeed. I found pleasure in my one-way train ticket. I brought everything I owned in the UP baggage car."

He shared in her happiness, and her heart filled.

"Here, I've found a place to belong. I have the dearest of friends in Sophia and Naomi—women who, like me, have gone against the grain of society's wishes and make real and lasting contributions to those around them."

He nodded, obviously in agreement.

"Here, I can be myself. Here, those who should love me most don't shame me with tears and lectures and chastisement. No one asks me to come to my senses and marry like I'm supposed to, before I break my mother's heart."

Henry tucked the reins in one hand and grasped her hand with the other.

Driving along in the sunshine of a glorious Monday morning, returning from another purposeful day in Almy beside the man she adored, her hand in his, almost made her believe Evanston had one more immense gift for her.

She closed her eyes, enjoying Henry's touch.

Almost like courting.

"Isabella." One more squeeze. "You are a fine dentist. You're skilled. Talented. Have you noticed the good you've done in Almy?"

She met the certainty in his handsome brown eyes. "Yes."

"Good. Believe me when I tell you that your value is not diminished because you chose a different path than what someone else wants for your life."

She turned his statement over and over. Weighing it, considering.

"It's the truth. You are astonishing. Don't let anyone tell you differently."

Such a simple thing, holding hands. Gloriously, wonderfully simple.

Astonishing, he'd said.

Talented.

Valued.

His words gave wings to her long-held determination to embrace her chosen path and ignore the naysayers.

"You fill a unique role, in Almy and in Evanston. You impact the health and wellbeing of many who won't allow a male dentist near. Who else would see to scared children? Their mothers, sensitive ladies, one and all, trust you."

Yes, she knew this.

He saw through every protective layer to her soul. He saw her for precisely who she was.

And pronounced her work worthy.

He deemed *her* worthy.

The magnitude of his gift settled upon her. How could she not love him?

Like wildflowers in warm summer sunshine, love for him multiplied, covering the hillsides with glorious color.

Where had this man been through the seasons of her life? Where, when she'd battled loneliness so acute she thought she'd die from it? What providential miracle had brought him into her life?

"If more men were like you, Henry Merritt, the world would be a better place."

He looked deeply into her eyes as he tugged on the reins. "Whoa."

Seconds passed as the team halted. He set the brake.

Her grin blossomed as he wrapped the reins about the brake handle.

She squeezed his hand between hers, loving this simple pleasure.

His grin replied. He nipped one finger of his driving glove, then two. He tugged the glove free and dropped it onto his lap.

He twisted on the seat, his long thigh pressed against hers. He brushed the backs of his knuckles softly against her cheek.

The friction of his barely there touch sent shivers racing over her skin.

He intended to kiss her!

Seconds passed. His pupils dilated. He took in her cheeks, her jaw, and settled on her mouth.

Sudden awareness of their mingling breaths, fast and shallow, rushed through her.

His knuckles gave way to the pads of his fingers. He traced the line of her jaw.

His reverent touch made her want to drift her eyes closed. She wanted to touch him, to feel the heat of his hand against hers, slide her thumb over his freshly shaved jaw.

Before she realized it, she'd touched his chin. With her riding glove firmly in place.

She groaned in frustration.

He chuckled. Beautiful teeth. White, straight, attractive.

With him, she'd shared her deepest heartaches. Rather than diminish her pain, he'd understood. She *wanted* his kiss.

How her heart craved him!

Slowly, slowly enough she could turn away—*never!*—he dipped his head.

Her heart pounded, anticipating the perfect moment when his lips touched hers.

His eyes drifted shut in that final moment. Electricity tingled along her nerves as his hand slipped behind her neck to cradle her head.

Heat speared through her middle at the first settling of his mouth upon hers.

Perfect.

His reverent kiss spoke volumes.

Far too soon, he pulled away.

She mewled in disappointment.

He chuckled, tipped his head a little more, and kissed her again. The heady rush of pleasure swept through her.

Now she understood all the fuss about kissing.

Especially when a kiss crowned the culminating moment of falling in love.

Everything had changed between them. *Everything.*

The kiss had sparked miraculous hope and thrilling possibilities, the beginning and the end. The beginning of the crowning relationship of her life. The end of doubts, wondering, and a hundred what-ifs.

She would've asked for another kiss, or simply taken it...

But he pressed his forehead to hers—or tried to. His hat brim collided with hers. Ribbons tugged beneath her chin as her hat slid askew.

She chuckled, and he laughed aloud. The masculine rumble deep in his chest was one of her favorite things about him.

With trembling fingers, she righted her bonnet and retied the ribbons.

"I forgot myself." Had she heard such transcendent joy in him? Ever?

How wonderful! She'd been the cause of his forgetfulness. "Forget yourself again, please."

Love had won, in the end, for Sophia and Chadwick, and sanctified the arranged union between Joe and Naomi.

Henry Merritt loved her in return!

She'd forever recall this first Monday of June, when their love story started a new chapter.

He tugged the brim of his hat into place and eased his hand from hers. "I would, but a rider's approaching." He released the brake and flicked the reins against the team's rumps. The horses pulled the wagon into motion.

She blinked, the world expanding from the pinpoint that encompassed only two, and noted the flowing Bear River and bridge not a hundred yards ahead.

As he'd said, a rider approached on a roan, visible through the riverbank foliage. "'Lo there!"

She knew him now. The Reverend Drescher, a German-accented preacher at one of the Evanston churches.

Henry waved in greeting.

"Dr. Pattison, Dr. Merritt—thank God I came across you this close to town."

"What's the problem?" Henry asked.

"My wife. Her toothache's bad enough she says she'd rather be in the travail of childbirth than tolerate the misery another moment."

· 10 ·

ISABELLA FOUND NAOMI in the medical clinic, cleaning after a procedure that had involved a good deal of blood. At the moment, it appeared she'd caught Naomi and Joe between patients.

"I simply must confide what happened today." Her heart overflowed with so myriad emotions. Relief. Happiness. Pleasure.

Naomi passed off the housekeeping duties to her husband and led Isabella by the hand into the back room, their private space where they kept medical journals and shared meals.

Months and months ago, Naomi had told her the sweetest story of Joe's first kiss in this room, followed by his proposal of marriage. The couple had known one another through a pair of telegrams and one life-changing surgery. Joe had known all he needed to. Naomi was perfect for him, and he for her.

Now Isabella's first kiss had brought her to a similar place. Who would've thought, last Christmas, that Dr. Henry Merritt would be the ideal man for her?

She sank into the chair Naomi offered at the table. Pleasant springtime air washed in through the open window. One quick peek outside confirmed no one would overhear from the alleyway.

"The most wonderful thing has happened. We returned from Almy to discover Mrs. Abigail Drescher waiting for us, presenting with what appeared to be an impacted wisdom tooth. Do you know her?"

"Indeed, I do. She was a witness when her husband officiated our marriage."

"Henry examined her, then invited me to also. We knew something wasn't right. We talked it through, he on one side of Mrs. Drescher and me on the other."

She delved into more medical details than she'd share with Sophia, enjoying the light in Naomi's eyes as her friend picked up on precisely what Isabella had. Through it all, Naomi's joy blossomed. Who in Evanston would understand as well? Doc Joe and Doc Naomi practiced medicine separately, together, and shared a marriage based on respect, trust, and love.

"Henry did the most astounding thing." Her heart tripped faster and expanded at least one more size. "He deferred to me. Without hesitation."

"Of course he did. Who found the missing piece of the puzzle?"

"We did. Together." Isabella laughed, the joy of coming together with Henry in a purely intellectual and utterly magical way effervescing within her. "He's bright, well-read, competent, and we've discovered our preferences and opinions coincide for the most part. Where we disagree, we've found common ground through discussion. He respects my opinion, and I respect his."

"I wondered how sharing that big dental office above the pharmacy would work out. I'm happy for you that it has."

"Working with him has been splendid." Listening to his innermost thoughts, holding them close to her heart... "It all feels right."

"I don't know what burr Henry had under his saddle from the hour you arrived in Evanston, but we've noted the changes. I believe he loves you." Naomi, with her patented blend of compassion and forthright comfort, clasped Isabella's hand. "Have you told him how you feel?"

Rather than answer the question, she opted to distract with a revelation. "He kissed me today."

Her friends knew, to Isabella, kisses conveyed promises. To kiss a man she didn't regard would be unthinkable. "I kissed him back. With equal interest."

"But you suppose Henry is freer with his kisses than you?"

She shrugged. "I don't know."

"Kisses are all well and good. Some men need words, or they miss the point." A moment passed. "Tell him how you feel."

She opened her mouth, found herself at a loss for words, and closed it.

"I know you, Isabella. You're one of my dearest friends. You don't give your heart easily, yet you're overflowing with love for Henry."

Yes, she did love him. Why risk everything by saying something?

"Your situation is highly unusual," she told Naomi. "Joe wanted you to be all that you are."

"From my observations, I believe Henry wants you for who you are."

Doubt tickled the back of her neck.

She'd believed in her parents' love, trusted their love and support would remain forever constant and unchanging. Her North Star.

But she'd lost her parents' affection. A grain at a time, through an hourglass, the currency of love had betrayed her because she wasn't what they wanted her to be.

If her own parents' love could grow dim and cold, how could she trust a man's affection to remain true?

Especially Henry, who'd wanted a traditional wife from the beginning.

He might love her for the moment.

How could she hand him the power to destroy her? Confessing her love for him, handing him that power on a silver platter, would give him the key.

But if she didn't, he couldn't reject her.

"He loves you," Naomi insisted.

She nodded, desperate to convey enthusiasm.

Much had damaged Henry's ability to love with abandon. He still carried scars from Lenora—a lady dentist.

What if he couldn't set aside those wounds, and trust again? Trust her, a lady dentist who wanted him to love her, forever and ever.

"Will you tell him how you feel?" Naomi believed one little step would close the gap. Maybe matters had been so simple for Joe and Naomi.

But for Henry and Isabella? Love hadn't been kind. Love hadn't been easy.

"I'll try."

•••

Henry wandered the city streets.

No amount of greeting friends and acquaintances lightened his mood.

He waved to Chadwick and Sophia peddling on the tandem bicycle Chad had built for his bride. Sophia rang her bicycle bell in rapid succession. Chadwick returned Henry's wave and called, "Good evening to you!"

The two of them were blissfully happy, their pleasure in bicycling evident for all to see.

Their happiness served to amplify his own misery.

He'd walked four or five miles, but agitation clung to him and vibrated in his bones.

The sun would set within the quarter hour, and the early June temperatures dropped quickly, but he wasn't ready to return to the Linden home. Frederick and Gertrude would be settling their child for the night. The sights and sounds of their blessed domesticity were usually a sweet reminder of everything he wanted and all he'd determined worth waiting for.

But after today's endearments, he'd had second thoughts.

Powerful, threatening reconsiderations.

He'd wanted, desperately, to cast aside his firm convictions to find a suitable wife—one who would make a comfortable home, one whose entire focus would be their family's happiness—even though he couldn't support that family. Yet. His income was still unstable and insufficient.

In the moment before he'd lost all sense and kissed Isabella, he'd stood at the proverbial fork in the road. He'd been tempted to abandon his carefully determined path. Where would that leave them?

Without meaning to, he found himself on Joe's street. Joe was on the porch.

"It's odd to see you alone on that swing," Henry said. "Is Naomi out?"

"We returned home to find a note from Mrs. Linden—you do know she's near confinement?"

A quick nod.

"Naomi won't be back for a while yet." Joe eyed Henry too closely. "Want to sit?"

"No, thanks." Discomposure drove Henry to pace. "I've ruined everything with Isabella."

"What happened?"

Regrets churned. Every time he closed his eyes, the delicate fragrance of violets and the softness of her lips taunted him. "I kissed her."

Joe waited. No sign of disappointment, no chuckle, no *I told you so*. How could Joe not understand the seriousness of this diversion?

"Now everything is at risk." Henry paced the walk from stoop to gate, turning back again. "Our business relationship, our friendship—"

"Not necessarily."

"Joe! My financial situation is finally improving. The fellows don't trouble her, not anymore. I enjoyed her company in the office, the drives to Almy. Everything was perfect."

Despite the intervening hours since the incident, he couldn't string together a coherent explanation. "I want to put it all back. I want everything the way it was."

Joe seemed content to listen without further comment.

"I need your insight, man. What possessed me to kiss her?"

"Do you want my thoughts?"

Maybe he didn't. Joe and Chadwick were firmly of the opinion that professional women made wonderful wives.

"I could pontificate at length, but I don't think you want to hear what I have to say."

How would Joe's crowing congratulations help? "You're right. I'm sorry, Joe. I must go."

· 11 ·

EIGHT MISERABLE DAYS after the kiss that spoiled everything, Henry realized the old adage was true. *Things can always get worse.*

Isabella, in her naturally happy manner, drilled and filled a cavity. Her patient was one of the UP engineers. This particular man was handsome and unfailingly polite.

She laughed with him, paused in her work to ensure he remained comfortable, and blast it all—remained quite immune to Henry's presence.

Now that she'd finished with the man's nearly perfect teeth, the fellow paid what he owed and lingered with her near the exit.

Henry tried, with varying degrees of success, to ignore the engineer. Without a patient of his own at the moment, he forced himself to read the periodical he held.

Weeks ago, he'd promised he wouldn't leave her alone with a male patient. If not for that vow, he'd have been out the door and down the stairs.

"Dr. Pattison," the patient—Mr. James?—pressed her hand between both of his. "I'm impressed with your work. My least painful experience in the dental chair in ... well, forever."

Must she laugh with him, listen intently to every word, and enjoy his company with ease?

Despite the fact that this man's attentions were a helpful development and unmistakably good news, Henry shoved down an unwelcome surge of jealousy.

Isabella was not his.

He didn't want her to be his.

Not now, not yesterday, not tomorrow.

Some things were simply not meant to be.

Mr. James grinned. He dressed well enough, and his polished manners probably appealed to ladies of all ages.

"Are you anticipating the statehood celebration events?" James still held Isabella's hand.

"I am, very much."

"Would you be so good as to save me a dance at the calico ball?"

"I'd be delighted."

Envy fermented in Henry's gut. Had Isabella looked at him that way?

What did James have that Henry didn't? Besides confidence as a dance partner and adequate income to take a wife?

"I'll count on it." He lifted her hand, kissed her knuckles, and lingered.

Right there, the man lost a solid five points in decorum. Decent men, good men, did not linger.

Henry kicked himself, again. He'd lingered. And he'd relived that lingering kiss one thousand times, at least.

That ill-fated kiss haunted him.

James still pressed his mustached lips to Isabella's hand, so Henry shifted forcefully, ensuring the chair squeaked. He thumped his boot to the polished floor.

Abruptly, James straightened.

Isabella didn't spare Henry a glance, so he went to the windows to pull down the new shades on each of four windows. The heat had become unbearable.

James cleared his throat. "The calico ball is a full month away, is it not? July 11? Today is the tenth of June. Such an infernal wait, don't you think?"

The flirtatious dolt ought to be on his way.

"The month," Isabella said, teasing in her voice, "will pass quickly enough."

"It will if I have the pleasure of seeing you again."

Two more points lost—no, make that three—for his presumption. She'd invite him to call if she wished. No gentleman invited himself, and no man called on a lady without an invitation. It simply wasn't done.

Though she believed she'd never wed, she had every right to welcome a suitor.

Hopefully James wasn't terrified of falling for a professional woman.

Isabella tossed a brief glare at Henry. He turned the page, unwilling to let her see he listened to every word.

The moments stretched, and Isabella did not extend the offer James wanted.

Henry fought to keep his expression neutral. Crowing in victory would prove most unhelpful.

The other man claimed his hat from the hall tree. He spun it in his hands. "Might I have the pleasure of accompanying you to the parade? We might have a picnic lunch and enjoy the music."

The paper had run a detailed list of the week-long celebration events to come. The marching bands planned a concert after the parade, a mixture of patriotic tunes and modern favorites.

"You're most kind to ask." Isabella's voice carried pleasure.

Henry should urge her to accept.

"If the parade and music performance don't suit you, I'd be honored to escort you to the calico ball."

But that kiss...

How could he maintain his distance and watch someone else court her? He'd figure it out, because he must.

"Thank you, Mr. James. I'll consider your offer."

"Very good." The man's relief was palpable. "Perhaps I'll stop by next week. Here."

"You may." Her tone cooled. "I might as easily mail a letter in care of the station."

His heart leapt. Isabella's disinterest in James might mean...

Nothing had changed. Though no longer in danger with creditors, he could not support a household on his current income.

If and when his financial situation were secure, he must make his selection of bride with care. He *needed* a real home.

No matter how much he wanted Isabella to be the right kind of bride, she wasn't.

•••

When her handsome, flirtatious patient left the office, Isabella listened to his footfalls on the stairs. *One, two, three...*

Thank goodness she'd heeded that little voice inside her and not given in to Naomi's pressure to confess her love to Henry. The past eight days had been horrid enough with her secret safely kept.

Ten, eleven, twelve.

Reasonably sure she and Henry were alone, she marched directly to him.

He looked up from his magazine, eyes widening briefly. What did he think she'd do?

As if dealing with a boy who'd fallen asleep with his book, she eased *The Dental Independent* from his hands and laid it on the table.

"Would you care to explain," she asked, unsure whether she'd laugh or cry, "what that was all about?"

He blinked. Had he any idea how clearly he gave himself away? Jealousy slanted his brows, quickly chased offstage by guilt's rampage. Last, but not least, determination. "I promised I'd not leave you alone with a male patient."

"You listened to every word exchanged."

"Yes. I'm your . . ." He circled his hand, as if the motion would conjure the missing word.

"Paid protector, I believe I said."

"Something like that."

"What happened to us?" That question had spun 'round and 'round in her head like a housefly trapped indoors, buzzing at all hours through eight interminably long days and nights.

To be fair, the first few were spent floating on a sea of tranquility. Henry had kissed her!

And then shut her out. He hadn't touched her, even with a friendly pat on the shoulder. He'd not offered his arm. She straightened, realizing he'd not so much as walked beside her.

He rose, as if towering over her made the question easier to address. "Nothing happened to us. We're still professionals. We still work in this office." He flung a hand toward the door through which her patient had passed. "Our names are still painted on the windows."

How, precisely, had she fancied herself in love with this man?

This aggravating, self-centered, petrified man?

How, exactly, did a single kiss ... in truth, that kiss had counted for at least two, if not three. How did three kisses, in the space of sixty seconds, terrify a man like Henry Merritt?

Finally! The question she'd danced around at two o'clock that morning, unable to identify.

She folded her arms and tipped her head up. "Please, Dr. Merritt, if you'd be so kind, do tell me how one little kiss brought you to your knees?"

"I, uh—" He splayed a hand over the precise location, anatomically speaking, of his heart. "I'm not—you didn't—"

"Prior to that occasion, eight days ago ..." One of her eyelids twitched. Once, twice, then picked up an annoying rhythm. "Eight." She cleared her throat. *Twitch.* "Days." *Twitch, twitch.* "Ago. Heretofore, I'd believed you a man with the constitutional fortitude of a bull elk."

His brows straightened. Stupefied. "Pardon me, Isabella. Is a question hiding in there somewhere?"

Twitch. She should've smacked him. Or pushed him backward into his chair.

Did the man think she'd simper in the corner, waiting for him to come to his senses? Did he believe she'd turn down an offer of companionship from Mr. James because the man she wanted found himself unnerved by The Kiss?

All excellent questions, but she'd do well to stick with the first.

"You kissed me, eight days ago."

He jerked his head to the right, as if he'd launched into a determined shake of the head, but instantly caught himself. He covered the brusque reaction by palming the back of his neck and massaging with force.

"And I kissed you back." With tremendous effort, she managed to sound at peace. After all, they were finally talking—and the annoying twitching in her eyelid had ceased. She'd do well to remain civil.

"Prior to that sixty seconds of affection, you'd been a dear friend. We talked about all sorts of scientific matters, the weather, the challenges our patients face. After those sixty seconds, you've been a changed man."

He opened his mouth. He honestly hadn't a clue what to say.

"Oh, yes. Definitely a changed man. Since that fateful morning, you've barely offered me a hand into the wagon or down from that dangerously high seat—"

"My mother taught me better manners than that."

She raised one brow and paused.

A little huff sounded. The fight left him.

"You've exercised great care to avoid touching me. Not intentionally, and certainly not unintentionally."

"How might I intentionally refrain from touching you unintentionally?"

A chuckle escaped before she composed herself.

"I still make you laugh." His pleasure faded, and the light in his eyes dimmed.

"Yes, you did." She tried to sweep her heartache under the rug before he witnessed it.

"Maybe," he whispered, "I ruminated everything you confided."

She'd churned over everything as well. Wondered, hour upon hour, what she'd said to chase him away.

"Maybe," he paused, "I startled, like a bird in the bush, and flew willy-nilly." Sadness and regret shone in the warmth of his brown irises. "Maybe I realized the emotions in my heart had serious . . . uh, hmm." He coughed. "Uh—feelings. Feelings connected."

Had that kiss made him realize he loved her?

"Maybe I realized I'm not the man you want me to be. And need me to be."

"Henry—"

"Maybe I realized that you're a woman carrying a bushel of ache in her heart. And maybe I looked at the situation closely and fear I'm not equipped."

Not equipped? "Henry." Her corset seemed tight as her heart expanded an extra size.

"Yes, ma'am?"

"I'm a woman who believes kisses are a special thing. Like gold dollars, they're not to be tossed away indiscriminately."

His Adam's apple slid down his throat and bobbed back up. Terror flickered over his expression.

"I say this, not as prelude to a marriage proposal—"

"Hey, I didn't think—"

"—but as an explanation." She spoke over his objection. "Yes, you and I are friends. We are dentists who work side by side at the same address. I comprehend that everything has changed between us, and yet nothing has changed."

She'd barely completed her statement when he broke in. "Do you intend to accept James's invitation? To the parade and music? Or the ball?"

"Why would I do that? The calico dress, petticoats, and unmentionables my mother ordered arrived yesterday by express."

He blinked, utterly confused. Such a dear man.

"Do you know what matches the yards upon yards of calico I'll wear to our calico ball?"

His confusion deepened. What adorable incertitude!

"Your undershirt, shirt, collar and cuffs, necktie, and sack suit. Your ensemble matches my costume."

"Uh . . ."

How had Mother reduced this eloquent man to a single syllable?

"I may have described you in my letter, but only so Mother could order a shirt, sans collar and cuffs. I have firsthand knowledge of men in Almy, near your size, who need a new shirt."

He dragged a hand over his face.

"Between you and me, no one will ever know if the suit remains in the crate, unworn." She tiptoed a step closer to whisper, "It's a handsome suit of clothes. Someone in Almy will appreciate it."

He seemed to follow the conversation, yet confusion lingered.

Perhaps she could put him at ease. "My mother might have a one-track mind, but I assure you, her gift of an entire set of clothing—yes, unmentionables for you, also—is by no means an expectation of marriage."

· 12 ·

"Must I wear this?" Henry tried to keep all traces of panic from his voice.

The calico suit of clothes Isabella's mother had commissioned lay across his lap. From the fine tailoring and the fabric's superior heft and finish, she'd paid a premium fee for the three-piece suit, shirt, collar and cuffs, necktie ... and drawers.

One week remained until Independence Day. He hadn't the time or resources to come up with anything different to wear.

Isabella's posture stiffened. Had he offended her?

"It's nice. Very nice. I've never seen a man's suit of clothes made from calico before." One shift in the mines, and no one would know it had once been blue-green and flowered. Someone would be grateful for the sturdy construction and multiple layers.

"It is a calico ball."

He nodded, his shoulders slumping. For this woman, he'd probably wear the blasted suit and express delight the whole time, if only she'd smile.

"And," she said, her voice lowered to a whisper.

They sat in the parlor of the boardinghouse, and for the moment, they were alone. The widowed boardinghouse proprietor held her role as chaperone for proper young ladies in all seriousness—even if she were younger than Isabella.

"And?" He leaned nearer, his knee bumping hers.

"And Mother took great care to ensure your clothing matches mine."

So she'd said, a couple weeks ago, when she'd mentioned the crate had arrived by express.

He fingered the polished, smooth cotton. In the fading light of the summertime sun, slanting through the west-facing windows, blinds, and lace curtains, the calico's flowers and vines intertwined in a small, repeating pattern. The flowers appeared blue, the vines green, and the background colored a mixture of the two.

"They match." He scrubbed his palm over his jaw, finding more stubble than he liked. He should've taken time to shave prior to calling on Isabella. "Guess that means your costume is this same . . . uh, print."

"My skirt and bodice have this small floral," she indicated the pattern on his shirt and necktie, "along the center front. The lapels of each are this plain sea green." She touched the collar and cuffs of his getup.

He knew green. But he'd never seen the sea. Somehow that shade of sky blue didn't seem right.

"The waterfall and center drapes incorporate the fine stripe of your trousers and coat."

They two would look like peas in a pod, matching halves of a single whole.

Wearing this suit would announce, loud and long, to everybody in the entire county, the state of their romance.

He'd look like a Vanderbilt in this suit of clothes. Not like the simple man he was.

She assessed him long enough his cheeks heated. "You don't like it."

"Now, I didn't exactly say that." Would she put words in his mouth now? Tell him how he felt?

She giggled. She clapped her hand over her mouth, the chuckles soon impossible to contain.

"Oh, Henry. I'm so sorry." Laughter spilled, bright and happy.

Relief eased in with her laughter. He'd escaped the embarrassment of wearing this laughing stock before everyone in the county.

"My mother seems—" she chuckled again—"unequaled in comprehending women's fashions. But this?" She held up the sleeve of the coat. "Do not misunderstand. Mother's dressmaker did superb work. But you're a man of subdued tastes. Plain wool. No highly decorative cotton for you."

He nodded. Plain wool for him. Plain brown or medium gray with a pale stripe. The two suits of clothes had done him plenty well for the past five years.

"You don't have to wear it."

"Thank you."

"I don't know what mother was thinking."

•••

In the week and a half since he'd begged off wearing the suit, a half dozen reminders had come calling. At least one had blown him ten miles off course.

First, Mrs. Roberts brought all five of her daughters into the office to see Isabella.

The matron had clucked her tongue, made comments about the expense of raising children, and asked for Dr. Pattison to send the bill to Mr. Roberts for payment.

Second, that sum due to Dr. Pattison haunted Henry as

he prepared to join Isabella with the Hugheses and the Chandlers to attend the Independence Day Parade, basket dinner, speeches, reading of the Declaration of Independence, and ultimately, hear the whole afternoon regaled by patriotic music.

On the hot noontide of the Fourth of July, small children waved American flags. Some were carried on the shoulders of their fathers. Others ran beside parents, enjoying the festivities.

Ahead, an approaching marching band led the parade with the time-honored tune "Yankee Doodle Dandy."

And he had Isabella on his arm, her white summertime bonnet upon her head, patriotic ribbons of red and blue matching the trim upon her smart suit jacket and skirt.

For the umpteenth time in the past week, he nearly lost the ability to breathe. If he did not change his course, he'd one day soon assume responsibility for this woman's dressmaker bills.

Yes, her father had paid for every costume until now. With marriage, all bills transferred to a woman's husband. No man with a grain of honor would allow his father-in-law to continue financial support.

He focused on the parade, the bright and cheery music, the flash of sunlight upon brass as the instruments swept past, carried by bright young men. The band represented two dozen sets of parents who had paid for music lessons and instruments.

How would he afford opportunities, as well as the necessities, of life?

Children squealed, clapping and cheering in their high voices.

Parents enjoyed them, for the most part.

Heady aromas of roasting meat filled the air. Street

vendors strolled the parade route with carts, selling cold beer, roasted nuts, and shave-ice snowballs flavored with brightly colored syrups.

I want, Daddy, I want!

How had he never noticed how much husbands and fathers spent on such luxuries?

As the parade wound up and the crowd moved as one down the street and toward the park where the basket dinner would he held, their tidy group of six passed the soda water fountain with its doors wide open.

Not a single stool waited empty at the crowded bar. So many thirsty patrons on this hot afternoon.

"Daddy!" a child yelled behind Henry and Isabella. "I'm thirsty! I want a soda water."

I want, I want, I want.

Street vendors had emptied their carts of beverages, sweets, and beers, and filled their pocketbooks with the money handed over by fathers.

Hadn't Isabella said her father had been overly indulgent?

Would she expect to spoil their children? Provide every opportunity, every music lesson, dance lessons—something Henry had missed out on—medicines, new clothing every month...

Right before them, an elderly man, dressed plainly, sold three cherry tarts to a well-dressed man. The fellow handed one each to his wife and his twin sons. The boys' grins revealed central incisors recently erupted, placing them within one year of their eighth birthday.

"Henry, are you well?" Isabella had been tugging on his arm, then she'd stopped.

The old man had pocketed his coin, nodded his thanks, and pushed his cart farther along the street.

The crowd had moved on, swarming around Henry and Isabella. Ahead, their friends turned back to see what delayed them.

"Henry?"

He swallowed, his mouth dry.

He swallowed again.

"Is it the heat?" She looked into the ice cream soda fountain. "Should we go in, out of the sun, sip a Coca-Cola?"

"No." What ailed him couldn't be fixed so easily.

He clung to the concern in her hazel eyes. She cared about him *now*.

But bottom line, he couldn't afford a wife. Not on his current income.

Precisely why he'd not been courting anyone and had intentionally delayed attachments since he'd floundered everything with Lenora.

How had he allowed himself to be swept along in the day-to-day unintentional courtship of Dr. Isabella Pattison?

He'd never intended to plant expectations.

He'd never expected to fall in love.

Why allow the brisk river of courtship to wash him downstream, ever nearer the inevitable?

He must save himself, immediately, or he'd find himself precisely where he could not be.

· 13 ·

"If not the heat, Henry, what is it?" Isabella shaded her eyes from the sun. At this angle, her white hat did little to protect her from the sun's rays.

"I can't do this." Agony deepened the lines in his lean cheeks. His brown eyes were pools of conviction.

Her skin flushed hot from crown to toe. Beneath many layers of clothing, her temperature spiked.

He referred to something far more important than the ongoing Independence Day celebrations.

"I must go." Henry paced four steps away, then turned, pacing back to her.

She'd pretend to misunderstand—until she locked herself in the oven of her boardinghouse room. She'd not dissolve into tears and hysterics in the middle of a celebration. Never would she be that woman who won what she wanted with tears.

"I understand." She forced the brightest of expressions. "The day is unusually warm. No need to stay."

Her breaking heart managed to pound harder, her pulse too loud in her ears.

From the direction of the park, a brass band struck up "The Gladiator March." She adored the popular John Philip Sousa piece. Focusing on the music barely held her together.

"I'm so very sorry." He looked anywhere but at her. Into the soda water fountain. At his shoes. He clicked open his pocket watch. Snapped it shut. "You understand, don't you?"

"Of course." Her smile widened, as did the fissure in her heart.

Didn't he care how greatly his rejection crushed her spirit?

Hadn't he listened when she'd explained her greatest heartache? How desperately she needed love and how unwilling her family had been to love her no matter what?

The street had grown quiet, the crowds having moved on toward the events at the park. Even Naomi and Sophia had left them alone for this conversation. They waited with their husbands in the shade of a tree at the end of the block.

In the growing calm, Isabella acknowledged the truth. She'd allowed herself to believe that this time, things would be different. This time, she'd magically prove worthy of love.

Forever and always, no matter what.

Conveniently, she'd not embraced *his* truth.

Henry's pacing halted several feet from her. "I told you how I feel, about my need for a secure home. Someone who will make our home comfortable within my income."

His stiffness pained her. "Yes, Henry, I heard."

But she hadn't. She saw that now. Somehow, that ill-fated conversation hadn't impressed upon her Henry's determination to wed the right kind of woman.

That woman was not Isabella.

For if she had truly heard, she never would have allowed the slimmest scrap of hope.

All the wishing in the world hadn't solved matters with

her family. She'd held on for years, fighting for common ground.

Why would Henry be different?

Tears threatened, and this time, they wouldn't remain hidden.

Henry stood with hands splayed, reflecting the hope and desperation in her own heart. "Even if I had adequate income—" A growl blending hopelessness and aggravation ripped from his throat. "*Even if.* Are you the woman I need, Isabella?"

Her heart tripped over itself, tearing in two. The irregular rhythm raced.

As if her broken heart spilled its deepest, most secret contents, clarity shone light on the most painful truth of all. She'd lost him. The one man she'd believed she could love and live with in happiness. The marriage that would please her mother and allow her to keep her dream.

The perfect solution—the proof that her sacrifice of timely marriage and motherhood, sacrifice of her family's love and support, had ultimately been worth it.

But Henry was so much more than a man she could to live with.

Henry was the one man, the only man, she could not live without.

He scowled. "Do you want to embrace homemaking? Raise children? Make the home your domain?"

He'd made himself clear. Now. And months ago. He'd told her the greatest, deepest desires of his heart. How could she ask him to give up his dreams?

Her family had asked, cajoled, and demanded she abandon her dreams.

After all she'd been through, the thought of leaving dentistry eviscerated her.

Even if she tried to remake herself into the woman he wanted, she would, inevitability, disappoint.

He *knew* she'd chosen dentistry over husband and children.

Why taunt her with prizes she would never win?

"No." Her voice broke. "I can't."

She could not abandon her career.

Not even for Henry.

• • •

At the breakfast table the following morning, Henry fought to hide his sour mood.

He'd made an enormous personal sacrifice, the hardest decision of his life. The rewards would last decade upon decade.

So why hadn't he slept like a baby?

True, the temperature had remained in the nineties overnight, and though the sun had been up all of an hour, the thermometer rapidly approached triple digits.

The single window in Henry's small bedroom opened six inches. The usual Wyoming wind had failed to blow. He'd lain atop the bedsheets and wished for winter's icy wind.

Through the thin wall separating his room from the Lindens', his inability to sleep had been exacerbated by the bawling child. And bickering between Mr. Linden and his wife.

So much for his long-held belief that Mr. and Mrs. Linden lived in their own Garden of Eden.

"Toast?" Linden passed the plate to Henry. "Ham?"

Henry accepted both, then picked up his coffee cup, only to find it empty.

"Gertrude," Linden snapped, "get the man his coffee."

Any husband who treated his wife like the enemy and strangers with kindness, deserved—

"I told you yesterday, we have no coffee." Heavily pregnant, the woman held her sobbing child on one hip. She blotted perspiration from her forehead with her sleeve. Red mottled her fair skin. She'd cried. Much. And recently.

From the beginning, Henry had wanted the Linden home to be like Dr. Ullman's home—that place where home and heaven were one.

"Can't you do anything right?" Linden stood, his chair crashing to the floor.

The child wailed louder.

She bounced the baby, urging him to quiet. He reached for the skillet on the stove, and she pulled his little hand away.

"It's your responsibility to keep necessities in the house." Without acknowledging his wife, Linden grabbed two pieces of ham from his plate and the remaining slice of toast. "Do yourself a favor, Dr. Merritt. *Never* marry."

The man slammed the door behind himself. Seconds later, the squeak of the gate's hinges carried through open windows.

Mrs. Linden turned away. Her body shook, probably fighting sobs.

What was the right thing to do?

"Mrs. Linden, please sit and eat." He hadn't a clue what to do for a miserable child, but he offered anyway. "I could take the child outside for a moment."

"Eat what, Dr. Merritt?" The usually sweet-tempered, hard-working woman showed her temper. "My husband ate my breakfast, and our child's."

The man needed a lesson in decency, and Henry itched to deliver it.

Instead, he pulled out his chair and held it for her. He'd not eaten more than a bite, and the single slice of toast and ham seemed insufficient for a hungry child and an expectant mother.

He was their boarder. Not a brother, not a friend.

What would Mother have believed right?

Better, what would Isabella do? She always knew the right way to approach challenges and how to offer help and kindness without offending.

"Please sit. Eat. Feed the child."

The boy wriggled, reaching for the toast on Henry's plate. He cried louder.

She sagged into the chair. The child grabbed bread in one hand and meat in the other. He bit into the toast and chewed. His cheeks shone, and his nose ran.

Mrs. Linden spilled fresh tears.

Henry reached to touch her shoulder but thought better of it. "How can I help?"

"You pay room and board. That's plenty."

No. A sorry excuse for a man had eaten while his child cried for bread.

As a boy, he'd known desperation, but never hunger.

Had Mother?

The child hiccupped. He sighed heavily and rested his head upon his mother. The child ate, unaware of his mother's hunger.

How long had it been since she'd eaten? How long since she'd eaten her fill?

"Has Mr. Linden gone to work?" If he were paid today—

"Union Pacific fired him for neglect of duty."

Henry's gut twisted.

No income. No affection in times of trial.

Not what Mrs. Linden had anticipated when she'd wed.

A good man, a decent man, did not walk away.

Truth slammed into Henry—as if he'd been caught unaware by an oncoming train.

A decent man did not walk away.

He, Henry Merritt, had walked away.

All because he'd been determined to protect himself, to ensure his own heart's safety.

What of Isabella? What about her protection? And her heart?

He'd brought this misery upon himself by his own selfish choices.

How had he deluded himself? Isabella wasn't merely the best woman for him. She was *the only woman.*

Linden's grievances were no less severe than his own.

He removed his pocketbook from his coat pocket and withdrew the bills. Every last one. He set them on the table.

Sometimes, the needs of the helpless ate at him.

"No, Doctor." Tears of anger and frustration streamed down her face.

"My mother worked tirelessly, desperate to make ends meet." He paused. "I'm sorry I wasn't aware. I won't make that mistake again."

He picked up one of the bills. "I'll walk to the market presently and return with groceries to see you and the child fed."

She hid her face in her child's hair. "Thank you."

Step one, rectify what he could, here.

Step two, face his own dazzling error in judgment.

· 14 ·

HENRY WORE THE horrid calico suit of clothes to the calico ball.

On the outskirts of the party, a few UP employees passed a flask around. One toasted Henry with a raised liquor bottle. "A fine suit you wear this evening."

Henry tipped his hat and trudged forward.

He raised his hat to matrons who whispered behind fans.

Only one person at this gathering held his interest. One.

He approached the pavilion proper, determined to find her.

Once he did, he'd lay his heart bare and confess the whole truth.

The orchestra completed a tune, followed by vigorous applause.

Mayor Gardner grabbed the opportunity, his speaking trumpet raised, to make an announcement. "I hold here," he bellowed through the device, "a telegram from Washington, District of Columbia!"

Commotion, mostly women hushing one another, melded with cheers and whistles.

"Dated yesterday, July 10, 1890. To: Honorable John W. Meldrum, Governor. Proclaim it to the people that Wyoming is a member of the Indestructible Union of American States—"

Applause drowned the rest of the mayor's amplified announcement, but Henry couldn't care about statehood or the calico ball or the enormous audience sure to hear most of his groveling.

Across the dance floor, he sighted Isabella on the arm of the UP engineer, Mr. James. Long evening rays slanted across the pavilion, casting her in golden light. The blue-green of her calico put him in mind of sunlight on the Delaware River.

Why had he believed he could live without this woman?

Certainty compelled him to abandon everything he'd clung to like bedrock.

The only thing he needed to know was that Isabella was the only woman for him. He didn't need all of the answers now. They'd find their way forward together.

He removed his hat and tucked it beneath his arm.

She turned, locating him instantly. She said something brief to James, who then looked in Henry's direction. He escorted her to within a few feet of Henry and disappeared.

Smart man.

Dully, he noted applause as the mayor finished with the telegram reading. The orchestra struck up the next dance number.

Isabella raised her chin. "That's a fine calico suit of clothes you're wearing, Dr. Merritt."

He smoothed his hand over the jacket, quick to find the gold watch chain he'd worn daily as a reminder of his chosen path. "It is a fine suit of clothes. My best."

Folks nearby lingered, preferring, apparently, to observe the couple whose clothing matched.

"Indeed, it is." Happiness, genuine and real, lit her face.

"I wear it because it matches your costume. We're a matched set."

Her countenance dimmed. "Fabric selected two months ago does little to convince me. My costume and your suit are nothing more than clothes. Clothes cannot explain who a person is inside."

Pain filled her words, her posture, her voice. He must fix this. "You captured my interest, Dr. Isabella Pattison, the moment I saw you on the street a year ago." She knew this story. But he'd not yet told her how he'd felt. "I was wildly attracted to you."

She slowly unfolded her arms. Good. She listened.

Someone nearby chuckled. Henry ignored his growing audience. He cared only for Isabella. The last months had shown they could talk things through and find a solution.

"We met," he told her, "and you captured my respect of your intellect. You put together odd glimpses of the puzzle and knew where I headed on Easter morning."

A soft smile touched her lips.

"You captured my heart the first time I saw you comfort a child."

Over the music, a nearby woman sighed. "No, Cletis. I won't dance with you. I'm listening to a swain plead his case."

Let the whole county watch and listen. They weren't Henry's concern.

He searched Isabella's face. "You affirmed what I already knew—you're compassionate, capable, and intelligent."

She lifted one shoulder in a shrug. None of this mattered to her.

"Isabella, you're the one I want by my side, every day of my life. How could any other woman give me encouragement, ongoing intrigue, and perspective in my life's work?"

Chatter among the onlookers swelled. More than one matron urged Isabella to concede and step into his embrace.

Still, she waited. And he knew why. He'd not yet apologized.

"I've been a fool. A miserable fool. I apologize, with all the sorrow in my heart. For all I said in fear and anger and all I should've said. And for hinting, even now, that you'd make a fine doctor's wife."

She nodded, the gesture so small, he'd have missed it if he'd blinked.

Moments ticked past as she looked into his eyes. He'd give every dollar in his possession to know her thoughts.

"What should you have said, Henry?"

What should he have said? His heart pounded, but those many somethings wouldn't come.

Finally, he repeated the important parts. "You're the one my heart desires. Yes, I want a home, love, and happiness. I'm a fool to look for those miracles anywhere else, with anyone else."

She waited, expecting more.

"I've realized, ultimately, that home is not defined by so strict a measure." He'd learned so many things in the past days. "How can anywhere be home without you?"

Did she understand?

An eternity passed, and finally she gave a brief nod. "And?"

What more was there? He wanted to pace, but forced himself to remain still.

"I've struggled to find answers." He ached in body, mind, and soul. Mostly in his heart. "Together, we can find the answers. We had an epiphany over a patient, but honestly, it was mostly you."

She nodded but crossed her arms again, shifting her weight away from him.

He floundered in the dark. If he failed this most critical exam of his life, he could lose her forever.

He took a step nearer. "We managed to afford the calico ball invitations on budget. Where we disagreed, we've talked it through and found common ground. You respect my opinion, and I respect yours. What troubles are so insurmountable that we can't solve them together?"

The ghost of hurtful things he'd told her flitted between them. He'd said he couldn't afford a wife.

He'd said he couldn't afford *her*.

His heart ached, knowing he'd contributed to the scars she carried from her banker brother-in-law's criticism and from her only sister's distasteful comments. And what of her mother?

"I'm a coward," he whispered. "I'm a coward," he repeated, determined Isabella hear his regret and apology despite the music and dancers and conversations surrounding them. "I admit it. I'm scared to take on responsibilities I doubt I can afford financially. But with you, I think, no—*I know*—we have a chance."

The gold watch chain slipped through his hand. He caught himself in time to avoid blotting his palms against the calico sack suit. Instead, he pulled a calico handkerchief from his pocket, dried his hands, and blotted his forehead.

Nervousness swelled, tightening the collar about his neck, forcing his heart to work doubly hard.

He'd imagined this conversation progressing on a more effective track. He'd apologized before, and she'd always been quick to forgive.

"Isabella?" He cleared his throat. Their audience grew impatient. *He* grew impatient.

She stood immobile, her arms folded tightly, and her posture rigid. Isabella's impatience outranked them all. Her expression filled with a marrow-deep sadness.

"Please give me one more chance to prove myself. Now that I know my own heart, I'll show you, every single day, that I can be trusted."

She turned her face away and tucked her chin.

What did she want? He'd give it to her, if only he knew.

Yes! She wanted partnership—he could give her that. "If you'll have me, I want a true partnership. I'll pay to have the sign painter come around. Merritt and Pattison Dentistry. No—Pattison and Merritt Dentistry."

Chuckles erupted from the crowd, but Isabella remained still.

But he'd thought . . .

Panic spurted through his veins. "I can't lose you. Not like this. Not again."

Slowly, she turned away, her body in profile.

This time, it seemed, he'd gone too far. Beyond forgiveness. Beyond second chances. His mind raced through every conversation, every secret she'd shared. What had he missed?

With the desperation of a drowning man, he cast about for help. He grappled in the crowd, at last discovering Joe—

I love you, Joe mouthed.

Not an uncommon showing of brotherhood, especially at a time like this—but . . .

Joe had thrown him a lifeline!

But—hadn't everything he'd said in the past ten minutes told Isabella he loved her? He'd spoken of love in every single way he knew how.

One more glance at Joe, who pointed at Isabella. *I love you. Say it!*

Relief, sweet relief.

He heeded the woman who held his heart in her dainty, capable hands.

"I love you, Isabella Pattison."

She looked up, her eyes sparkled . . .

"I love you with everything here," he tapped his temple, indicating his mind.

Her delight died beneath a bucket of cold water. She opened her mouth as if she intended, finally, to contribute to the conversation.

Good thing he wasn't done.

"And I love you with everything here." He tapped his fist over his heart. "You are precisely the woman I've searched for, my perfect match. The one I want, the one I need to make my life whole. Will you have me?"

Fear slammed into him, knocking his confidence sideways a good ten miles.

One beat passed, then two.

He'd never intended to propose! *No, no, no!*

Proposals did not go well for him, especially in public. This wasn't the time nor the place. He'd only intended to confess, in specific words, that he loved Isabella.

"You best say yes, Dr. Pattison," a young, feminine voice called over the crowd, "or I'll leap into his arms myself."

Laughter tittered among the women. A few men's baritone chuckles mixed in.

Isabella closed the distance between them, four ladylike steps, and stood immediately before him. He fancied her scent of violets reached him.

She searched his eyes.

What *more* was there? He'd explained himself. He'd apologized and begged forgiveness. He'd admitted she was the more capable problem solver between them. He'd asked for a future with her, including her fondest dream: continuing as a dentist. He'd confessed his love—in front of every soul in Uinta County. He'd foolishly asked her to wed him. All in a ridiculous calico suit of clothes!

"Before I say yes," she said, "I need to know what you intended by 'will you have me.'"

He blinked. Startled. Memories poured in, her heart-breaking tales of a family whose love she couldn't feel, people who she'd chosen to leave.

"I hesitate," she said, "to give my answer before I know if this means we're to go forward courting or continuing on as before..."

"Isabella, I..." His mouth dried, his tongue sticking to the roof of his mouth. Was she giving him a chance to retract his proposal? Did he want that chance?

"Or," she asked, "do you mean to ask me to be your wife?"

No! He didn't want a do-over. Insecurity in this lovely woman's eyes told him everything he needed to know.

He'd ensure she had no chance to misconstrue his offer.

With his hat still tucked beneath his arm, he lowered to one knee. Lit from the west, by the setting sun, she looked like an angel.

"You are an angel, dearest Isabella. You own my heart, my body, my soul. You own my life, because without you, my life has no meaning. I love you more than I loved my parents and brother. You are *everything*."

Tears overflowed, streaming over her cheeks. He wanted to kiss them away. But he had one more thing to ask.

One question, upon which everything hinged.

The question that had caused him as much pain as his broken heart could bear. He must ask once more.

Clarity stole in, banishing doubt.

The error, in the past, had been not in asking the question, but in asking it of the wrong woman.

With Isabella, everything, including this most important question, was absolutely right.

"Will you, my Isabella, do me the esteemed honor of becoming my wife?"

Applause erupted. Commotion, too, as matrons shushed those who dared utter a word. They wanted to hear the good dentist's reply!

If they'd been able to hear, they'd know Isabella hadn't said a thing.

But Henry witnessed the truth in her eyes as more and more tears flowed. Happy tears.

She nodded, her sweet smile conveying everything within her heart. She stepped into his arms, took his freshly shaved cheeks between her hands, and kissed him.

· 15 ·

ON THURSDAY, JULY 17, 1890, *The Chieftain* published the first edition following the Calico Ball.

The headlines: WYOMING STATEHOOD CELEBRATIONS, CALICO BALL SUCCESS.

The final event of Uinta County's celebration of statehood for Wyoming was a gala ball in the style of a calico ball. Mayor Gardner invited a committee composed of the city's professionals to this very purpose. Under the direction of the city engineer and bridge builder, a team of craftsmen constructed the large dance floor and pavilion. Determined the most romantic public place in town, three upcoming weddings have already been scheduled for the coming week.

Entertainment included music by the city orchestra, dancing, refreshments from J. P. Adam's Bakery, and Dr. Henry Merritt, DDS. Dr. Merritt regaled the crowd with pleas for love and commitment from his lady love, Dr. Isabella Pattison, DDS. The display concluded with an official engagement. The nuptials are scheduled to be held at the pavilion on Friday, August 1. As all were present at the moment of engagement, all are invited to celebrate the marriage that afternoon.

The Chieftain is pleased to report the financial success of the occasion—the calico ball, not the engagement (according to those who heard most clearly, the financial success of the soon-to-be-wed couple is under question). Dr. Naomi Chandler, MD is to be thanked for her selection of this theme.

The Council of City Professionals delivered 291 ladies' costumes, 300 various ladies' undergarments, 188 sunbonnets, 94 aprons, 107 men's shirts, 87 men's neckties, 20 calico handkerchiefs, 1 men's union suit of calico, and 1 finely tailored suit of clothes of superior calico construction.

Ticket sales netted an unexpectedly generous dollar amount. $292 was put into the hands of the Widows Union, an elected body representing the families of men and boys who perished in the disaster last November. The Widows Union will ensure the needs of survivors will be met. Food, clothing, firewood. And transportation, should any wish to remove to locations with family nearby. Sheriff Preston reported no difficulties in delivery of calico and cash.

It is possible more donations will trickle in this week. If so, Dr. Merritt and Dr. Pattison will deliver again to Almy next Sunday.

As a lasting memorial to the extraordinary work of the Evanston Council of City Professionals, the pavilion will remain a monument to the people of Evanston, and the county of Uinta, and the people of the great state of Wyoming.

Epilogue

SIX WEEKS AFTER the most publicly attended wedding in the history of Uinta County, Dr. and Dr. Merritt attended an intimate supper party hosted by their closest friends.

"Or," Chadwick asked, "do you prefer Mr. and Mrs. Merritt?"

Isabella emerged from a hug with Naomi and Sophia to note Chadwick shaking Henry's hand in the way of closest of confidantes.

Henry chuckled. "Best ask my wife. After all, my name hasn't changed."

Isabella tapped her chin, pretending to consider. "From you, I'll answer to anything. But I prefer missus."

"Has a lovely ring to it, hasn't it?" Naomi squeezed Isabella's hand once more. "It's wonderful to have you home. Don't you ever leave us for a month and a half, not ever again."

"Missed us, did you?" She'd been walking on clouds, even when at "home" in Los Angeles. But Evanston was *home*. To return brought satisfaction.

Henry's hand settled at her waist. Make that *immense* satisfaction, with her husband at her side. Anywhere, with him, would be home. But she'd missed her friends.

Noting the warmest of welcomes for Henry from Joe and Chadwick, Naomi and Sophia, she amended that distinction. Definitely *their* friends.

"Do come in out of the cold." Sophia shooed the group into the dining room, closing the front door against the glorious mid-September day. On the warm side, actually.

The house—make that the meal Chadwick had prepared—smelled delicious. Aromas of roasting meat and bread blended with the sweet-tart of fruit. Her stomach rumbled.

Soon they were all seated around the dining room table. Had it been only last spring that she'd sat at this dining room table, one of five, and content?

Three men at one end and three ladies at the other put Chadwick and his wife properly seated at the head and foot of the table, the Chandlers on one side, and the Merritts on the other.

She couldn't help but smile! *The Merritts.* How she liked the sound of that.

Dishes were passed, the meal enjoyed, and conversation begun well.

"I propose a toast." Joe raised his wine goblet, his free arm draped across the back of Naomi's chair. "To new lettering on the Merritt and Pattison dental office windows. Drs. Merritt and Merritt, Modern Dentistry."

"Hear, hear!"

Isabella sipped. The new sign, to properly reflect her new marital status, was most welcome, indeed. Not quite ready to return to the patients Dr. English had managed in their absence, Henry and Isabella had merely observed the new signs on their way to their new residence, arranged for by Naomi and Sophia while the newlyweds were on their wedding trip.

The small rental would do, as long as necessary. Isabella liked the idea of living two doors down from the little house where Doc Joe and Doc Naomi resided.

Henry set his wine goblet down and leaned near to kiss her cheek. How she loved this man. *Her* man.

"I can't wait another minute," Sophia said. "Tell us, Henry, how your visit with Isabella's parents went. Do they approve?"

He laughed aloud, meeting Isabella's eye. How she loved the happiness sparkling in his beautiful brown eyes. "Very well."

Her cue to tell the story. "My parents, having been forewarned by telegram—" she'd sent it the day of the wedding, only at Henry's insistence (she couldn't give them time to arrive in Evanston and spoil her happiness, now could she?)—"met us at the station and took to Henry instantly."

He stroked his thumb along the nape of her neck. She loved his familiar touch and that he seemed incapable of being near without touching her. In this intimate setting, he could. And did.

"Tell them," he whispered near her ear, "what you discovered."

After all she'd disclosed to her dearest friends, they'd want to know. "I—*we*—discovered our first evening in my parents' home wouldn't be a quiet one. Florence and Dudley, and the children, were present." She'd worried about Henry, bombarded with the entire family at once. "It turns out they love him." Emotion surged, filling her throat. She pressed a palm to her collar bones.

Henry stepped in. "And they love Isabella, very much."

She nodded, still amazed to discover how wrong she'd been. Happy tears filled her eyes. One glance at her husband—*husband!*—and he picked up the conversation.

"It seems," he said, "Mrs. Pattison ceased writing letters to Isabella, not because of failing love for her daughter, but because she loves her so completely. She feared she couldn't write without offending, and having been chastised by Dr. Pattison—father, not daughter—who urged his wife to allow their daughter to choose for herself, she did the next best thing. Mrs. Pattison loves new clothing more than anything else. So she commissioned and shipped new costumes, coats, shoes, etcetera, as wordless declarations of ongoing love and support."

Henry had been immensely relieved to discover the spending and excess were Mother's doing.

She squeezed Henry's hand. "I'd believed Mother's stylish clothing was her way of ensuring I caught a man's attention. I hadn't realized she'd meant to express love."

How wrong she'd been about many things.

"Wonderful," Naomi said, with happiness. "What of your sister and her silly husband?"

Isabella shared a look with her husband, her smile matching his own. "Let's say Dudley will come around."

"Oh?" Sophia set down her water goblet. "Need I inform him of a thing or two?"

"No, no. Nothing like that." Isabella couldn't help laughing. "He did bring his impressionable children to meet us and dined with us, too."

"But?" Leave it to Sophia to discover things left unsaid.

"I learned Dudley had heard Florence crying on more than one occasion."

Both Sophia and Naomi spoke at once. "And?"

"Perfect, obedient Florence believed Mother loved me best." She'd learned a thing or two about a mother's love.

Joe clapped Henry on the shoulder. "Did you thank your mother-in-law for the calico suit of clothes?"

"Indeed. She takes full credit for bringing about our wedding."

"What about me? I introduced you!"

Laughter enveloped them all.

"She's not angry?" Joe knew human nature, as well as human anatomy. "I suspected she'd fuss about missing the wedding."

"Mother seemed willing to overlook a great deal of things, as her fondest wish has been realized."

"Your marriage." Sophia supplied.

Henry kissed Isabella's temple. "Our marriage."

"Mother expressed affection for Henry with that ridiculous calico sack suit long before she knew more than I had a man for whom I wished to provide one calico shirt."

Laughter filled the dining room and overflowed Isabella's heart. She simply couldn't contain her flourishing happiness.

Much good had come from a wedding trip to Los Angeles. Introducing her husband to her parents had uncovered irrefutable truth.

Her parents hadn't stopped loving her.

She'd made a faulty assumption and allowed the error to cause years of pain. In hindsight, she could see how foolish she'd been.

"Proof" of her parents' failing love, in the full light of disclosure, became irrefutable demonstrations of undying love.

Watching her parents, at their advanced ages, showed how much in love they still were. To Mother, marriage meant happiness and fulfillment. No wonder Mother had wanted her daughter wed.

"I hesitate to mention it," Naomi said, already apologizing, "yet I know you'd rather hear this from us . . ."

"What is it?"

"While you were away, a lengthy article ran in the newspaper." Naomi shared a heavy look with Sophia.

"You must tell me about it." Nothing Fisher said could hurt her. Everyone local whom she loved sat at this table, hale and happy. "Henry and I haven't subscribed to the rag in months."

"A witticism." Sophia grinned. "One we found much satisfaction in."

"Do tell." Isabella wanted to hear this.

"It appears Mr. Fisher's eyes are opened." Sophia sat a little straighter, preparing to recite. "'Why shouldn't the girl who as a graduate is resolved to set the world on fire, be ultimately satisfied to start a flame in somebody's heart, if he's all the world to her?'"

Warmth, akin to full sun in July, spread through Isabella. "Indeed, why not?" In this room, with the man she loved and her four best friends who wholly comprehended the capacity of embracing the best of both worlds, no discussion was required.

"Hear, hear." Naomi raised her glass. "First glimpse of wisdom from Thomas Fisher to date."

Joe tapped his knife against a crystal goblet. "Speech, speech!"

Henry laughed. "I gave the finest speech of my life for the entertainment of the people of Uinta County." His touch settled on Isabella's shoulder once more. "Have you a speech for our intimate friends?"

Love radiated from her husband, more than enough to fill the holes within her. "Thank you," she told him once again, "for bringing balance into my life. Now, instead of happiness and laughter, I have you to laugh with and to share in my happiness."

If she'd given him laughter and happiness, he'd provided

her peace and simple joy. Two elements she'd been desperately missing. How well he completed her life, brought meaning, and ultimately proved the one thing she'd most needed since determining to pursue dentistry as a career. "With you, Henry Merritt, I see the sacrifices I made for dental school were utterly worth it."

"Thank you, Mrs. Merritt."

How she loved this man. He'd made her an equal partner in every way. He not only asked her opinion, but wanted her thoughts. He often deferred to her judgment, for as he'd said, she was the better problem solver.

"Without dentistry, without that path, we'd never have met." She'd told him of this insight on their first full day as man and wife, while traveling in a private compartment from Evanston to Los Angeles, a wedding gift from the Hugheses and the Chandlers.

But more had simmered in her heart, refining to a pure truth that begged to be shared. "My entire life, your entire life, prepared us to be in the right place at the right time, our very natures, formed by our experiences, making us an ideal match for one another. I wouldn't trade the journey—or the unexpected destination—for anything."

One soft clinking of crystal doubled, then quadrupled. She'd spilled her innermost thoughts before their friends!

Her smile softened, ripe with comprehension of all Henry had braved to make her his in front of the entire county. No matter what he'd said, the man was the furthest thing from a coward.

He leaned near. "They expect a kiss."

The soft tinkle of crystal, music to her ears, brought her back to her groom.

She met him halfway. This brush of lips, warm, familiar, was special beyond measure. This kiss sealed every word spoken, from her wedding vows to her deepest, heartfelt realizations. A promise of so much more to come.

"Whoever said female professionals couldn't have it all was not only mistaken. They are unenlightened."

"I'll kiss to that." Henry's kiss caused her brimming heart to overflow.

Applause filled their ears as she looped her arms about her husband's neck. Who cared if they kissed while seated at the supper table? She imagined she'd seal many a realization this way. In the office (probably without patients present), at home, and with their friends.

A journey of discovery had brought her to Henry, and a beautiful path lay before them, together.

"I'll kiss to that, too." So she did.

A Note from the Author

Dear Reader,

Thank you for visiting Wyoming Territory with me as citizens celebrate the accomplishment of statehood! Many tidbits within this 1890 story come straight from the annals of history.

I've provided links to many sources on the Internet, including my own articles, should you like to explore the background and setting.

First—Victorian snow cones? Come on! History confirms this treat's availability, decades prior to 1890. A *full twenty years* earlier than this book is set, theaters sold flavored "snowballs" during summer months (and urged patrons to finish consuming the treat during intermission). Folks *expected* cold drinks in July.

Second—Running water? Indoor bathrooms? In southwest Wyoming Territory? Yep. 100 percent accurate (after all, it's a hub for the great east–west railroad).

Before I fell in love with history, I wasn't aware that "professional women" (in "men's educated" work, not prostitutes) were frowned upon, nationwide. Women weren't welcome in dentistry. Lucy Hobbs Taylor, the first woman to graduate from a dental college wrote, "People were amazed when they learned that a young girl had so far forgotten her womanhood as to want to study dentistry."

A female's delicate constitution couldn't possibly withstand the rigors of the man's sphere, nor did women possess the brain power to succeed. Words attributed to Dr. Henry Merritt, DDS (the DDS degree had been around a good long while by 1890), and highly embellished by newspaperman Thomas Fisher, came from an article published in 1889 by dentist W. R. Spencer. Yes! (Many, but not all) men in professions and trades detested the encroachment of women on their private domain. (Read: *Boy's Club. Girls Stay Out.*)

How could I resist writing professional women who sought education and the right to work in their chosen field, despite cultural demands that women must be nurturing mothers and make a comfortable home for their husbands?

How things have changed in the short one hundred-plus intervening years.

Consider science! The conversation between Henry and Isabella, about the germ theory in human mouths, came straight from science of the day. Willoughby Miller, an American dentist in Germany, noted the microbial basis of dental decay in his book *Micro-Organisms of the Human Mouth*. This generated an unprecedented interest in oral hygiene and started a worldwide movement to promote regular toothbrushing and flossing (in German, in 1889; English in 1890).

In many ways, things haven't changed all that much. As mentioned briefly in the historical note before this novella, dentistry was surprisingly advanced for 1890. The use of laughing gas (nitrous oxide), amalgam (white) fillings, gold foil fillings, a power drill/dental engine (foot treadle), injections to manage pain (even though needles and syringes were not sterile). And quite modern dentures for those whose teeth had required extraction. (Frontier dentistry was something else altogether.) Toothbrushes and toothpaste were mass-produced in factories and readily available.

Would dentists have given away their work (a "dental dispensary")? In the nineteenth century, medical dispensaries gave medical care and medicine to those who couldn't afford to pay.

Enough dentistry. Let's talk calico balls!

Calico balls were popular in nineteenth-century United States communities. When I stumbled across references to a "calico ball" in a vintage newspaper, I was intrigued and scoured more until I was able to gather a picture of the phenomenon. Just as people had leap-year Balls (*Sophia's Leap-Year Courtship*), debutante balls, Independence Day balls, and mask balls (Mardi Gras), they often selected calico balls. Common elements included new dresses (or neckties or men's suits) constructed of calico fabric (not always a small floral print), to then be (sometimes) donated to the needy after worn—*once*—at the occasion and the price of tickets collected for similar good-will purposes.

Yes, they used speaking trumpets, and cities had civil engineers and builders, marching bands, and Coca-Cola at soda fountains.

Come see the wardrobe of Dr. Isabella Pattison, DDS, on Pinterest—part of a Pinterest board exclusively for this novella. The images inspired my writing and will provide a crisp image of the history (in different categories—easy to find!) within this story.

You're invited to check out more true-to-history details: sled runners for farm wagons, men's proper suits of clothes, collars and cuffs, ladies costumes (or dresses—which is it?), reasons why men lift their hat (don't pinch the brim!), Old West races, and why men must never call on a woman without her invitation to do so.

Evanston, Wyoming, is a real place, as is the historic mining town (now a ghost town) named Almy. I've included as much accurate history as possible in Uinta County (significantly larger in 1890 than now). As none of Almy's mining calamities coincided with the timing of this novella, I made one up. William Crompton and his two-story brick residence in Almy are real historical characters used fictitiously.

Winters in the 1880s were uncommonly severe compared to decades both before and after. Some blizzards, like the Schoolhouse Blizzard, Great White Blizzard (NYC), and the Snow Winter (Laura Ingalls Wilder), are familiar to many. My use of the severe Wyoming winters, from 1887 to 1890, including the "Cow Killing Winter" of 1889 to 1890 (in the Bear River Valley of Wyoming) is accurate. Wyomingites are wonderfully resilient.

Do you wonder about other historical attitudes, elements, or events I've not mentioned here? You're welcome to contact me through my website or email me directly (Kristin AT KristinHolt DOT com). *(Note: Kristin is e-free;* spelled without an 'e'*).* I enjoy hearing from readers and reply to all (reasonable) messages.

I'd enjoy connecting with you on social media. See easy links to Facebook and more on my website.

Kristin

Hi! I'm Kristin Holt, *USA Today* bestselling author of Sweet Romances (G- and mild PG-rated stories) set in the Victorian American West. You may have recognized Dr. Joseph Chandler, MD, and his mail-order bride, Dr. Naomi Thornton, MD, from *WANTED: Midwife Bride (Mail Order Bride Collection: A Timeless Romance Anthology)* or, perhaps, Chadwick Hughes and his not-quite-mail-order bride, Sophia Sorenson (attorney), from *Sophia's Leap-Year Courtship. Isabella's Calico Groom,* contained within *Calico Ball: A Timeless Western Collection,* rounds out my set of three novellas, each with a "professional woman": a doctor, a lawyer, and a dentist.

All three titles are available from Mirror Press and

Timeless Romance Anthologies, *USA Today* bestselling indie publisher of Clean & Wholesome Romance anthologies and collections.

While secular in nature, my titles are appropriate for all audiences and appeal to selective readers and fans of Christian historical romance.

I write frequent articles about the nineteenth-century American West on every subject of possible interest to readers, amateur historians, and authors, as these tidbits surfaced while researching for my books. I also blog monthly at Sweet Americana Sweethearts.

I love to hear from readers! Please drop me a note or find me on Facebook.

You're invited to join a fantastic Facebook group for authors and readers of Western historical romances: Pioneer Hearts.

Meanwhile, please stop by www.KristinHolt.com and say hello.

Kristin

Timeless Regency Collections:

Don't Miss Our Timeless Romance Anthologies:

www.ingramcontent.com/pod-product-compliance
Lightning Source LLC
LaVergne TN
LVHW021755060526
838201LV00058B/3100